Cast of Characters

Captain Henry "Cuckoo" Goyles. Formerly a schoolmaster, now an escape specialist, who is assigned the difficult task of sorting out the puzzling events at Campo 127. His closest friends are:

Captain Roger Byfold. A professional soldier and tankman, already enlisted when war broke out; and

Lieutenant Tony Long. The youngest of the three, captured after a bridge he blew up fell on top of him.

Captain Alec Overstrand, Major Martin "Hefty" Grimsdale, and Captain Hugo Baierlein. Three more accomplished escapers.

Colonel Lavery. The B.S.O. (British Senior Officer) who oversees his fellow prisoners.

Colonel Baird. A New Zealander and head of the Escape Committee, which is also composed of:

Colonel Stanlislaus Shore, an American airman, and

Commander Oxey of the Royal Navy.

Captain Benucci. The suave, dapper, sinister camp commander, a staunch member of the Fascist party.

Colonnello Aletti. A professional soldier, nominally Benucci's superior but who defers to him in matters of politics and intelligence.

Cyriakos Coutoules. A Greek soldier who is suspected of being a German spy.

Tenente Ercolo Mordaci. A translator, of the Carabinieri Reali.

Plus many other of   Allied and Italian, who inhabit Camp   lay in this story.

Books by Michael Gilbert

Close Quarters (1947)
They Never Looked Inside (1947; in America, *He Didn't Mind Danger*)
The Doors Open (1949)
Smallbone Deceased (1950)
Death Has Deep Roots (1951)
Death in Captivity (1952; in America, *The Danger Within*)
Fear to Tread (1953)
Sky High (1955; in America, *The Country-House Burglar*)
Be Shot for Sixpence (1956)
Blood and Judgement (1959)
After the Fine Weather (1960)
The Crack in the Teacup (1966)
The Dust and the Heat (1967; in America, *Overdrive*)
Game Without Rules (1968; short stories)
The Etruscan Net (1969; in America, *The Family Tomb*)
Stay of Execution (1971; short stories)
The Body of a Girl (1972)
The Ninety-second Tiger (1973)
Amateur in Violence (1973; short stories)
Flash Point (1974)
The Night of the Twelfth (1976)
Petrella at Q (1977; short stories)
The Empty House (1978)
Death of a Favourite Girl (1980; in America, *The Killing of Katie Steelstock*)
Mr. Calder and Mr. Behrens (1982; short stories)
The Final Throw (1982; in America, *End-Game*)
The Black Seraphim (1983)
The Long Journey Home (1985)
Trouble (1987)
Young Petrella (1988; short stories)
Paint, Gold and Blood (1989)
Anything for a Quiet Life (1990; short stories)
The Queen Against Karl Mullen (1991)
Roller-Coaster (1993)
Ring of Terror (1995)
Into Battle (1997)
The Man Who Hated Banks (1997)
Over and Out (1998)
The Curious Conspiracy (2002; short stories)

The Danger Within

by Michael Gilbert

Introduction by Tom & Enid Schantz

Rue Morgue Press
Lyons / Boulder

ISBN: 978-1-60187-009-4

Rue Morgue Press
87 Lone Tree Lane
Lyons CO 80540

Printed by Johnson Printing
Boulder, Colorado

PRINTED IN THE UNITED STATES OF AMERICA

The Escapes of Michael Gilbert

The Danger Within, Michael Gilbert's sixth novel, first published in Great Britain as *Death in Captivity* in 1952, relies heavily on his experiences as a prisoner-of-war in various prison camps in Italy during World War II. While serving with the Royal Horse Artillery in North Africa in 1943, Gilbert was investigating a farm which he believed to be in Allied hands. While he was in the farmhouse his driver heard a burst of automatic fire coming from the building and immediately drove off, leaving Gilbert to fend for himself. Gilbert was officially reported as missing in action, presumed dead. Instead, he was captured and, along with scores of other British officers, flown to Italy.

He was one of the lucky ones. British enlisted men who were taken prisoner in North Africa didn't fare as well, with hundreds of them dying from thirst and disease in desert prison cages where they were left to rot, according to Gilbert's fellow officer Tony Davies, who also served with the artillery and who was to join Gilbert in numerous escape attempts during the coming year.

Gilbert and Davies were reunited at Camp P.G. 66, a transit camp at Capua near Naples, where prisoners were kept until places were found for them in permanent camps. The first few weeks in the camp were called the "wire happy" days when the captured men first learned what it was to be a prisoner, a caged animal. After absorbing that initial shock, the captives grew accustomed to their status and began doing things to make their lives as comfortable as possible.

And to plan their escapes.

Gilbert, gaunt and bespectacled, looking very much like Captain Henry "Cuckoo" Goyles in *The Danger Within*, insisted to Davies that they needed to be in top physical condition when they made their attempt. Fortunately, Red Cross packages began arriving at this time, replacing the meager fare they had been fed in the North Africa camps—disgusting ersatz coffee made from dried lupin seeds, macaroni soup, bread, a little cheese and dates. The Red Cross rations, on the other hand, provided a balanced diet and did much to keep the men fit.

As part of their daily fitness regimen, Gilbert and Davies made sixty brisk circuits of the camp, just inside the barbed wire, each night between 7 and 9. Tunneling at this camp was not possible and, besides, it was unclear how long they would be there. Instead, the two decided that their best chance for a successful escape would be to jump from the train that would transport them to their permanent camp. They figured that once they got clear of the train they would walk 80 miles to the Adriatic coast, steal a fishing boat and head for Yugoslavia, where they could make contact with the partisans. They squirreled away as much food as they could spare from their rations but planned to live off the land as much as possible. To this end, they traded bits from their Red Cross packages to get lira from the Italian guards.

The Italians were easy to deal with in this matter. And, anyhow, they couldn't understand why the prisoners were so anxious to escape and get back to the war. The Italians also couldn't tell Germans from English, so the idea was to pass themselves off as German soldiers since badly spoken Italian seems very much the same whether it comes from a German or an Englishman. Fortunately, it was easy to alter their own uniforms to make them look like the Africa Korps uniforms they already resembled. What they lacked were the peaked forage caps worn by Rommel's men. These they managed to get from some black South African troops in a neighboring compound, who presumably had taken them off of dead German soldiers and had been, oddly enough, allowed to keep them. It cost them two weeks worth of Red Cross rations, their own British berets, and, most importantly of all, a string beads—to the South Africans the most important part of the transaction— which they were able to obtain by having another English prisoner steal them from some other South Africans.

After six weeks in the camp, Gilbert and Davies were notified that they would be among 40 prisoners who were to be transferred to a permanent camp at Chieti, near Pescara on the Adriatic, about 100 miles from their present location. The prisoners were placed in second-class compartments in groups of six along with an armed sentry. The train left Capua at 6 p.m. heading first south to Caserta near Naples, then northeast over the mountains. The train proceeded uphill in the darkness at a steady 30 miles an hour. Once the train began to accelerate, the two knew that they were on a down gradient and it was time to make their move. Another prisoner who was in on the plan distracted the sentry by offering him a cigarette. At that moment, Gilbert pulled the window down three feet and jumped, Davies following nearly immediately, stealing one last look at the sentry whose surprised face was illuminated by the match lit for his cigarette. Davies landed on a small road alongside the track and immediately began to scramble to safety up the hillside. Gilbert was nowhere in sight. The train braked and sentries on the flat van at the rear of the train began shooting in his direction but soon gave up. Obviously, there was no way that a handful of soldiers could find two men in this kind of terrain in the darkness and the train soon recommenced its journey as the remaining prisoners cheered and sang "God Save the King."

After the train was out of sight, Davies and Gilbert both shouted for each other but apparently the two were out of earshot and each decided the other had been either recaptured or killed by the jump. The two proceeded on their separate ways, Gilbert sticking to the original plan of walking to the Adriatic while Davies decided the best idea was simply to get as far away from the jump site as quickly as possible. For the next couple of days the two moved across the countryside, fooling most of the Italian soldiers they encountered, although Gilbert was eventually recaptured by the Italians. Davies' phony uniform was his eventual downfall. At one point, he encountered a German patrol and decided to bluff his way through, at which point he was stopped as a suspected deserter. A closer look at his uniform elicited a laugh from the German officer in charge who immediately identified Davies as one of the two escaped English prisoners.

"You know," the German said, "the funniest thing about this whole business is that the Italians have called out at least a division to look for you. You are classed as highly dangerous and to be recaptured at all costs. What a joke! You dodge the whole lot of them and walk straight into me. Funny, isn't it?"

The Italians Davies was turned over to also thought the affair was funny, but for different reasons. He was told: "You go through the hell of Africa, the beastliness of fighting, you are fortunate enough to be captured and to leave all that behind you. You come to our lovely country, and then, at the first opportunity, you risk your life so that you can get back to the war. You must be crazy!"

Crazy or not, the two were even more determined than ever to escape again. Gilbert told Davies, "At least we've learned a lot. We shan't make the same mistakes a second time."

For their efforts, the two were court martialed (an odd but standard procedure for attempted escapees) along with the hapless sentry who received two years at hard labor for accepting a bribe, even though the English officers told the court that he had been merely derelict in his duty. The court sentenced Gilbert and Davies to 30 days in solitary confinement, a sentence that struck neither as being particularly onerous since it meant that they would enjoy one of those precious things that all prisoners lack, a bit of privacy, and besides the solitary confinement cells weren't all that small. Or all that solitary, for that matter. It turned out that two of the three cells were already occupied and so Gilbert and Davies were placed in the same cell where they immediately began preparing for their next escape attempt by getting the guards to help them perfect their rudimentary Italian. The worst part of their incarceration was an infestation of body lice.

They also had a bit of fun at the expense of their jailers by doing a little sentry-baiting. One night, Gilbert positioned his head and shoulders in front of the cell's window and proceed to whack an out-of-sight mattress with a board while Davies, safely hidden from view in another corner, shrieked in pain. When the sentries showed up with their officers to show them how the prisoners were attempting to kill each other both men were tucked quietly in their beds, apparently sleeping the night away.

Near the end of their confinement, a Swiss delegation arrived in camp to insure that the Italians were adhering to the Geneva Convention rules for prison camps. The camp had been tidied up and punishment cells were discreetly disguised. Gilbert and Davies waited until the Swiss team was passing close to their cell and then began banging on their cell door, crying out: "*Acqua, Acqua.* For the love of God a little water." The Swiss somehow didn't hear but the Italians did and they were not amused.

The Italians, in fact, were often not amused at the way the English prisoners made fun of them. For the most part the Italian citizenry were proud of their own soldiers, affectionately referring to them as *I Nostri piccoli,* which translates to "our little ones." This term never failed to amuse the British, who ridiculed the Italian troops as "more shout than shoot." It was obvious to everyone that most of the Italian soldiers were not happy about being drafted, but once in the army they fell in love with their uniforms and the accompanying pomp. In *The Danger Within,* the prisoners make fun of the guards in order to trick them as part of their escape plan.

Once out of solitary confinement, the two reported to the camp's escape committee and then presented a talk to about 300 prisoners on their failed attempt to escape. The talk was entitled "The Principles of Marine Insurance," and the Italians never seemed to question why so many men would be interested in so specialized a topic. Toying with the guards remained one of the most enjoyable ways to pass away the time in the camp. Even though Gilbert spent only five days at Campo P.G. 21 (not counting that month in solitary confinement), he obviously based Campo 127 in *The Danger Within* on Campo P.G. 21, which Davies described as "a series of one-story buildings arranged in rows on either side of a large dusty expanse" surrounded by a 15-foot high wall with guard towers situated at each corner and halfway along each side. Each tower had a searchlight and a machine gun.

"There were no less than four tunnels in progress at that moment," Davies wrote in *When the Moon Rises,* his 1973 account of the escape attempts he made with Gilbert. "Italian security guards were extremely active, and the 'Ferrets,' *carabinieri* (Italian soldiers) working in pairs, spent the entire day inside the compound, searching every inch of ground and buildings for signs of tunneling activity." Often the prisoners only had two minutes warning to conceal their labors before search teams arrived.

Although the escape plans in *The Danger Within* center around tunnelling, it was one of the few methods in which Gilbert himself was not directly involved. His first camp at Capua did not lend itself to such methods and he wasn't at Campo P.G. 21 long enough to do any tunnelling. Tunneling at this next stop was out of the question, since the prison consisted of a single three-story building with basement in the middle of the village of Fontanellato five miles north of Parma. It was a prison designed to house *Molto Pericoloso*—troublemakers and habitual escapers. It would take all of Gilbert and Davies' ingenuity to break out of this place.

Unlike the *Fascisti* in charge of Campo 127 in *The Danger Within*, the Italian officers at Fontanellato were professional soldiers who treated their prisoners well. They knew—and respected the fact—that it was a prisoner's duty to escape just as it was their duty to prevent those escapes. One of the amenities that the Campo 49 lacked was a place for the prisoners to exercise, other than a weekly walk under heavy guard outside the walls. These walks not only provided the prisoners with fresh air and a little exercise, they also provided them a knowledge of the local geography which was to prove invaluable. Eventually, the Italians allowed the prisoners to build an exercise field outside the building. It was heavily guarded and enclosed by a barbed-wire fence. Since the ground was too rough for regular exercise, the prisoners were allowed tools to level the field.

The prisoners soon saw a possible means for escape and carefully constructed a small trench, roofing it over and disguising it each night. When it was finished, the British organized a game of rugby. When the scrum fell on top of the trench, two men climbed in and were roofed over hidden from view by the mass of bodies. At roll call, the two men were reported to be asleep in sick bay and before the guards could reach their supposed resting place, two of the prisoners who had already been counted rushed in and occupied their bunks. The two men in the trench made it to the border where they could see the inhabitants of a Swiss village from their perch before they were recaptured.

By this time, the war was going badly for the Italians. The Allied invasion was going very well and it was expected that Italy would soon be out of the war. That, however, meant that the Germans would take over and this is what the prisoners most feared. Although a full-scale tunnel was not possible in Campo 49, the prisoners managed to cut into the stone walls above the basement to create a hiding place in case the Germans should try to seize control of the prison. In that event, the hole could be pushed through the wall, allowing the prisoners to escape at ground level.

Then on the evening of July 21, 1943, the prisoners heard shouting and cheering from the guards' quarters. Mussolini and the Fascist regime had been toppled. Soon villagers joined in the cheering, tearing down Fascist posters and smashing plaster busts of *Il Duce* to bits. The atmosphere had changed greatly, but as the days passed the prisoners' status remained unchanged. Finally, on September 9, the Italians cut a hole in the fence surrounding the exercise field and within a few days the prisoners marched out, free at last but far from out of danger. The Italian guards threw away their guns and went into hiding, fearing reprisals from the fast approaching German troops, who were determined to hold the northern regions of Italy.

Villagers gave the newly freed men clothes and food. Most of them chose to head for the Swiss border and interment until the end of the war. Gilbert and Davies wanted nothing to do with that option. One other prisoner, Toby Graham, joined them in their decision to head south instead toward the advancing Allies. They were about to embark on one of the most remarkable journeys in the history of warfare, most of it along the 600-mile backbone of Italy, the Apennine mountain range. It was an ordeal that no doubt partially inspired Gilbert's 1985 novel, *The Long Journey Home.*

The three men dodged German troops for next several weeks, aided by Italian peasants who opened their homes and barns to the former prisoners. Some days they fared better than others, but Gilbert was always determined to make the best of their situation. "Any bloody fool can eat and sleep rough," he said, so the threesome quit their trek each day in time to find a suitable resting place, staying with peasants and avoiding the more prosperous homes which they feared might belong to unrepentant Fascist sympathizers. Eventually they made it through Tuscany and into the province of Marche, where they found refuge in a monastery. Gilbert and Graham talked to the Father Superior, mostly in Latin, and were invited to stay there to wait for the Allied arrival. Gilbert favored the idea but Davies and Graham pointed out that the Allies were still 200 miles away and that the Germans could still recapture them. The three continued on their journey but at one point, disagreeing over the route, Toby went his separate way.

The three miraculously met up again, along with another escapee, a South African named Hal Becker, just a few miles from the Allied lines. But the closer they got to the Allied lines, the more Germans they had to get through. Finally, they reached an open valley near those lines. It looked safe enough but they decided it would be best to go in pairs. Michael and Toby took off and made it without any difficulty. Ten minutes later Becker and Davies followed. Halfway across the valley, shots rang out and Becker was killed. Davies ran on and jumped over a crest only to fall into the hands of a German patrol. He was a prisoner again. Gilbert and Graham, on the other hand, made it safely to the Allied lines. Of the 400 officers who marched out of Campo P.G. 49, only a tenth made it to freedom. The rest were killed or recaptured by the Germans within days. Davies was sent to Moosburg POW camp in Germany, later famous for its "great escape" and brutal aftermath. Davies succeeded in escaping that camp as well but was recaptured near Prague where he spent the rest of the war.

Gilbert, who died in 2006 at the age of 93, went on to become an attorney and one of the most honored mystery writers of the second half of the twentieth century, Graham became a history professor at the University of Toronto, while Davies settled down as a country doctor. If such a thing as the "greatest generation" exists, these three—and their comrades—surely stood at the very front of its ranks.

Tom and Enid Schantz
Lyons, Colorado
August 2007

Editor's note: This introduction is but a poor summary of the events related in Tony Davies' *When the Moon Rises* (Leo Cooper, 1973), a book that cries out to be made into a movie.

Chapter 1

The Camp—Evening and Night

1

"Is it true, Captain," asked Colonel Lavery, "that Pantelleria has been invaded?"

"Quite true," said Captain Benucci. He added without a great deal of conviction, "After heroic resistance our gallant troops, greatly outnumbered, were forced to yield. Many laid down their lives but their deeds live on. Our *Duce* will not forget them."

"Quite so," said Colonel Lavery. "I believe you had something you wished to discuss with me."

"It arises from the invasion of Pantelleria. That affords me, so to speak, my context for what I wished to say. From now on there may be other assaults—small assaults, you understand—on outlying islands in the Mediterranean. Your troops may even land in Sicily."

"So," said Colonel Lavery.

"Frankly, if they make such an attempt, I do not think that many will survive it. Our German allies are there in great strength. However, there may be temporary successes. All this may serve to inflame the prisoners. They may try to organize something." He paused for a moment and added, "Something stupid."

"We have some very high-spirited officers here," agreed the Colonel.

Captain Benucci seemed suddenly completely serious. He turned his head so that his black eyes looked directly into the Colonel's washed-out blue ones, and he said, "If any such thing were encouraged, you yourself would incur a terrible responsibility."

"Yes," said the Colonel.

He looked out of the little window, across the bare, stamped earth of the exercise ground, at the red brick boundary wall. Without troubling to move his head he could see three platforms. On each of them stood two

11

men. One man controlled a searchlight, the other a machine gun mounted on a tripod. He visualized, for a moment, an unarmed crowd attempting to scale the walls. When he turned back he found that Captain Benucci was still looking at him.

"I demand your full cooperation," went on the Italian. "Otherwise I shall not answer for the consequences. If any untoward incident were to take place, no one would regret it more than myself."

"On the whole," said the Colonel, "I'm inclined to agree with you."

Silence fell again in the wooden, cabinlike room.

Shrill in the distance sounded the yelps of the Italian soldiers as they herded the last of their obstinate flock into the five big huts. From the Italian quarters a bugle was blowing for evening mess.

It was the Colonel who broke the silence.

"Is that just a general warning," he said, "or have you any concrete suggestions?"

"Two suggestions," said Benucci. "First, I was told—I do not know if it is true—I am naturally not in the confidence of the people concerned—that there might be some attempt to rush the walls. The people who made such an attempt might rely on the fact that the sentries would hesitate to shoot down unarmed men. Such a suggestion is fallacious. They would shoot them."

"I can assure you that I know of no such plan at the moment."

"Even if the ordinary soldiers might hesitate to do their duty, I am giving orders that, during the hours of darkness, one of the pair on each sentry platform shall be a member of my own regiment, the carabinieri. That order will come into effect tonight."

"Very well."

"Secondly, I must insist that the rule is observed *without exception* that no one shall move from hut to hut after evening roll call when the huts have been closed. After all, it is not a difficult rule to keep. Each hut is self-contained. Each hut has dormitories, latrines and kitchen. The camp was designed with forethought."

"It was indeed," said the Colonel. During the short period of his captivity, he had been confined, in varying degrees of discomfort, in a museum, a station hotel, a castle and a monastery. Campo 127 was easily the best camp he had ever seen.

"There is no reason at all to leave the hut from the time it is locked after evening roll call, until after breakfast, when morning roll call has been completed. If a prisoner should be sick, you have your own medical man in each hut. Even if he should die"—Benucci showed his white teeth for a moment under his clipped mustache—"he will keep till morning."

"Oh, quite," said the Colonel.

"Yet, in spite of this, during the last two months there have been three cases of prisoners being found outside their huts after dark—for trivial reasons, in each case."

The Colonel nodded. He knew that a certain amount of "visiting" went on.

"In each case the guards have shot high, as a warning. Those were their orders. The orders have now been changed. They will shoot to kill."

"Yes, I understand," said the Colonel. As always, with Benucci, he wondered how much of it was truth and how much propaganda. He remembered the last case of "visiting" only a few days previously, and a quite impenitent Roger Byfold saying, "As a matter of fact, I'd just gone over to make up a fourth at bridge in Hut A: one of them spotted me on the way back and the silly bastards spent five minutes shooting all round me."

"I quite understand," he repeated. "I'll give something out. Is that all?"

"That is all." Captain Benucci clicked his heels and walked stiffly out of the room. The Colonel went to the window and watched him, as he strutted away toward the main gate of the camp, a solitary, dapper little figure.

It was nine o'clock of a perfect summer evening. The sun had disappeared, at last and reluctantly, behind the buttress of the Apennine Mountains which ran up to the west of the camp. It left behind it that deep blue, almost green, light which the sky drew from the hidden Adriatic.

It was the moment in the day which the Colonel liked best.

The last of the five big huts was locked, and the last of his obstreperous four hundred children were locked away inside them. He, a few senior officers, his Adjutant and half a dozen camp officials had rooms in the end of the sixth hut, which held the camp offices, the stores, the library, the barber shop—dignified names for tiny partitioned cubicles.

As a privilege the outer door of this sixth hut was not locked at night. It was, incidentally, a privilege that the Colonel was determined to maintain.

He shuffled the papers on his table into some sort of order, for his bedroom was also his office, and went to look for his Adjutant.

2

Room 10 in Hut C—which was the end room on the south side, next to the kitchen—had a neat label on its door headed "Smokey Joe's." Underneath, in the same meticulous handwriting, were six names, in two sets of three:

MAJOR GRIMSDALE
CAPTAIN BAIERLEIN
CAPTAIN OVERSTRAND

CAPTAIN GOYLES
CAPTAIN BYFOLD
LIEUTENANT LONG

It was the only room in the building which had as few as six names on its door, and this exclusiveness was due entirely to the forethought of the Italians. Reckoning that if he had six dangerous criminals to watch it was easier, on the whole, to have them together, Captain Benucci had ordered the six to occupy a single room at the end of C Block. It was almost the only order of Captain Benucci's which they had obeyed with enthusiasm.

All of them were notorious escapers. All of them had spent long hours undermining Italian property, destroying Italian buildings, cutting up Italian furniture and threatening Italian self-respect and peace of mind. All of them had been, at least once, at large in the Italian countryside, pursuing the will-o'-the-wisp freedom in a variety of unlikely disguises.

Cuckoo Goyles, Roger Byfold and Tony Long—they worked as a trio, finding the concord which often comes from three discrepant natures— had jumped from a train, and spent fifteen days of unspeakable discomfort in the Apennines before convincing themselves that there was no future in night marching in mountainous country. Alec Overstrand had been out three times, on the last occasion in the company of Martin Grimsdale, when, dressed as Rumanian commercial travelers, they had got as far as Bologna before arousing the suspicions of the ever alert railway police. Hugo Baierlein, who was later to prove one of the outstanding escapers of the war, had already made a remarkable four-day journey by freight train from Caserta Hospital to Chiasso on the Swiss frontier. He had actually crossed the frontier and had been shunted back again into Italy, to fall into the hands of the customs guard.

Although Room 10 had six beds in it, only three of them were occupied. Grimsdale, Baierlein and Long were all, at that moment, concluding a seven-day spell in the punishment block for organized insolence to Captain Benucci.

"It may be different in the big world outside these walls," Roger Byfold was saying, "but in a prisoner-of-war camp, there's no doubt about it. Crime does pay."

Alec Overstrand, who was copying a map onto a small roll of waterproof silk, nodded his agreement. Cuckoo Goyles, lying on his bunk absorbed in a phrase book of modern Greek, said nothing. Only the electric light glinted on his steel-rimmed spectacles as he moved his head.

"In the Union of Soviet Socialist Republics," went on Byfold, "which a prison camp in many ways resembles, a man's status and consequence are measured by the amount of living room he is permitted to occupy. Here we are, six of us, none of us of great seniority, yet comfortably lodged in a room designed to hold eight, while all around us similar-sized rooms are full to overflowing with eight, ten or even twelve less fortunate prisoners. We enjoy the additional chance—almost, I might say, the certainty—that, from time to time, our numbers will be even further depleted by the vigilance of Captain Benucci or the offended dignity of Il Colonnello Aletti—"

"Do you suppose he's anything to do with the Hotel Aletti in Algiers?"
Byfold considered the matter. "It's possible," he said at last. "He has, now you come to mention it, a certain resemblance to a hotelier. Not a very high-class hotelier. The proprietor, possibly, of one of the less well-known eating houses in Soho."

"It's all very well shooting a line about your criminal reputation." Goyles looked up from his book. "It hasn't got you a room all to yourself yet."

"Like Coutoules?"

"The little rat." Overstrand's rather heavy red face took on a look of distaste. "Why don't we string him up and have done with it?"

"Stringing up's too good," said Byfold. "I should recommend slow immersion in canteen vermouth—head first, of course."

"He's not such a bad little beast really," said Goyles. "I had quite a long talk with him the other day."

"You're out of this world, Cuckoo," said Overstrand. "He's an informer and a stool pigeon."

"How do you know?"

"Didn't the caribs go straight to Desmond's tunnel last week—and hadn't Tony seen Coutoules snooping round the trap door only the night before?"

"Coincidence," said Goyles. "Desmond's such an ass. He's been leaving sand all over his bedroom floor for weeks."

"Coutoules can't do much more harm, anyway," said Byfold. "Not now that he's tucked away, all by himself, in a little room in the senior officers' block. And no one ever talks to him now—except Cuckoo here."

"Schoolboy stuff," said Goyles calmly. "What's the use of sending him to Coventry, even if he is a stool pigeon? If you talk to him you may get something useful out of him."

He returned to his studies and silence fell.

Ten minutes later he looked up and said, "Can anyone think of any situation in which it might be useful to know the modern Greek for 'Please inform me, sir or madam, whether the cabinet of easement is nearer to the Cathedral or the Railway Terminus'?"

No one could.

3

Other parties were also discussing Cyriakos Coutoules.

Colonel Lavery said to his Adjutant, "I'm worried about Coutoules, Pat."

"It's he who should be worrying, sir," said the Adjutant.

"Yes, I know. He's not exactly popular. That's one of the things I was thinking about."

"Are you expecting trouble?"

"Well—not at the moment. Byfold and that young ass, Overstrand, have both threatened to lynch him. But it's nothing more than a threat—as yet."

"You mean—?"

"What do you think would happen if two or three of our hotheads—and we're not short of hotheads—"

"Who'll get hotter as the war comes closer."

"Exactly. Well, supposing some of them try to rush the walls. And the guards, instead of being distracted by whatever distraction is offered, are wide awake, and turn a searchlight on them and shoot them down. And suppose someone starts a little story that 'they had no chance because Coutoules tipped off the Italians—' "

"It might be sticky," agreed the Adjutant. "Tell me, sir, do you really think he's an informer?"

"I don't know," said the Colonel. "It's so easy to imagine these things. We know nothing about him. He just says he was landed in Sicily to do sabotage. He's got Greek Army papers, only no one here knows enough about the Greek Army to say whether they're genuine or not. We can't check up on his home background—regiment and school and so on—as we could if he was a British officer. That makes him automatically subject to suspicion."

"One couldn't condemn him on that sort of thing alone," said the Adjutant. "But Desmond Foster's tunnel—that was a bit too coincidental to be nice."

"I wasn't too happy about that," agreed the Colonel. "But tunnels get found in hundreds of ways. The Italians may have known about it for weeks and just chosen that moment to pounce. If that had been all there was against him I shouldn't have worried."

"Has something else happened, sir?"

"Yes. Something I haven't worked out yet. Coutoules came to me this afternoon and practically begged me to put him back in one of the main huts."

"He *what?*"

"Yes, I know. It didn't seem quite natural to me. After all, he's got a room to himself in our hut here. Almost anyone in the camp would give a year's pay for a private room."

"Besides," said the Adjutant, "he must know he's not popular. So why does he want to go and put himself back into the lion's den?"

"Exactly. There's no doubt he did want to, though. No doubt at all. I've never seen anyone more anxious in my life. Practically went down on his knees."

"Did he say why?"

"Not really—just a lot of talk. He didn't like being alone."

"Do you think he was play-acting?"

"I didn't get that impression," said the Colonel. "If you want my real opinion, I think he was scared stiff."

4

The punishment block lay in the northwest corner of the camp, alongside the carabinieri office. With the camp guard quarters and other Italian administrative huts, it lay outside the inner line of defenses that guarded the camp proper. This was one of its advantages, and it was not entirely by chance that three such hardened escapers as Tony Long, Hugo Baierlein and Hefty Grimsdale should have been guilty of the simultaneous offenses which had landed them in the cooler together.

As nine o'clock struck Tony Long was standing on his bed looking out of the single barred window of his cell. He was reflecting, in a detached way, on the problem of escape from a prison camp. Campo 127 was not an easy place to escape from. It had been designed, as Captain Benucci had pointed out to Colonel Lavery, with a good deal of forethought. Miracles apart, there were only three ways of getting out of any camp. You could tunnel under the walls, you could climb over the walls, or you could walk out of the gate.

All of these methods had their own drawbacks. The real disadvantage of tunneling was the length of time it involved. What with the constant watchfulness of the Italians, their security checks and their sudden searches, any tunnel was almost certain to be spotted in the end. To suppose that you could keep it entirely hidden for the six or eight months necessary to reach the open was like gambling on the same number coming up six or eight times running at the roulette table. It could happen, but it didn't very often.

To get over the walls was a proposition of much greater risk but carrying with it that fundamental chance of success which must attend any bold and unexpected maneuver. Three months before, a particularly well-organized effort of this sort had been completely successful. The camp lights had been fused and, in the few seconds that the darkness had lasted, four officers armed with hook ladders had crossed the wall midway between sentry and sentry and had disappeared. (It is true that all of them had eventually been recaptured and were now in the fortress prison of Gavi for their pains.)

Lastly there was the gate. To crash the gate was a project which needed expert disguise, nerve and plenty of luck. At 127 you needed a double portion of luck, for there were, in fact, two gates: an inner gate and an outer gate, and a very elaborate security system of passes and checks existed between the two, which no one had yet entirely succeeded in defeating.

Standing at his window, that evening, Tony watched the system at work. A small open laundry van came across the prisoners' compound and approached the inner gate. Despite the fact that it was driven by one carabiniere and had another seated on the back, the sentry abated nothing of his caution. He checked both passes and then went round and thrust his long "needle" bayonet through one or two of the largest bundles. The carib in the back said something and the driver laughed. The sentry walked across to the telephone, and spoke to the guardhouse. Not till he had had a reply would he even open the inner gate. At the outer gate, although it was in full view of the inner one, and not more than thirty yards away, the whole performance was repeated.

Tony sighed, shifted his weight onto his other foot, and wondered how long it would be before it was dark. He had blond hair and a Nordic, rather serious face, which looked deceptively youthful: only his mouth and chin had the hard lines of a generation which had been brought up to war.

By half past ten most of the light was out of the sky, but it was eleven o'clock before he moved.

The first thing he did was to take out a short piece of wire which appeared to form part of his bed and thrust it through the ventilator between his cell and the next. He jerked it once or twice and then pulled it out, and put his ear to the ventilator.

He could hear Baierlein's voice quite distinctly.

"Not yet. The outer gate guard is on the other side, looking this way. I'll knock when he changes over."

Ten minutes later a quiet knock sounded.

Tony put his hand up and appeared to be fumbling with one of the bricks which formed the sill of the window. Then he put his other hand up, and twisted one of the bars. Then bar and brick came clean out of the window. The whole operation took less than thirty seconds.

The gap left by the removal of the bar was not much more than twelve inches, but it was enough.

Tony climbed from the bed onto the sill, put a long arm through, caught the gutter above the window, and pulled.

A minute later he was on the roof of the punishment block, hidden in the deep shadow behind a buttress.

Baierlein, in Cell 2, turned to Grimsdale with a smile and said, "He's up."

"Should be all right now," said Grimsdale. "They won't see him so long as he keeps still."

"They certainly won't hear him," said Baierlein. "Not with that filthy row going on."

In the camp office next door a loudspeaker, full on, was relaying a dance band from Radio Roma.

The two men lay in silence in the dark cell. Each was deep in his own thoughts. There was an occasional rustle as Baierlein turned on his bed to look at the illuminated face of his watch.

Outside, the saxophones laughed and sobbed and the high trumpets screamed.

5

"Three hearts," said Tag Burchnall.

"Pass," said Billy Moxhay.

"Four hearts."

"Three hearts give us game, you know."

"Oh, so it does. Sorry, I'm sure," said Rollo Betts-Hanger. "Pass then."

"Pass," said Billy Moxhay. "Good fun this afternoon, wasn't it?"

"First class," said Rollo. "I thought we were a bit weak in the scrum."

"Definitely weak."

"We want a bit more weight."

"A lot more weight. Aubry and Peter don't push their weight at all."

"We really need a first-class man behind them. Someone who can lock the back row."

"What about—oh, sorry. I didn't know you were waiting for me. I thought you were pondering. I'm playing the queen. I was going to say, what about Grimsdale? He's a Hibernian, isn't he?"

"I asked him—of course. He won't do it."

"Won't play rugger?"

"That's what he told me. He said he'd always been made to play at school and in the Army. In a prisoner-of-war camp he was going to please himself."

"Must have been pulling your leg. Why, he played for Middlesex, didn't he?"

"The truth of the matter is," said Rollo, "that he spends so much time over this escaping stuff that he hasn't got time for anything else."

"Of course, in theory, I'm all for escaping," said Jerry Parsons. "It's one's duty, and so forth. But the fact of the matter is—oh, it's me again, is it?—the fact of the matter is that no one ever really gets anywhere. It isn't as if there was any chance even of getting out of this camp—to say nothing of getting out of the country—and when anyone does try, what happens—"

"They cut off the showers," said Tag Burchnall. "You can't trump that, Billy. Hearts *are* trumps."

"That's what I mean. They just make everyone uncomfortable."

"Still," said Tag, "one doesn't exactly want to stand in their way. One wouldn't want to do a Coutoules," he added.

"I can't think why someone hasn't taken the little beast right apart," said Billy Moxhay. "I should have thought the S.B.O. ought to take it up. All that's happened to the little blot is that he's got a room of his own. I'm trumping that."

"You can't trump that card," said Tag. "I know it looks like the knave of hearts but it isn't really. It's the three of clubs."

"I thought the other knave of hearts was the three of clubs."

"No, that's the knave of hearts. It's turned down in the corner. That makes ten tricks. Game with one overtrick. Eight hundred on the rubber."

Scores were carefully checked and eight small figs were pushed across the table.

The president of the Old Hibernian Rugby Football Club cut, and the cards were dealt again.

6

At two o'clock Hugo Baierlein turned over on his bunk and sat up. He had many of the talents of the true escaper. One was the ability to sleep anywhere and wake on demand.

He got out of bed, picked up a chair, put it on the table which was under the high barred window and climbed onto it. He maneuvered the bars in much the same way that Tony Long had done in his cell and after a few minutes he also had the middle one loose. He then put his arm and shoulder out, reached up and scratched very gently on the iron gutter.

He waited, and scratched again, until he heard the muffled sounds which indicated that Tony Long was on his way down. He gave him a few minutes and then crossed to the ventilator.

He heard Tony's voice, still puffed from his descent.

"Went very well. He couldn't see me, of course: I was just behind the parapet. Don't think he was suspicious. Just jumpy. He spends most of his time in the box with his back to us, but he comes out every half hour, just before the sergeant arrives on his rounds. I've written down the time."

"Good," said Baierlein. "I'll make a note of that myself."

"You'll have to be damned quiet getting up," said Tony. "You haven't got a ruddy great dance band to cover you like I had. I'll give you the word when to start."

Five minutes later Baierlein was on the roof.

It was cold enough to make him feel glad of his double layer of underclothes.

He was lying alongside the low parapet which divided the flat roof. His wrist watch was strapped with its luminous face on the inside of his left wrist. In his right hand he had a tiny black notebook and pencil. His job was to note down every movement of the sentry on the main gate and of the pair on the northwest guard platform.

He faced the prospect of approximately two and a half hours of immobility.

Under the full Italian moon, which paled even the arc lamps round the perimeter, the camp lay black and sharp. Every few minutes a searchlight from one of the guard platforms blinked its frosty carbon-blue eye and swept across the enclosure.

Baierlein lay safely in the long black shadow of the parapet. His eyes were on the gate sentry. He saw exactly what Tony had meant. The chap was too slack to stand his post properly. He preferred to lounge in the comparative comfort of the box. Only, every half hour, just before the sergeant of the guard announced to the world the start of his rounds by throwing open the guardroom door, the sentry left the box, crossed the gateway, and stood facing the punishment block.

In that position alone was he a danger.

Baierlein glanced at the watch face, and made a meticulous note in his book. It was for moments like this that he lived—and was nearly to die, once or twice, before he finally hobbled across the Swiss frontier at Gott-madingen eighteen months later.

7

On the guard platform at the northeast corner Ordinary Soldier Bian-celli stamped his feet and prayed for his relief. He hated guard duty at the best of times but he hated it still more now that, in place of his friend, Moderno, he had this unspeakable, unsociable Marzotto beside him. His dislike was not personal. It was the dislike of a member of an ordinary corps for the member of a privileged corps. He, Biancelli, was a soldier. A soldier of the King. Marzotto, although he styled himself "of the Regi-ment of Carabinieri Reali," was a policeman. He took his orders from Captain Benucci, who took them from some colonel of carabinieri at dis-trict headquarters, who took them, in the long run, from *Il Duce*.

Biancelli was distressed both by his discomforts and his responsibilities.

In the old days, it had been simple. If you saw an English prisoner escaping you shot at him. Now things were more complicated.

He looked sideways at Marzotto, who avoided his gaze.

As an ordinary soldier he was not told much about how the war was going, or what was happening in the camp he was guarding. But he could not help being aware of certain undercurrents of feeling: certain possi-bilities.

He stamped his feet again and watched the sky lightening impercepti-bly toward morning.

Chapter 2

The Camp—Morning

1

The camp came to life slowly.

In Hut C the first sound was usually the clatter of the orderly cook as he hurried along the passage to light the kitchen stove and heat the coffee which, with a slice of Red Cross biscuit, made up the normal prisoner-of-war breakfast.

At eight-thirty the Italians were due to open the huts and conduct their morning roll call. It was an operation which might take anything from fifteen minutes to an hour according to the temper and efficiency of the Italian officer conducting it and the degree of cooperation which he succeeded in obtaining from his charges. During roll call no one was allowed to leave his room.

Opinion varied from hut to hut as to whether it was better to heat the breakfast coffee before or after roll call. There were advantages either way. In Hut C, at that time, for reasons which will appear, the cooking was done as early as possible.

Immediately roll call had been concluded and the last Italian had left the hut quite a lot of things happened. None of them, in themselves, was significant or suspicious: but the total would have added up to the same answer in the mind of any experienced prisoner.

Certain officers, lying on their beds beside windows, hung out towels to dry. One prisoner fixed his shaving mirror to a nail beside the window and seemed to be experiencing some difficulty in tilting it to the exact angle he required, for the mirror could be seen, for some minutes, winking like a semaphore in the morning sun. In a room in Hut C a tall major, wearing the green flashes of the I Corps, sat at a table filling in what appeared to be a chart of the interrelated royal dynasties of England and Hanover, and a stream of visitors came and went with items of information which he found helpful in his strange, self-imposed task.

All over the camp, from each of the five big living huts, from the senior officers' quarters, from the orderlies' billet, from the barber shop, from the canteen and the shower baths, the quiet, invisible network floated out, like a thousand spiders' webs of gossamer over an early morning field. A subaltern in the Royal Corps of Signals—in peacetime a professor of history at Oxford—who was sitting in a deck chair against the wall of the camp theater, found himself reminded of Oman's description of Craufurd and the Light Brigade at their watch on the Portuguese frontier: "The whole web of communication quivered at the slightest touch." He himself had a tiny part to play: the outer main gate was under his observation. If it opened he would drop his book. If anyone dangerous came through he would stand up. The gate remaining shut, he was able to continue his studies in peace.

The object of all this organization, the heart of the labyrinth around which this watchful maze of attention had been constructed, lay in the kitchen of Hut C.

In the middle of the kitchen, set in a six-foot-square slab of concrete let into the tiled floor, stood the stove. It was a huge caldron, shaped like a laundry copper, and it still hissed and bubbled from its morning coffee making. Apart from a few shelves, almost the only other fitting in the room was a pair of hanging clothes driers of a sort not uncommon in old-fashioned kitchens, made of slats of wood, and suspended, on two pulleys each, from the ceiling. These were covered, as usual, with prisoners' private laundry, underclothes, stockings and sports outfit. The only odd thing about them—and no doubt the matter was so obvious that it had never occurred to the Italians as being odd at all—was that the racks appeared to be a trifle too well-made for their function. However great the weight of damp laundry to be hung on them, it seemed an unnecessary precaution to have bolted the pulleys right through, at both ends, to the solid beams of the roof. Nor did it seem strictly necessary that the racks, instead of being raised by a single pulley, should be operated at each end by a small double block and tackle. The obvious is rarely apparent.

At five minutes past nine, four officers entered the kitchen. Two of them went to the clothes racks and lowered them to their fullest extent so that they hung just above the stove. They then took out, each of them, a short length of wire rope with a hook at both ends. One hook went over the pulley, the other round one of the four legs of the stove. No word was spoken: nor was any word necessary since they had been performing this particular operation twice every day, for several months.

Each man took up the slack on his pulley. There was a moment's pause. Then, in tug-of-war parlance, they "took the strain."

For a moment nothing happened.

"Ease a little on the left," said the leader. "You're jamming her."

Suddenly, with no perceptible jerk, smoothly as a hydraulic press, the whole of the concrete slab came up out of the floor, with the stove fixed to it. When it was about three feet up, the leader gave the sign, ropes were fastened and, as silently as they had come, the men departed.

The stove, despite its ascension, continued to bubble and hiss merrily.

Such was the entrance to the oldest existing undiscovered tunnel in a camp whose Commandant had boasted that no tunnel was possible.

One had only to see it in operation to realize why it had escaped all searches. Like the African elephant in its native jungle, it defied detection by its immensity. The Italian security police, as they probed and searched with antlike zeal each night, running steel spikes between bricks and tapping on floors with leather hammers, were looking for something altogether different—something smaller and slighter. A trap door which consisted of a single slab of concrete, six feet by six feet, and over two feet deep: a trap door which weighed nearly half a ton and needed four men, assisted by double pulleys, to lift it, was something outside their ambit. It evaded search by being too big to see.

(It might as well be admitted that only a fluke had rendered its construction possible. The Italians had made the mistake of letting the prisoners into Campo 127 a fortnight before it was really ready—a fortnight during which construction work was still proceeding on the shower baths and the drainage. Despite all their precautions it had proved possible to get hold of cement and certain tools, and the Escape Committee had immediately ordered the construction of this monster trap. The original base of the stove, a lighter piece of work, was taken out, broken into pieces, and dropped into the water storage tank. The new base was cast in one piece and the lifting apparatus installed. Before the camp had even been completed, therefore, the foundation stone for a way out had been well and truly laid.)

Overstrand and Byfold were already dressed for work.

It was their job, every morning, to open up the tunnel, connect the electric lighting system, see that the hand pump and airline were in order and that the trolley, which ran from the trap door to the digging face, was working without hitch. With the tunnel now more than a hundred feet long these details were becoming of increasing importance. When they gave the word that all was ready the first shift of diggers would go down and the trap would be lowered on them. They would dig for four hours and would then be replaced by an afternoon shift.

Although they had dressed for tunneling often enough not to feel self-conscious about it, both Overstrand and Byfold might have presented, to the unaccustomed eye, somewhat remarkable figures. From the waist downward, they were clothed in that useful army garment known to the quartermaster as "pants, woolen, long," the ends tucked into the tops of their socks, of which they wore two pairs. Their top halves were covered by skintight football jerseys (of no known club—they were part of an issue of sports kit by the Protecting Power, and were alleged to be the colors of the Zermatt Wanderers). Both wore balaclava helmets and were shoeless.

"Where's Cuckoo?" said Overstrand.

"He's along there already," said Byfold. "Check the security, would you?"

Overstrand looked out of the window, and noted the position of various towels, shutters, refuse bins and deck-chair loungers.

"Seems all right," he said. "Let's go."

They made their way along the empty passage and into the kitchen. The stove hung suspended in the air.

A pair of steel spectacles gleamed from the darkness of the entrance shaft under it.

"I thought you were never coming," said Goyles. "I've connected up the light. It looks all right from this end. There are twelve bags of sand waiting. We'll have to get them out before digging starts."

All three of them had climbed down the ladder and were standing in the bottom of the twenty-foot vertical entrance shaft. The tunnel itself, rather less than a yard square, ran away from the east side of this shaft. A slight bend hid the working face of the tunnel from a person standing in the shaft.

"I'll go up," said Overstrand. "Give me two minutes and then start checking the pump."

He placed himself face downward on a small flat trolley which ran on rails up the tunnel and propelled himself forward with his hands. Trolley and man rounded the bend and disappeared.

Goyles looked at his watch.

"Ten to nine," he said. "The shift will be here in ten minutes. Let's have these bags up and get the disposal squad busy."

"Why did God make sand so heavy?" said Byfold. He had tied two sacks together, hung them over his shoulder, and was climbing up the ladder.

Goyles had nothing to say to this and had turned his attention to the pump. He looked at his watch again. Overstrand had said "two minutes" and this was about the time it would take an experienced tunneler to reach the face. A novice would need five.

At eight minutes to nine Goyles started operating the homemade pump. At three minutes to nine he stopped. Byfold had got most of the sacks of sand up and was starting his last trip.

One of the weaknesses of the system, thought Goyles, was that there was no means of communicating with the worker at the face. Even if you shouted, which would have been unwise, your voice by some trick of acoustics could not reach him. Something to do, no doubt, with the blanketing qualities of sand. A telephone from the shaft to the face would be a luxury, but might in the end save—

"Hullo," said Byfold, "what's happening to Alec? I've got all the bags clear. The shift's about due."

"Nip up and tell them to wait," said Goyles. "We'll give him a few more minutes. The trolley may have stuck."

As Byfold's stockinged feet disappeared out of the top of the shaft, Goyles stared anxiously up the tunnel. If Overstrand really was stuck he would have to go after him and since there was only one trolley he would go on his elbows and knees. This was all right, of course. In fact, during the first fifty feet of the tunnel, before the rail had been laid, it had been the normal method of progress. But it meant an awful waste of time, and every minute that the trap stayed open could be dangerous.

He peered again up the tunnel.

Where there had been a faint glimmer of yellow, it was now completely dark. This did not necessarily mean that the light at the face had failed. Overstrand's body and the trolley between them would blanket it effectively.

He became aware that Byfold was saying something.

"—how long to wait."

"I don't know," said Goyles. "I think I'll have to go and see—no—hold it. Here he comes."

Two feet appeared in the gloom of the tunnel and they heard the rumbling and creaking of the trolley on its homemade tram lines.

"How is everything?" said Goyles.

And then, even in the dim light of the shaft, he saw that Overstrand's face was white.

"What's happened?"

Overstrand climbed off the trolley and stood up. He wiped his hands together, separating his fingers and rubbing them through each other as if to get the sand from between them.

"Part of the roof's fallen in at the top," he said, speaking slowly.

"Has it—?"

"No. It's not right through. There's no daylight showing. I think it's held up by the foundations of the theater. It's difficult to see. You know we thought we were about under it."

"I see," said Goyles. It didn't sound too alarming. "We'd better get the shoring-up started straight away. I'll call off this shift and we'll have a word with—"

He was aware that Overstrand was staring at him.

"It's not just a collapse," he said. "There's someone in it."

"What's that?"

"There's someone in it. I could see his feet sticking out. I got some of the sand away. I think it's Coutoules. He's dead."

"You're sure of that?"

"Of course, I'm sure," said Overstrand. He seemed to be trying to work up a little honest anger to counteract the effect of what he had seen. "You can tell that just from seeing his feet. I dug to his face to find out who it was. What are we going to do?"

It was noticeable that although both Overstrand and Byfold were regular soldiers it was usually Goyles who assumed the command in any real crisis. He did so now.

He wasted no more time on Overstrand but climbed halfway up the ladder and said to Byfold:

"Get this shift away, Roger. Tell them there's a bit of the roof come down and there'll be no digging until we've got it shored up again. Then will you send someone for Doc Simmonds and—ask Colonel Baird to step along."

Byfold started to say something, took one look at Goyles' face, and changed his mind.

2

Colonel Baird was head of the Escape Committee. He was a New Zealander, had commanded an infantry battalion and had been acting commander of a brigade at the time of his capture in the desert. He was a thick, grizzled, slow-speaking man: not a person you took liberties with.

He strolled into the kitchen three minutes later, slashing with his home-made flywhisk.

Both Overstrand and Goyles were up by this time, and standing beside the trap, and he listened to what they had to say.

"It sounds to me like a two-man job," said the Colonel. "You found him, didn't you, Overstrand? Well, that's enough for a bit, I reckon. You go and change. You two—you'll have to get that Greek out. It's not going to be easy. I suggest you push the trolley ahead of you to the face. When you get there you'll have to get either side of it and scrape the sand away with your hands until you can pull the body back onto the trolley. It won't be exactly safe, that bit. Do you think you can manage it?"

"I expect so," said Goyles. "The lights still work. Overstrand says that the collapse is pretty well held up by the foundations of the theater hut— we're underneath that now."

"Stroke of luck," said Baird. "We might be able to save it yet. We don't want to lose *this* one if we can help it. Down you go now. I'll guarantee you ten minutes but don't take longer if you can help it."

Goyles couldn't pretend that he enjoyed the crawl up the tunnel but by the time he reached the face curiosity had the upper hand. He had never been in a tunnel fall before. The shift of the previous day had dug about six feet beyond the existing shoring: it would have been the first job for that morning's shift to shore it up with the short lengths of wooden bed board of which a stock was kept in the shaft. Sometime in the night a large neat section had fallen out of the exposed roof. It had not quite filled the tunnel and over the top of it you could see the empty space it had fallen out of and the bricks and cement which were the foundations of the theater hut. Underneath the fallen sand, somehow, incredibly, was the body.

The actual operation of getting him out proved surprisingly easy, though far from pleasant, with every incautious movement bringing down a fresh trickle of sand from the cavity above.

Somebody—presumably Overstrand in his first effort to identify the body—had already scraped away a lot of the sand on one side. Goyles, lying beside the truck, was able to dig, one-handed, into the pile on the other side. The difficulty was disposing of what he dug, but in the end he simply piled it on the trolley and Byfold, lying behind him, pulled the loaded trolley back and scattered the loose sand up and down the tunnel.

In the end, when the body was nearly clear—it was Coutoules all right— they edged the trolley in under his legs, retreated to the shored-up por-tion, and pulled. There was a further, alarming fall of sand but the body came away with the trolley and the worst was over.

Five minutes later they were back in the kitchen of Hut C. Colonel Baird said, "If my hair's white it's you two who are responsible. Do you know you've been forty minutes?"

"Time stood still, sir," said Goyles impenitently.

The body of Coutoules lay under a blanket in the corner of the room. Overstrand, who had changed and returned, lent them a hand and the four of them lowered the trap.

Up to that moment they had been too busy with the pressing necessities of the moment to give much thought to the problem which the figure under the blanket represented.

The awkward silence was broken by the arrival of the doctor.

"He's over there, Doc," said the Colonel. "It's Coutoules."

The doctor turned back the blanket, and then said, "I should like a little more light if I'm going to make a proper examination. Can he be moved?"

"I was thinking the same thing, sir," said Goyles. "We're rather a sitting chicken if anyone should come." The pulleys were still fastened to the stove and there was a good deal of bright, newly excavated sand on the floor, as well as four full bags which they had not yet had time to dispose of.

"All right," said the Colonel. "But have you thought how you're going to move him out of this hut?"

No one had.

"Get him into the nearest bedroom for the moment—that's yours, isn't it, Goyles? Then clear up in here as quickly as you can. I'll fix something up to get him out. We'd better take him into Hut A. Meet us there, would you, Doctor?"

Goyles and Byfold picked up the body. Now that they were out of the tunnel they were beginning to feel glad of the blanket over it. They carried it in and laid it on the floor of their room.

"Get hold of about twelve reliable types," said the Colonel, "people from this hut, if possible. We don't want a lot of coming and going. Tell them to put on some sort of gym outfit—and hurry."

The power of Colonel Baird's name was such that in less than five minutes a dozen puzzled but willing gymnasts had been assembled.

Colonel Baird gave them instructions.

Ten minutes later the sentries on the walls were diverted at the sight of seven of their prisoners galloping from the end of Hut C with seven other prisoners mounted on their backs. The procession galloped past Hut B, down the alleyway between Hut B and Hut A, and from there out onto the sports ground, where a spirited tourney took place, each pair of riders trying to unseat the other. It did not surprise the sentries because nothing that the British did had the power to surprise them. In the general excitement it may have escaped their attention that, while seven pairs had started out, only six had arrived at their destination.

The seventh rider was being dismounted from his perspiring horse in the dining room of Hut A.

"I don't want to do that again in a hurry," said Byfold. "I thought he was going to slip just as we got opposite the sentry platform—and the feel of those arms round my neck—ugh."

"All right," said Colonel Baird. "Put him down on the table, will you. You can do your stuff there all right, Doctor? Byfold, I don't think we need you and Overstrand any more. Fewer people here the better, really. Warn the watchers that something is going on in this hut and we want the longest possible warning if any Italian heads in this direction. Oh, and you might see the Adjutant and ask the S.B.O. if he'll step over here. Warn him not to hurry straight here—the sentries are very quick at picking up things like that—and I don't know whether they've fallen for that bareback circus act or not. Suggest that he might make his morning round in this direction in about ten minutes. You stop behind, Goyles. I want a word with you."

The Colonel lowered himself onto one of the dining-room chairs—it had been built to Italian barrack specifications and was inadequate to his bulk—and Goyles sat down too, glad that he had his back to the things that were going on on the table behind him.

"Now, boy," said the Colonel and he said it so kindly that Goyles felt suddenly guilty of nameless crimes, "tell me what happened."

"There's not an awful lot to tell really," said Goyles. "We opened up the tunnel, this morning, in the usual way, just after half past eight. The routine is that three of us go down first."

"Yourself, Overstrand and Byfold."

"Well—not necessarily. Any three out of our room. We happen to be the only three of us there at the moment. The others are in the cooler."

"I see. And you get things ready."

"That's it. We've all been in on this tunnel almost from the beginning and we know our way about it. We check the lighting and the pump and go up on the trolley to see that the shoring is holding up and there haven't been any falls during the night and we organize the disposal of any sacks of sand that the afternoon shift have left from the day before."

"I see. And this morning—by the way, do you open it yourselves?"

"No. That wouldn't work. It's a four-man job to open or shut the trap, and it might have to be shut in a hurry. The same four chaps always do the opening—they live in the room next to ours—and they have to stand by the whole time the trap's open in case there's a panic."

"I'll have a word with them in a moment," said the Colonel. "What's next?"

"I went down first and connected up the light. Then Overstrand and Byfold arrived. Overstrand went up the tunnel and—found Coutoules."

"Just like that," said the Colonel. "Quite simple, quite straightforward, and plain bloody impossible."

"I agree with you, sir," said Goyles stiffly, "but that's what happened."

"I'm not disbelieving you, boy," said the Colonel. "How was he lying when you found him?"

"I didn't actually find him," said Goyles. "Overstrand did that. He says he tried to unearth him. He scraped the sand far enough to see who it was, but I don't think he moved the body. When Byfold and I went up to get him back he was lying, half on his side, half on his face. His hands were in front of him, as if he was trying to scrape his way out. Enough sand had come down on him to pin him, though. He wouldn't have had a chance. He must have died quite quickly."

"He didn't die all that quickly," said the doctor from behind them. "Take a look at his face."

In life Coutoules had not been a particularly handsome little man. Now, in death, his lips were lifted from his teeth in a grimace of pain and his brown eyes, from which the doctor had carefully wiped the sand, were open and staring.

Footsteps sounded in the passage outside and they all got to their feet as Colonel Lavery came in. In fact, Colonel Baird, being a full colonel, was the senior officer, but Colonel Lavery was, by appointment, Senior British Officer in the camp and formalities of that sort were observed.

"Please sit down," said Colonel Lavery. "What—oh, I see. A tunneling casualty."

"Yes," said Colonel Baird. "I expect that's right. But it's not quite as straightforward as that. Goyles, would you tell Colonel Lavery what you just told me."

Goyles repeated his story. It took longer this time, because there were a lot of details which he had to explain to Colonel Lavery which Colonel Baird, as head of the Escape Committee, had understood without explanation.

When he had finished, Colonel Lavery turned to the doctor.

"Can you tell us anything now?" he said. "It might help to clear things up. At the moment, I can't see—"

"Certainly," said Dr. Simmonds. He was an unexcitable Scot who had left a first-class job in Edinburgh to look after the simple ailments of a Lowland regiment in the Western Desert. "This man died of asphyxiation. He's been dead, in my opinion, rather less than twelve hours. Certainly nine or ten. I can't be more precise."

Everybody looked at his watch and did sums.

"Ten o'clock now," said Colonel Baird. "That makes it that he died about eleven o'clock or midnight last night."

"The whole thing is impossible," said Colonel Lavery. "Unless there's been a conspiracy of silence in Hut C—" He looked speculatively at Goyles. "As I understand it, it takes four men to open this trap, and four men to lower it. Will someone tell me how Coutoules got into that tunnel? I'm leaving aside altogether the question of how he got into the hut. So far as I know, at lockup last night, he was in his own room in our senior officers' hut—"

No one found anything to say.

"I'm perfectly aware," went on Colonel Lavery steadily, "that Coutoules was not a popular character. It was, in fact, at your suggestion,

Baird, that he was removed from Hut C and was segregated in a small room in our hut."

Colonel Baird nodded.

"If I might suggest it," he said bluntly, "we're putting the cart before the horse. There's no doubt *how* Coutoules died. Anyone who wasn't used to tunneling, blundering along in the dark—particularly not realizing that the last six feet hadn't been shored up—would be more than likely to bring the roof down on top of himself. I should say that the chances were in favor of it. How he got into the tunnel I know no more than anyone else, but the fact is that he *did* get there—and I expect the truth about it will come to light sooner or later. It usually does. So I suggest we stop worrying about what can't be helped and tackle the immediate problem. What are we going to do with the body?"

"We shall have to tell the Italians," said Colonel Lavery sharply. "We can't keep a death quiet forever—besides we should be putting ourselves hopelessly in the wrong."

"All right," said Colonel Baird. "We hand over the body, I agree. But do we have to say where we found him?"

While Colonel Lavery was thinking this one out Colonel Baird went on.

"Because if so, I'd like to put it on record that we should be making the enemy a present of the only undiscoverable tunnel in the camp."

"I can quite see we don't want to do that," said Colonel Lavery.

"Let me be quite frank about this," said Colonel Baird, "and strictly I ought to turn these two young men out of the room before I say this, but I expect they can be trusted to keep their mouths shut—"

The doctor grunted, and Goyles nodded.

"I don't really visualize this tunnel being used for an escape—not a normal escape. We all know that the British have taken Pantelleria. The Eighth Army will be in Sicily soon—and Italy after that. Suppose the Italians pack up. Have you thought yet what the Germans are going to do—about us, I mean?"

"I've asked myself the question a dozen times," said Colonel Lavery. "I haven't liked any of the answers either," he added.

"All right," said Colonel Baird. "Let's take the obvious answer. The Germans aren't going to let go the sixty thousand prisoners in Italy that it cost them all that sweat and blood to take—not if they can help it. One morning we're going to wake up and find the *Wehrmacht* on these walls, and a train in the station getting up steam to take us all to Krautland. Tell me how much you'd pay, then, to have an absolutely foolproof tunnel waiting and ready?"

"Yes," said Colonel Lavery.

"Not just a rat-hole which a dozen men might squeeze through with luck, but a decent, wooden-lined, three-foot-by-three, guaranteed back door. With proper organization we could empty this camp in one night—

and the British lines might be at Naples by then."

"Yes," said Colonel Lavery again. "You're absolutely right. What do you suggest?"

"I suggest," said Colonel Baird, "that we dig a hole right here and bury him. Let the Italians look for him."

"And what if they find him," said Colonel Lavery, "as they may very well do? Murder's a criminal offense, even in a prisoner-of-war camp. Would there be anything to show that we hadn't suffocated him first and buried him afterward? They know very well he was unpopular in the camp. There have been threats. It wouldn't be too pleasant if they started to hang someone for a murder which we knew had never been committed."

"It's nasty either way," said Colonel Baird.

"There's just one thing about that," said the doctor. "If they examine the body properly they can't maintain that he was suffocated and buried afterward."

"Do you mean the sand in his nose and mouth? There's nothing to show that wasn't put in after death, is there?"

"Have you looked at his hands?" said the doctor. "He was alive when he went under that sand all right. He's pulled one of the nails clean off his right hand and the other three nails nearly off, trying to scratch his way out."

There was a short silence.

"If it comes to that," said Colonel Lavery, "I suppose we might have faked even a detail like that, but—"

"Could I make a suggestion, sir?" said Goyles.

"Certainly."

"Why don't we bury him in *another* tunnel? There's one started in this hut. It isn't, actually, a very good tunnel. It hasn't gone more than about twelve feet and I think it's been a bit lucky to survive so far—"

"You suggest," said Colonel Lavery, "that we put him in this tunnel, pull down some of the roof on top of him and call in the Italians—pretending it's a normal tunneling accident."

"Something like that, sir."

"What do you say about that, Baird?"

"I think it's a damned good scheme," said Colonel Baird. "I don't think this other tunnel's got a hope in hell of getting anywhere. The Committee thought twice about letting them start even. The trap's much too obvious for one thing. If we've got to throw away a tunnel, this is the one to discard."

"All right," said Colonel Lavery. "The less I know about it in my official capacity, the better. I'll leave the details to you."

Chapter 3

Second Interment

1

The Hut A tunnel started from the bathroom.

A square of tiles had been taken up, and the tiles had been cemented onto a wooden tray-shaped frame. The work had been done neatly enough and, in its original state, it had probably made quite a satisfactory cover. Unfortunately it suffered from the frailty of its construction. Daily use had cracked and chipped the edges of the tiles, so that its outline was becoming distressingly apparent to the eye. Also it had developed a slight, but detectable, wobble.

For this, and other, reasons the tunnel had been allotted low priority by the Escape Committee: in particular very little material had been made available for shoring-up. Things had gone well enough while the diggers were actually under the foundations of the hut, but now that they were striking out into the sand of the open compound progress was becoming increasingly difficult. That they had got as far as they had was almost entirely due to the enthusiasm of the tunnel's proprietor and only beget-ter, Brandy Duncan of the Black Watch.

There was another reason for its slow progress, and Brandy expressed this bluntly to Goyles. "They're such a hopeless crowd in this hut," he said. "No bowels."

"I know what you mean," said Goyles.

"They spend their days sunbathing, and their evenings filling up their stamp albums and playing roulette and complaining about the food. I ought to be sick at you for collaring this tunnel, but by God, I'm not. Book a place for me and Andy in your outfit and you can have this tunnel and welcome."

Goyles thanked him and reported back to Colonel Baird. He had known that morale in Hut A was low, but hadn't realized how far it had slipped.

Colonel Baird wasted no time.

"We'll want someone to go down the tunnel and do the actual damage. I think it had better be Byfold—he's the nippiest of you. Get him over here with his tunneling outfit. Duncan and Anderson can open the trap for us. Doctor, will you give Goyles a hand and fetch the body along?"

So, in haste and with no rites, the second interment of Coutoules took place. The watchers were alerted round Hut A. Brandy Duncan and his friend Lieutenant Anderson opened the trap door in the bathroom floor and helped Byfold down with the body. Laboriously it was handed along to the far end of the tunnel.

To Byfold's eye the whole thing looked shockingly makeshift. To start with, the shaft went down a bare seven feet—as opposed to the twenty feet in their tunnel—so that the roof had very little clearance from the surface. So long as they were under the hut, this did not matter because the concrete foundations of the hut themselves formed a roof to the tunnel. The last six or eight feet were a different matter. It was like going along a rabbit hole.

Alone, it would have been tricky. With Coutoules in too it looked both dangerous and impossible.

When the body was at last in a position at the end of the tunnel which resembled, as closely as possible, the position in which it had been found, Byfold crawled back to the shaft for further instructions.

He was running with sweat.

"Now you'll have to fake the accident," said Colonel Baird. "One thing, though, you'll have to take care not to open a hole right up to the top. A partial fall is what we want."

"I don't think that's possible," said Byfold. He was irritated and exhausted and his eyes were full of sand.

"If it can't be done," said Colonel Baird, patiently, "the scheme's a washout. Think, man. If you make a hole that can be seen from the top, a sentry will spot it happening and we'll have Benucci here in five minutes. What do you think he's going to say when his doctors tell him that Coutoules has been dead for twelve hours?"

"Hm," said Byfold. It really hadn't occurred to him before to wonder what the Italians would say. So long as his own tunnel was not in jeopardy he was quite happy.

"I think," said Duncan, diffidently, "that it could be managed. If you were to take one of the uprights from the shaft"—these were about nine feet long: they had come out of the rafters of the theater hut—"I think you could squat down in the safe part of the tunnel and work the end of the wood into the roof. You ought to be able to bring down a good slab that way, without too much danger—"

"Try it that way first," said Baird.

The upright to which Duncan referred was one of four which ran up each corner of the entrance shaft and supported the trap. They were all embedded in the earth at the bottom and screwed into a framework at the top, on which the trap itself rested.

It took a little time to get one out but they did so in the end, and Byfold grasped it in his hand, lancelike, and crawled once more along the tunnel until he was in sight of Coutoules' boot heels. He hoped it was for the last time. He had not loved Coutoules in life; in death, he felt, he was seeing a good deal too much of him.

He propped himself on one elbow, made sure that he was himself still under the firm foundations of the hut, and edged forward the piece of wood which he held.

The roof of the tunnel, which had looked only too ready to collapse, proved, of course, tiresomely difficult to dislodge. He thrust his wooden spear lengthways into it and wriggled it about. A thin dusting of sand fell from the roof and the wood came out and fell with a soft thud, on Coutoules' rump.

Byfold swore and began all over again. He saw that he would have to dig the roof out in a series of steps.

Jab, jab, jab.

His arm was aching, he was sweating all over, and the sand had got into his eyes again.

Why to God do we ever trouble to shore up a tunnel, he thought, if it takes all this trouble to bring it down.

He dug the end of the wood in once more and revered downward. There was a soft, rushing noise, quite unlike anything that had gone before and the air was full of falling sand.

When he raised his head he saw that he had done an almost perfect job. The whole of the roof at the far end of the tunnel had come down. The body was completely buried. There was no daylight showing, but judging by the depth of the fall he guessed that there was very little left between the roof of the cavity and the surface.

He crawled back to the shaft, propped the wooden upright loosely back into position, and climbed out.

Cyriakos Coutoules was reinterred.

2

"I do not understand, Colonel," said Captain Benucci. "You say that this Greek died in the tunnel, but you do not know who was with him."

"I didn't say I didn't know," said Colonel Baird. "I said I wasn't going to tell you."

"And why is it you who reports this to me, and not Colonel Lavery?"

"As you are well aware," said Colonel Baird, "I am in charge of all escaping enterprises in this camp. And if you want to make anything out of it," he added, "go ahead."

"It is not I who will want to make anything out of it," said Captain Benucci. "If a man has been killed it is a matter for criminal process."

"What do you mean—been killed?"

"Been killed or died—what difference for him? He is dead. In any event I suggest that you, by your own admission, are his murderer."

Colonel Baird slowly turned dark red. Then he said, in a voice which he made not even a superficial effort to control, "Will you explain what you mean by that?"

"I take the words from your own mouth. You are the organizer of these childish enterprises. You encourage men to risk their lives in underground burrows and in suicidal attempts to climb the walls. If they fail, as they must, and men get killed, then you are responsible."

"I see," said Colonel Baird. "I thought for a minute you were being personal."

The two men were standing in the bathroom of Hut A. The trap door was open. The body of Coutoules had been recovered and removed. The room seemed to be full of the dark blue uniforms of the carabinieri. Behind Captain Benucci was the chief interpreter, *Tenente* Mordaci, known to the camp as Dracula on account of his gross figure, his large red lips and his habit of wearing a long, silk-lined cloak. With Mordaci was his assistant, Paoli, a youthful, girlish-looking under-lieutenant, who was known as "The Boy" and whose alleged relationship with Mordaci was a source of unfailing ribaldry to the prisoners.

Outside, one party of soldiers was beginning to break down the roof of the tunnel and another was roping off the area. Photographs were being taken.

"You tell me, Colonel," went on Captain Benucci, "that the diggers—the nameless diggers—of this tunnel came to you this morning and reported this matter to me. They say that Coutoules was the last man in the tunnel last night—and must have been pinned down by a fall of sand—unknown to his friends."

"Yes."

"That they became alarmed when they found that Coutoules was missing this morning—reopened the tunnel, and discovered his body."

"Yes," said Colonel Baird again. He felt that the less he said at this juncture the better.

"And Coutoules was a member of this—tunnel-digging gang?"

"Yes, he was."

"Curious. I should not have thought, from what I have observed, that he was of that type."

"Life is full of surprises," said Colonel Baird. "Do you want me any more?"

"Not at the moment," said Captain Benucci.

They hated each other with the instinctive hatred of different sorts of animal.

Colonel Baird walked thoughtfully back to his own quarters. There was something about the way in which the situation was being handled that he did not like at all. It was difficult to put a finger on it. Previously, when an escape attempt had "broken" or had been discovered before it could "break" the Italians had behaved in a different and much more predictable manner. There was a purposefulness about their moves this time, an altogether un-Italian lack of excitement. It almost looked as though what had happened had not come as a complete surprise to them.

Colonel Baird liked it not at all.

3

When Byfold and Goyles got back to their room they found Tony Long sitting at the table. "Hugo and Grim are out too," he explained. "We only got seven days this time. Just petty criminals. What on earth have you been up to while I've been away?"

Goyles and Byfold told him what had happened.

"Thank God Colonel Baird stuck his toes in over our tunnel," said Long. "It should be through in six weeks—less if we hurry. The other scheme's not unpromising either."

He reported the results of his and Baierlein's observations the previous night. "Both cell windows are wide open," he said. "It took two months to do but it's a beautiful job. The stone that holds the bottom of the middle bar has been loosened so that you can slide it right out. The bar then drops away from the top socket and leaves you quite enough room to squeeze through and get out onto the roof. Grim was too hefty, but Hugo and I did it easily. Once up on the roof you need a short wooden ladder. Pick your moment when the gate sentry's in his box, and it would be money for old rope."

"The real difficulty," said Byfold, "would be making sure that we all got put in the cooler at once."

"There's a bigger snag than that," said Goyles. "The first part's all right, but what about the next? We should need all the usual kit—money, food, and so on. How are we going to get it into prison with us?"

The three men formed one of those close prisoner-of-war friendships which, if analyzed, would have been found to be based on community of interests and dissimilarity of character.

Their own accounts of how they came into captivity afford a sufficient commentary.

Roger Byfold was a regular soldier. He had left Sandhurst at about Munich time to join a lancer regiment already under orders for the Middle East. He had been there when war was declared. He was a tankman and a professional soldier and desert warfare had suited him down to the ground. Indeed, he had done very well at it, as the white and purple ribbon on his battledress bore witness, until one day everything went wrong. "Just a normal patrol. Can't help thinking it must have been Friday the thirteenth and I never noticed it. First my wireless went dead. Then I broke a track. Told the rest of the troop to complete the 'recce' and pick me up on the way back. I heard afterward they lost their way and were lucky to get back themselves. Got out and mended the track and found we were in a mine field. First news of this was when we blew the other track off, and half the suspension with it. Nothing much left to do. Waited for the troop all day. When they didn't turn up, we tried to walk back. Got picked up by the Krauts early next morning."

"Bad luck," everyone agreed, "but just the sort of thing one expected in armored warfare."

Henry Goyles was a schoolmaster, the son of a solicitor. He was a good bit the oldest of the three. When war broke out he joined the ranks of a gunner regiment where his precision of thought and speech, his occasional absence of mind, and his large round steel spectacles had earned him the name of "Cuckoo"—a name which had followed him through the army and accompanied him into captivity. He must have been quite a good gunner, because in 1941 he got one of the few and much-coveted commissions into a regular horse artillery regiment, and he reached his battery in time for the Auchinleck offensive. If he was frequently frightened in the course of the next three months he managed to conceal it as well as most, particularly when he could devote his mind to a purely technical problem.

This was eventually his undoing.

"It was rather an advanced sort of O.P.," he explained. "We got there before first light, in Bren carriers, and then everybody who had come with us seemed to fade away. I was just thinking that we were rather out in the blue, and perhaps we ought to pull back a bit, when suddenly I saw a most beautiful target—the type of thing you get on the ranges at Larkhill, but never expect to see in real life. It was a German staff car, which had broken down, just behind a sort of hump. They thought they were hidden, but I could see them all right. A pinpoint target, you understand, with flank observation. Really, a fascinating problem. Being out to one side, you could see the effect of the charge zone very clearly. I bracketed for line, and I bracketed for range and I worked out the angle and the factor and then I put over a beauty—I think it landed on the radiator cap. I had noticed someone come up behind me just before I gave the order to fire, and I turned round and said, 'What about that for a shot?' And," concluded Goyles sadly, "it was a German with a tommy gun."

"Very bad luck," everyone agreed, "but just the sort of thing which was always happening to forward O.P.'s."

Tony Long, the youngest of the three, was a born irregular. He took to any form of Special Service like a duck to water. To look at him you might have thought that he was one of those serious, polite, hard-working, athletic boys who make the best regimental officers. To a certain extent, this was true. What you would never have guessed was that he was at heart a bandit and a killer. He had arrived at Campo 127 after three years of miscellaneous and improbable enterprises.

"The last one really was rather mad," he said. "I landed on the coast of Sicily with one sergeant and a bag of bombs. I had to blow up two railway bridges. Moreover, I did blow them up. Unfortunately, something went wrong on the last one and we brought down a good deal of the bridge on top of ourselves. When I came to, I found the sergeant was dead and I had broken an ankle. I got picked up two nights later."

"Extremely bad luck," everybody agreed. "But what else can you expect if you go about behaving in such an unorthodox way?"

4

"You want to do what?" said Colonel Lavery, surprised for once out of his usual calm.

"Just a precaution, you understand," said Benucci.

"Everybody's fingerprints!"

"We must take everybody's, otherwise the check will not be complete."

"The orderlies too?"

"Everyone," said Benucci firmly.

"I don't think you can do it," said Colonel Lavery. "I don't think the Geneva Convention allows it."

"The Geneva Convention governs the conduct of the captor toward his prisoners of war," agreed Benucci. "In this case it is not a question of prisoners of war. An unexplained death has taken place. Indeed, the matter has ceased to be entirely under my control."

"How do you propose to set about it?"

"It should not take very long. The pads have been prepared and if you will issue the necessary orders, I will have it carried out at roll call this evening."

"I shall report the whole matter to the Protecting Power," said Colonel Lavery.

5

"Really," said Rupert Rolf-Callender to his friends in Hut A. "I mean to say—fingerprints. What next?"

"If you feel so strongly about it, why didn't you refuse?"

"Really, Terence, I couldn't start a brawl."

"If you want my opinion," said Captain the Honorable Peter Perse, "it's all on account of this stupid tunnel. I always told Duncan it would be discovered, and of course it has been, and now there's going to be nothing but unpleasantness, you see if I'm not right."

"I've never known them to behave quite like this before," said Terence Bush. "Usually, they harry the hut a bit when a tunnel's discovered and then forget about it. They haven't done a thing this time except shut up that actual bathroom—they haven't even turned the showers off."

"I don't think they're really worried about the tunnel," said Rolf-Callender. "It was finding that chap in it."

"How did he get there?"

"As a matter of fact, I can tell you that," said Bush. "He was put there. I got it from Chris Martin in Hut C. Apparently Colonel Baird got a lot of them to put up a sort of gym display to cover up carrying the body across and Chris was in it. They put Coutoules on Byfold's back and galloped him across."

"Do you mean to say," said the Honorable Peter with some indignation, "that they simply dumped him on us? Why can't Hut C stick to their own rotten bodies? Here we are, cut down to one bathroom between eighty of us—"

"Shocking."

"What can you expect?" said Rolf-Callender. "Those cloak-and-dagger types are all the same. It isn't as if they'd got a chance in a million of getting anywhere. If they had, one might do something about it. But no one's ever got out of this country yet and no one's ever going to. All that happens is that they dig these footling holes in the ground, which get discovered, and everyone else is made uncomfortable. If they *do* get out they spend about three nights in the open and then get caught and come back and have thirty days in the cooler and think themselves no end of chaps."

"In any case," said the Honorable Peter, "we've only got to sit tight a few more weeks and the Eighth Army will catch up with us. Is anyone going to spin the wheel tonight?"

"Not tonight," said Rolf-Callender. "Have you forgotten? We're rehearsing tonight. We'll use the dining room after supper's been cleared away."

"We shall probably find someone starting another tunnel there," said the Honorable Peter bitterly.

6

Baierlein, Overstrand and Grimsdale were walking round the perimeter of the camp, just inside the trip wire, which guarded a six-foot forbidden zone at the foot of the wall itself. Every fifty yards inside the wire a notice board bore an imaginative piece of English prose which ran, "Passage and demurrage strictly forbidden." If anyone stepped over this wire the sentries shot at him.

Baierlein and Grimsdale were busy reporting to Overstrand the result of their recent imprisonment. Their conclusions were much the same as Long's had been.

"It's easy enough," said Baierlein, "provided you're a stock-size person, to get out onto the roof. If Grim's going to do it, it will mean loosening another bar."

"What about the gap between the roof and the wall?"

"Ten feet," said Baierlein. "You need a short ladder for that bit, but could make it out of the double bedsteads in the cell. They're enormous things—the side pieces are over ten foot long. That isn't the real trouble though—"

"It's the kit," said Grimsdale. "What's the use of getting over the wall if you find yourself, dressed in battledress, with no food and no money and no papers in the middle of Italy?"

"I had wondered," said Baierlein, "if we mightn't arrange to have the stuff brought in to us. I know we shall get thoroughly searched when we go into the cooler, and I agree that it would be unnecessarily risky to try and smuggle much escaping kit in with us. One might get away with money and maps and compasses, but nothing really bulky."

"If we're going cross country we should want some sort of covering— a blanket, or at least an overcoat, and a knapsack to carry hard rations."

"To say nothing of the rations themselves."

"Exactly," said Baierlein. "Well, my idea was, we take in the small stuff hidden on us, and get the orderlies to smuggle the rest in bit by bit, in the food."

"It would need a bloody big apple pie to hide an overcoat in," said Overstrand.

They paced on for some minutes and had made a complete circuit of the camp before Overstrand spoke again.

"I've been thinking," he said, "that we ought to look for something more immediate."

Neither of the others said anything.

"I've been in nearly two years," went on Overstrand, "and that's one hell of a sight too long. Now we've had this trouble over the Hut C tunnel I don't see it going ahead very fast. They may decide to seal it up altogether for a bit. There are too many snags in this cooler business to make it worth going flat out for—that's my view, anyway. I think we ought to try something more straightforward and less—well, less fiddling."

Baierlein and Grimsdale looked worried. They were both genuinely fond of Overstrand, but they knew that he was apt to be unreliable where his emotions were involved.

"Had you anything particular in mind?" said Baierlein.

"As a matter of fact, I had," said Overstrand. It's something that Desmond Foster is doing—"

"He can't be starting another tunnel already."

"It isn't exactly a tunnel. It's top secret, of course, but he couldn't mind my telling you two. This is how it goes—"

7

"Five women," said Rupert Rolf-Callender, "and twelve men. Thirteen, if you count Flush."

"Was he a man?"

"It says 'Flush—a spaniel.' "

"How are we going to manage about Flush?"

"First things first," said Rolf-Callender. "We'll start with the girls. Peter, you'll have to do Elizabeth."

"Must I?"

"Certainly you must. The part's made for you."

"Why do I always have to do girls?"

"To be quite honest," said Rolf-Callender kindly, "I don't know. It isn't as if you were pretty, in any sense of the word, and the trouble we had keeping the backs of your legs shaved for the run of *Bitter Sweet* is a thing I prefer to forget. Nor is your voice precisely virginal. It's something to do with the bones in your face—"

"Who's going to do the father?"

"I think we shall have to ask Abercrowther."

"You can't have a Mr. Barrett with a Scots accent."

"We shall have to put up with it. He's a damned good actor. Do you remember how good he was in the Monty Woolley part in *The Man Who Came to Dinner?*"

"All right, put him down. Where is he, by the way?"

"He's dining out tonight," said Bush. "What are you going to do, Rupert?"

"I rather thought I'd try Robert Browning."

"My God, Rupert, do you mean to say I've got to make love to you *again?*"

"You did it very nicely last time," said Rolf-Callender complacently. "Now all these brothers—Octavius and Septimus and so on. They're really only stooges. We'd better let the Adjutant do one of them, then he'll make no trouble about letting us have the theater hut for rehearsals."

"Whatever happens," said Bush, "we've got one absolutely guaranteed laugh here." He was turning over the pages of the acting edition.

"What's that?"

"At the beginning of Act III. 'Elizabeth (rapturously) "Italy! Oh, it's hard to take in even the bare possibility of going there. My promised land, Doctor, which I never thought to see otherwise than in dreams." ' "

"That should bring the house down," agreed Rolf-Callender.

Chapter 4

The Scapegoat

1

"Dr. Simmonds," said Benucci, "you are a man of experience."

"That would depend on what you mean by experience."

"Medical experience."

"I should say so, yes."

"You are not a regular military doctor."

"Oh, no. Certainly not."

"You are a civilian doctor. You hold the degree of F.R.C.S."

"It's not exactly a degree," said Dr. Simmonds cautiously. "Anyway, I expect it's in my record somewhere. What's it all about?"

They were in the camp Commandant's office. Besides Benucci, the chief interpreter and Dr. Simmonds there was a fourth party present, a thin civilian in black coat and striped trousers, with that neat beard which appears to be the hallmark of professional eminence in Latin countries.

"I must introduce Professor Di Buonanvilla of the medical faculty of the University of Florence."

The professor rose to his feet and bowed. Dr. Simmonds half got up, made an indeterminate noise, and sat down again.

"It is because we wish to proceed correctly in this," said Captain Benucci smoothly, "that I have afforded you—Dr. Simmonds—this opportunity of examining the body of Lieutenant Coutoules. Also because I understand that you were the best qualified in the camp to make this examination."

"Very good of you," said Dr. Simmonds. He was not quite sure what a professor in the faculty of medicine did. "If this gentleman is a practicing doctor, I have no doubt that his conclusions will be the same as my own."

"No doubt," said Benucci. "That is exactly what we wish to establish. I should perhaps have explained that the professor is consultant to the police force at Florence. It is for his experience in this type of work that we have asked him to assist us. He does not speak English himself but I will ask Lieutenant Mordaci to read you a translation of the statement he has prepared. If there are any questions you wish to ask, pray use the services of the interpreter."

Mordaci read from the statement in front of him. It was a long statement. It started with a description of the body of Coutoules as the professor had seen it at two o'clock on the afternoon of its discovery. It contained some sound observations on rigor mortis, post-mortem bruising and the tendency of blood to drain outward from the center of a corpse after death. Dr. Simmonds, who had the essential disinterested honesty of the expert, found it hard to disagree with any of its conclusions. These were: that Coutoules had died some time one side or the other of midnight, but not earlier than nine o'clock on the previous evening; that death had been due to asphyxiation; and that the body had been moved and handled after death.

"Have you any comments to make, Doctor?" asked Benucci, when the statement had finished.

For form's sake Dr. Simmonds asked a few questions and Mordaci translated them, and retranslated the professor's answers. He asked the professor if he had noticed a bruise on the back of Coutoules' neck. The professor had noticed it. He suggested it might have been made by a stone in the fall of sand. Dr. Simmonds agreed that it might. It was quite clear to him that the professor knew his job—as he would be likely to do if he was, in fact, a police consultant.

"Well, Doctor," said Benucci again, at the end of it, "what are your conclusions?"

"I'm not sure that I follow you."

"It seems plain to you that Coutoules was moved after death?"

"That's a matter of argument and inference. Not a matter of fact."

"If we accept it," said Benucci, "is it not logical to surmise that Coutoules was smothered first, and placed in the tunnel afterward, in order to conceal the truth about his murder—and his murderers?"

"You mean that you think he was killed in one of the huts and put in the tunnel afterward?"

"It is not a question of thinking," said Benucci, in an ill-natured parody of the doctor's professional manner. "It is a question of evidence."

"But that's absurd," said Dr. Simmonds. "Did you look at his hands?"

"Not particularly."

"He must have died under the sand. Why, he'd pulled half his nails off trying to claw his way out."

The last few exchanges had been in English. The professor had clearly understood nothing.

"Ask *him*," said Dr. Simmonds.

There was an awkward moment of silence while Mordaci looked at his senior officer for guidance.

"Put the question, Lieutenant," said Benucci evenly.

Mordaci said something in Italian.

Dr. Simmonds did not listen to the answer. He was looking at the professor's face. His expression was enlightening. He started to say something, then changed his mind; started a second sentence, and broke off in the middle of it.

Benucci said, "The professor says that he does not attach any particular significance to the state of Coutoules' hands."

2

The Escape Committee met in Colonel Baird's room. Baird sat on the only chair: the other two members of the committee sat on his bed. They were Colonel Stanislaus Shore of the U.S. Air Force and Commander Oxey of the Royal Navy. No one had been able to discover by exactly what administrative muddle these two had been sent to a camp for British Army officers, but everyone was very glad to have them. Colonel Shore, in particular, was a three-dimensional character in his own right. He was the only prisoner of war in Italy who had ever forced an officer of carabinieri to carry his luggage for him to the station. The fact that he was drunk at the time had detracted nothing from the performance.

It was Colonel Shore who was speaking.

"I certainly find it difficult to figure out exactly what they're up to," he said. "They've never made a fuss like this before over a dead body. You remember when they shot Colley and his two friends when they tried to rush the gate—we didn't hear anything more about *them*, did we? They were buried and forgotten inside a week. Forgotten by the Italians, I mean. I suppose someone's got the facts notched up somewhere to sort out after the armistice."

"Or those men who jumped the train—" said Commander Oxey.

"I think this is a little different," said Colonel Baird. "Those others were all killed escaping. For some reason the Italians refuse to be convinced that Coutoules was."

"That doctor from Florence," said Shore, "and the fingerprinting and all those photographs they've been taking around the dig. Maybe I've got a suspicious mind, but the whole thing's beginning to look to me like the beginning of a frame-up. It has the smell of one. They want to pin the murder onto someone and I don't believe they're fussy who they choose."

"Who *did* kill Coutoules?" asked Oxey.

This direct naval question produced a silence.

"I'm damned if I know," said Colonel Baird. "On the face of it, the thing's impossible. The only sort of solution that holds any water is that he was knocked off sometime that evening in Hut C, and dumped in the tunnel."

"If that's so," said Shore, "an awful lot of people are telling an awful lot of lies."

"It might be a good thing, to find out," said Oxey. "We don't want the wrong person hanged."

3

"Now, Captain Byfold," said Benucci, "I should strongly advise you to speak the truth."

"I doubt if you'd recognize it if you heard it," said Byfold. Nevertheless, he was neither as comfortable nor as confident as he sounded. He was in the camp Commandant's office. The Commandant, Captain Benucci and Lieutenant Mordaci were seated. Since there were only three chairs in the room it followed that the rest of those present—Captain Byfold, Under-Lieutenant Paoli, two camp guards and three or four carabinieri—were standing. They seemed to have been standing for a long time. Byfold wondered what would happen if he suddenly sat down on the floor.

"Were you a member of the party who were engaged in digging a tunnel from the bathroom in Hut A?"

"As I have said a dozen times before, that's not a question I can be made to answer."

"If it was simply a matter of escaping, no. This is a question of murder."

"Who says that it is murder?"

"The facts say so. For the last time, Captain Byfold, did you work in that tunnel?"

"For the last time, I refuse to say."

"Are you aware that your fingerprints—and only yours—have been found in several places on one of the pieces of wood which formed the upright of the framework in the shaft of that tunnel?"

"If you say so."

"I do say so. A piece of wood, Captain Byfold, which formed—I use the past tense—which formed one of the uprights. It had been removed from the framework of the shaft, and very carelessly replaced. It had plainly been put to some use in the tunnel."

"Very possible," said Byfold wearily. "Woodwork is used in a tunnel you know. It has a variety of uses—"

"A variety of uses." Benucci smiled. It was not a very pleasant smile. "Might I inform you also—I do not wish it to be said at some future time that we have concealed anything from you—might I therefore inform you that photographs taken in the tunnel show a number of marks in the roof—and that these marks have been measured and match exactly that piece of wood to which I refer. What do you deduce from that, Captain Byfold?"

"You tell me."

"I suggest that the wood was used to bring down the tunnel on Coutoules—while he was, perhaps, unconscious—"

"That's a perfectly filthy suggestion."

The Commandant said something, and Mordaci translated. Byfold gathered that the Commandant was asking what his answer had been. He therefore said slowly and loudly in his best Italian, "All that has been suggested is quite untrue." The Commandant looked up at him for a moment, but said nothing. He seemed to be almost asleep.

"You still refuse to admit," went on Benucci, "that you were a member of this tunnel gang?"

"It's obviously not much use denying it," said Byfold. "You seem to have made up your minds about it. I suppose it hasn't occurred to you that I don't even live in that hut."

"Indeed," said Benucci—"and you never visit it either—after dark?"

Byfold had nothing to say to this. It seemed silly to say that he had visited the hut once only, after dark, in order to play a rubber of bridge. Also he had been afforded a sudden glimpse of the care with which the case against him was being constructed—a fractional lifting of the curtain—and it gave him a cold feeling in the pit of his stomach.

"You must not imagine we are blind, Captain," went on Benucci. "Because we do not always take action, it does not mean that our sentries have not got eyes—and tongues."

The Commandant asked a question and Mordaci translated.

"The Commandant asks if you were a friend of Coutoules."

"No. Certainly not. I hardly knew him."

"Then you disliked him?"

"I didn't dislike him—I hadn't much time for him."

Mordaci did his best with this idiom and the Commandant nodded, and asked another question.

"Why was Coutoules disliked?"

Byfold who had seen this one coming answered it more or less truthfully. "It was thought that he had been giving away information about the prisoners to the authorities—to you." Mordaci again translated and Byfold was interested to see that the Commandant looked genuinely surprised. Benucci remained impassive. Either the suggestion was not news to him or possibly he had a better command of his face.

"Thank you," he said. "That is all, Captain Byfold." He motioned with his hand and one of the carabinieri threw open the door. As the two guards hustled him out Byfold saw Benucci lean across and say something to the Commandant. He seemed to be pleased with himself. The Commandant had relapsed into a stupor.

4

Colonel Lavery refrained from saying "I told you so" when Colonel Baird reported to him that evening.

"They seem to be making a dead set at Byfold," he said. "It's easy to be wise after the event, but if I'd thought they were going to push the case so hard I'd have taken some elementary precautions."

"I don't think it's just Byfold," said Colonel Lavery. "I think the truth of the matter is that they want a scapegoat."

Baird said, with unusual bitterness, "Since when have they become so fussy about a death? And I don't only mean escaping. You remember last winter when the Red Cross parcels didn't arrive for two months and we had to live on a minus quantity of Italian rations. How many prisoners did we lose then, from starvation and near starvation? And young Collingwood, with blood poisoning, that they wouldn't even let a doctor look at, until it was too late. If they want to investigate anything let them start on that."

"I expect that the approach of the British Army is making them progressively more tenderhearted," said Colonel Lavery. "What are you proposing to do now?"

"I suggest we wait and see if the case against Byfold comes to anything. It may be just bluff. Something for the record, as you suggest. Meanwhile we push on as fast as possible with tunnel C."

Colonel Lavery looked anxiously at the homemade calendar on the wall. It said "July 5th."

"How soon do you think you can be ready?"

"It isn't just a question of digging," said Baird. "If that's all it was we'd have nonstop shifts and be out inside a week. It's the shoring-up of the tunnel, and above all, the old, old problem of getting rid of the sand. I've got an idea about that. If it comes off we might be out in just over three weeks—say twenty-five days."

"I hope you're right," said Colonel Lavery, "because if my reading of the situation is correct, that could be all the time we're going to get."

5

"Life," said Rupert Rolf-Callender, "is getting perfectly intolerable."

"Grim," agreed Terence Bush.

"They'll be asking us for another bed board soon."

"It'll be a nice change if they ask for it," said Rolf-Callender. "Last time they just took it. I can't lie on my bed now without bits of me sagging through the boards. I feel like a lot of shopping in a string bag."

"You look perfectly disgusting," agreed the Honorable Peter Perse who slept underneath him. "There's another of those damned penguins."

Through the open door of their room in Hut A they watched in disapproving silence as a large subaltern—a stranger, from Hut C—waddled down the passage. Waddled is the exact description of his gait, since he seemed to find his legs unnaturally heavy, and lifted them one after the other with just the tentative deliberation of a young penguin learning to walk. The ends of his long drill trousers were tied tightly round his ankles, and the calves of his legs seemed to be suffering from a form of shifting elephantiasis.

"Where does he put the sand?" asked Bush, when this remarkable figure had passed out of sight.

"In *our* tunnel," said Rolf-Callender.

"What?"

"It's a fact. The Eyeties have posted a sentry on the outside end, but they just sealed down the bathroom and left it. The bright boys have got the trap open again and are filling the tunnel up from this end."

"Do you mean to say," said Bush, "that those types from Hut C are digging sand out of *their* tunnel and putting it into *our* tunnel?"

"It's all very well talking about *our* tunnel," said the Honorable Peter, who was a fair-minded man, and also enjoyed provoking people. "I can't remember you doing much about it when it was actually being dug."

"Maybe not," said Bush, "but if this caper is discovered—God, there's another of those penguins—" he got up and shut the door pointedly—"if it is discovered, it's this hut that's going to suffer. With Benucci in his present frame of mind I can see him shutting off the water *and* the electric light."

The others agreed that this was highly possible.

6

"We're definitely interested," said Overstrand to Desmond Foster, "but we'd like to know a little more about it first."

"Particularly that bit about the lights," said Baierlein.

"All right. You know Tim Meynell?"

"The Sewer Rat?"

"That's him." They referred to an enthusiast from the Royal Engineers who had dug a way for himself from the camp latrine into the main sewer and had propelled himself along it on an inflated rubber mattress in a number of indescribable journeys of exploration. He had never succeeded in reaching the open and the only result so far of his pioneer work had been that his friends ostentatiously walked upwind of him.

"Well, he went down last week to have another look at the main pipe—he's got an idea of forcing a grating inside the Italian quarters—and he reckons he was just about here—" Foster demonstrated on a plan of the camp which he had drawn—"when he suddenly ran into this new electric cable."

"New?"

"Oh, definitely. He'd been that way two months before, and it wasn't the sort of thing you could miss seeing. A great insulated cable, obviously new."

"That sounds interesting," said Overstrand. "You think—"

"Well, it's pretty obvious, isn't it? Between the time he was down before, and that time, those four chaps got away over the wall by fusing the lights. You know how it was done."

"They cut the overhead wire with a pair of shears on a stick, didn't they?"

"Yes. And it's hard for them to guard against that sort of thing. There are too many places where you can get at the overhead wire—from the roof of the theater for one, or anywhere along the south wall, if you're prepared to take a bit of a chance on it—or from the cooler. Obviously, if they wanted to prevent it happening again, either they had to change all the overhead wiring or else—"

"Or else," said Overstrand bitterly, "or else, like the triple bastards they are, they might install an alternative *underground* wiring to all the sentry boxes, so that the next lot who tried to fuse the lights and rush the wall would only fuse *one* of the systems—the other would come into operation, and the results would be sticky."

"Just the sort of clever, slightly sadistic, thing Benucci would think up," agreed Baierlein. "It's got his signature all over it."

"And you think that this cable is the alternative system?"

"It looks like it, doesn't it?" said Foster. "It was put in a few weeks after the last attempts, and you can see from its direction—" he demonstrated again on the plan—"it runs out from the main toward the outer wall. I don't see what else it can be."

Overstrand and Baierlein turned this over for some time in silence. They were walking with Desmond Foster round the perimeter, since this offered the only chance of complete privacy to conspirators.

"The idea being, I take it," said Overstrand, "to cut *both* systems at the vital moment."

"Yes."

"I think it sounds rather hopeful," said Baierlein. "It's got just that element of the unlikely that brings a scheme off. Have you thought about the ladders yet?"

Foster looked the least bit embarrassed.

"As a matter of fact we have," he said, "only you must most solemnly promise not to say a word about it to anyone. There's going to be a certain amount of feeling about this, when it's found out, but I don't see what we could have done. There simply wasn't another piece of wood in the camp of the right length."

"Of course, we won't say anything," said Baierlein. "What's it all about? You sound as if you've robbed a church."

"Well, it's not quite as bad as that," said Foster. "I'll tell you."

7

"Are you coming out for a kickabout this afternoon?" said Tag Burchnall. "We thought we might start with a scrum practice and have a pickup game afterward."

"I hope there's not going to be any nonsense about allowing baseball on the rugger pitch," said Rollo Betts-Hanger. "I hear the sports committee have been approached."

"Baseball. Surely we haven't sunk to that."

"I don't know," said Betts-Hanger. "It's quite an interesting game when you look into it. People in America get quite keen on it, I believe."

"I've no objection to them playing baseball, as long as they don't do it on the rugger pitch."

"Someone was arguing," said Billy Moxhay, "that July wasn't the right month for rugger. Perfect nonsense, I thought. Rugger's an all-the-year-round game. As I pointed out, the only reason chaps don't play rugger during the summer in England is because the ground's too hard. Here the ground's hard all the time, so it makes no difference."

"Quite right," said Burchnall. "Has anyone seen Jerry—"

At this moment the door burst open and Jerry Parsons arrived at a gallop. His face was red and he appeared to have lost his voice. His friends stared at him in amazement.

"I say," he said at last. "Do you know what?"

"End of the war?"

"Revolution in Italy?"

"Extra issue of Red Cross parcels?"

"No, I say, this is serious," said Parsons. "They've simply gone and pinched them—"

"Pinched what?"

"The rugger posts."

A horror-struck silence was broken by Burchnall.

"This is the final, ultimate limit," he said. "They can't do it. I've a good mind to go straight to the S.B.O."

8

At about five o'clock that afternoon—the fifth of July—a garment of comparative peace lay over the camp. The sun still held much of its noon power and most of the prisoners were lying on their beds in their huts or toasting themselves quietly in the open.

A jazz band was practicing in the theater hut, and a lethargic class was being lectured to in the open space between Huts D and E on the logistic problems involved in Hannibal's campaigns.

Even the sentries seemed to feel the weight of the afternoon and they were dozing as openly as they dared on their platform.

The history don was lying back in his deck chair and wishing that he could have been spending the afternoon in a punt on the Cherwell. He was watching, with half his attention, a large covered lorry of the Italian Army type, which had stopped in the road outside the main gate and was now maneuvering backward and forward in an apparent endeavor to turn in the narrowest part of the road.

It had got halfway round now and was facing directly toward the outer gate.

It started to move.

The sentries on both gates ran forward and threw the gates open. The van accelerated.

A towel whisked out of a window. The professor jumped to his feet and dropped his book.

The van was inside the camp now, and coming on fast.

In one of the end rooms in Hut C a bell rang three times urgently. Four men left their bunks with a jump and disappeared through the door. As the last of them reached the kitchen they could hear the Italian Army lorry squealing to a stop outside, and a high-pitched scream of orders as the hidden carabinieri leaped from the back of it.

"They'll have to take their chance," said the leader of the four, and as he spoke the stove was already on its way down.

There was a thumping of feet outside the hut and the passage door burst open.

The stove was back in position now and one of the men was doing some quick work with a broom.

"We shan't be able to get out of here," said the leader. "Pretend to be hanging up clothes—and for God's sake, Peter, push that wire further down inside your shirt. I can see the end of it from here."

There was a second of silence, followed by a mutter of Italian voices, among them Benucci's.

"They're in Goyles' room."

"Don't whisper," said the leader, "and try to look as if you were auctioning it."

There was another silence, and they heard Byfold's voice.

"I demand to be taken to Colonel Lavery."

"I fear that Colonel Lavery has no jurisdiction in this case."

"Then I protest."

"You may make your protest to the criminal court that tries your case." Benucci's voice had lost a lot of its suavity. He sounded vindictive and triumphant.

There was a further stamping of feet. The hut door slammed and the lorry drove away.

Chapter 5
Goyles Is Given a Job

1

At ten o'clock on the morning following Byfold's arrest Goyles knocked on the door of Colonel Baird's room and was asked to come in. When he saw that Colonel Shore and Commander Oxey were there, he apologized and prepared to back out.

"Come right in," said Colonel Baird. "This isn't a committee meeting. Have you got some news for us?"

"That's what I wanted to ask you, sir," said Goyles. "Have you heard anything more about Byfold?"

"Not a thing. Just a typical Italian trick." He slapped angrily at a fat black fly on the wall. "They might have been kidnapping him, not arresting him, the way they went about it."

"I expect they thought there would be a riot if they walked in and took him," suggested Commander Oxey.

"Might have been, at that," said Colonel Shore.

"What's the worst they can do to him?" asked Goyles, putting into words for the first time something that had been worrying him all night.

"They can't try him, can they—he's a prisoner of war?"

"I wouldn't be too sure about that," said Baird. "I remember a case in one of our camps—it happened in the prison cage at Asmara, when I was temporarily in charge of it—a lot of real, dyed-in-the-wool, last-ditch Nazis got the idea that one of the other prisoners was a traitor. I don't know if he really was, or if it was just that he didn't say 'Heil Hitler' smartly enough when spoken to. Anyway, they ganged up on him, and one night, after lights out, they held a set-piece trial and found him guilty, and strung him up. They didn't even pretend to be sorry about it—told everybody what they'd done."

"What happened to them?"

"The three ringleaders were shot," said Baird shortly.

"I see," said Goyles. A sudden, quite terrifying, idea had occurred to him which he took a good deal of pains to suppress.

"I'm afraid," went on Baird, "if they convince themselves that they've got a good case, there's no doubt they could—well, they could make things very sticky for Byfold."

"Even though they know he didn't do it?"

"*We* know he didn't," said Baird. "And if the worst comes to worst we could tell them the truth. But why should they believe us even then? We might have been making the whole thing up to save Byfold's skin."

"Yes," said Goyles. "And, of course, we'd lose the tunnel—"

"It wasn't only the tunnel I was thinking of," said Baird. "I think it's a good tunnel, and it might be a very useful tunnel. But if it came to a direct showdown—tunnel or Byfold—I guess I know which way we'd vote. But it isn't. We could lose both of them, quite easily, if we played this wrong."

"There's only one possible thing to do," said Commander Oxey. "To my mind, it's clear as day. We've got to find out what actually happened, who killed Coutoules, and why and where—and how his body got in that tunnel."

Colonel Baird turned to Goyles.

"Would you like to take that on?" he asked.

Goyles looked considerably startled.

"The Committee would back you, of course. It's not the sort of thing they could very well undertake officially. You're a friend of Byfold. It would be quite a reasonable assignment for you. We'll give it out that anyone who's got any information about Coutoules—where they saw him last—whether they noticed anything suspicious—that sort of thing—is to contact you."

"Yes—but," said Goyles. He was trying hard to see himself in the role of special investigator. "Of course, I'll do anything I can," he added, "only don't hope for too much. Have you got any general idea about it at all? I mean it seems quite crazy."

"On the face of it," said Colonel Shore, "it *is* crazy. That's what ought to make it easy to solve. If it was ordinary, there might be half a dozen solutions, and you could never be sure that you'd get hold of the right one. With a crazy problem like this, if you can find *any solution at all*, it *must* be the right one."

"Something in that," said Commander Oxey. He had a deep respect for the American's intellect—a respect based subconsciously on the fact that Colonel Shore looked like Gary Cooper, who was the only American film star of whom the Commander approved.

"We were talking about it when you came in," said Baird. "We hadn't got very far, but for what it's worth you can have it. We thought that the general idea—the shape of the thing—was that Coutoules was an informer. We thought that either there were people in the camp who knew a lot more about this than we did, or else—and it would amount to the same thing in the end—who *thought* they knew a lot more than we did. They get together—it must have been four of them at least—and kill Coutoules quietly—by tying a wet towel over his face, or holding his head in a pillow or something of the sort. Then they do more or less what we did in the other tunnel—open it up, drag him down, and pull a bit of the roof down on top of him—having first filled his mouth and nose with sand."

"What about what the doctor said—about him having been alive under the sand, and trying to scratch his way out?"

"It's not a pretty idea at all," said Baird. "But having gone that far is there any reason they shouldn't have gone a bit further, and faked that detail too after he was dead?"

"I suppose not," said Goyles doubtfully. "I take it this means they must have been people out of our hut."

"Not necessarily. They must have known how the tunnel worked, but they needn't necessarily have been from the hut itself. People wander in and out of each other's huts pretty freely, don't they, till lockup time?"

"Do you know," said Goyles, diffidently but firmly, "I don't believe it."

Colonel Baird and Commander Oxey looked quietly up at him and Colonel Shore said, "No? Tell us why, then."

"It just doesn't seem to me to be the sort of thing that could have happened, sir. I don't believe that any group of people could have got Coutoules off somewhere, and killed him, and taken him into Hut C, and put him down the tunnel, and—done all the other things you mentioned, sir—without *someone* knowing about it. Why, you can't blow your nose in this camp without at least three people coming along in the course of the day and saying how sorry they are to hear you've got a cold. As for murdering someone and hiding the body—it's just not on."

"Right," said Baird. He didn't sound annoyed, only interested. "What's your idea?"

"I haven't got an idea yet," said Goyles, "but I've got a question that I think wants answering. It seems to have escaped notice in the general excitement, but it's just this. Why wasn't Coutoules missed on roll call that morning?"

This took a moment or two to sink in. Then Colonel Shore slapped his leg softly and said, "That's quite a point, isn't it?"

"Yes," said Commander Oxey. "Why wasn't he missed? What happened on roll call that morning in our hut? You've got the room next to him, Baird."

"I'm trying to think," said Baird. "So far as I can remember it was an ordinary morning roll call. They must have been a little late, because I remember I was up and dressed and I don't get out of my bed a minute before a quarter past eight."

"I think they were a bit late, that morning," agreed Commander Oxey. "I'd finished my daily dozen—as often as not they open the door when I'm in the middle of them."

"I'm always asleep anyway," said Colonel Shore. "So I can't help you."

"Well, say they arrived at twenty to nine. It was the little boy—Paoli—who was taking roll call. He looked in my room, said 'Good morning' or something like that—he had a carib with him, I think, but the carib didn't come in. Then—by God, you're absolutely right—*they didn't go into Coutoules' room at all*. I didn't consciously notice it at the time, but I'm sure you're right. They just turned about and marched off down the passage."

"Coutoules had the room next door, didn't he?" said Goyles. "That's the last one in the passage."

"That's right. We two were always the last to be inspected."

"It's funny either way," said Colonel Shore. "If your recollection's right, it's odd enough that they didn't look in his room on that one particular morning—"

"They might have skipped it because they were late—"

"Well, they might. On the other hand if Baird is wrong—it's some days ago, and he might have been thinking of some different morning—well, it's funnier still. If they deliberately refrained from looking in Coutoules' room on that one morning, then either they did the thing themselves, or they were in the know about it being done. It's quite a thought, isn't it? Suppose Coutoules *was* an informer, but his bosses were finished with him. He wouldn't be much use to them after he'd been spotted. And suppose there was another reason for them not persevering with Coutoules—because they'd got a second, *unsuspected* informer in the camp. So what happens? A party of prisoners decide that it's time Coutoules was liquidated for his treachery. The second informer tells the Italians. The Italians say, 'Splendid. Suits us. So far as we're concerned he's safer dead.' So they just sit back and let it happen. The only detail they forgot was that they weren't supposed to know about it at roll call next morning. It was quite an easy thing to forget. None of us remembered it until a minute ago."

"Yes," said Baird. "Yes. But do you see what it *means*? It means that the Italians must know all about the Hut C tunnel."

The three men looked at the New Zealander. It was Goyles who spoke first.

"Not necessarily, sir. If Colonel Shore is right, they might have known that Coutoules was going to be killed that night, but they might not have known where he was going to be put."

"Take it a step further," said Commander Oxey. "They might even have known that he was going to be put into *a* tunnel, without their informer knowing which tunnel, or exactly where the tunnel was, or how it worked."

"That does explain one thing," said Baird. "I always thought they were being unnaturally smart about the way they tackled the Hut A tunnel. It wasn't like them at all. All that photographing and fingerprinting. But if they knew Coutoules was going to be murdered and planted in some tunnel or other for them to find, it makes much better sense. They'd have had the whole procedure worked out in advance."

"Duns Scotus and the Medieval Schoolmen," observed Colonel Shore unexpectedly, "used to devote many hours to arguing the question of how many angels could balance on the point of a needle. As they were unable to decide either on the size of the needle or on the amount of parking space required by an angel, no very exact conclusion was ever arrived at."

"Moral appreciated," said Baird. "If you're willing to take this thing on, Goyles, the first thing you'll have to do is to ferret about and find out who saw Coutoules last that evening. Anything else that might be helpful, too, of course."

"I can take what steps I like?"

"You've got carte blanche, so far as we're concerned. And we'll give you any help we can. The first thing, I suggest, is that we'll put it round the grapevine that anyone with information should see you. There's one other thing. If you should chance on anything—" Colonel Baird paused, and looked at his two committeemen—"particularly anything that affects the security of the escape arrangements, we should like to know about it first."

"Not the S.B.O.?"

"We shall pass it all on to Colonel Lavery, of course," said Baird. "We'd just like to have first cut at it, that's all."

Goyles went straight back to his own room, which was empty, and lay down on his bunk with a pillow behind his shoulders, an attitude which he normally found helpful to thought.

He had quite a lot to think about.

He realized that he was in a position which, as a reader of detective novels, he had often imagined himself occupying without ever really expecting to do so. He had been invited to investigate a murder.

The position was, in many ways, a remarkable one.

His suspects, although numerous, were closely gathered together, within the walls of one small piece of the earth's surface, measuring not more than two hundred yards in any direction. It was a community, moreover, which was relatively without privacy. What he had said to the Escape Committee on this point had been exaggerated, but not greatly. The inmates of a camp like this really did know everything about everybody else: partly because they came of a class which is trained to be observant and partly because they had plenty of spare time in which to observe. One result of this was commonplace. The most closely guarded escape plans had a disconcerting habit of becoming common property overnight.

Again, it was an investigation with no possibility of competition from the regular police force. Indeed, any official action which there might be would be likely to prove unhelpful, if not actually hostile.

Lastly, and above all, Goyles was aware that he was now deputy of the most powerful authority in the camp. It was true that Colonel Lavery as S.B.O. was the administrative head, and his regime in normal matters was accepted without undue demur. On the other hand, the twenty-five or thirty per cent of the prisoners who were actively engaged in escaping owed a strong, almost a fanatical allegiance to their own elected committee. It was powerful because it was practical. Even its sanctions were practical. There had been a prisoner who had voiced too loudly and too often his dissatisfaction at having to give up a bed board for the lining of a tunnel. One day he had found himself without any bed at all. His protests had been quite unavailing and he had slept on the floor for a week, until space could be found for him in a new room.

Goyles was sure, therefore, that any help he might require would be forthcoming to the limit of human endeavor.

Nevertheless, he was far from sure as to what exactly his first move ought to be. He lay on his bunk and devoted his quite considerable mental powers to the problem. He imagined that the soundest plan was always to begin at the beginning. Accordingly he turned his thoughts to the evening of July 1st, and ran through in detail, first his own movements, then the movements of everyone whom he had encountered; lastly, anything that he had heard of the movements of others.

He meditated until the lunch bugle blew.

It was that evening that his first informant appeared. He was a subaltern in the Royal Engineers: his name was Tim Meynell, and his subterranean activities, as has already been mentioned, had gained him the unkind nickname of the Sewer Rat. He was a thin, stringy, serious person, with the faraway look in his eyes of one who works with blind forces and knows that the cube root of the function of a power of seven may make all the difference between inertia and total oblivion.

"I say," he said. "I believe you are the person who wants to know about anything out of the way which anyone has seen or heard. Is that right?"

"Well," said Goyles. "In a way I suppose it is. Come for a walk."

They started on a circuit of the camp.

"I don't know if this is going to be any good to you—"

"Any detail, however small," said Goyles, feeling like all detectives of fiction rolled into one.

"It isn't anything really to do with the evening Coutoules disappeared, but it was so funny, I thought you might like to hear it. It was about four weeks ago. I was down the main drain—it goes along about ten yards this side of that path there—" he pointed to the path which bisected the camp and ran out at the main gate—"I must have got a good way along it—further than the dividing wire, I should think—"

"You must have been almost under the carabinieri quarters."

"Yes, I think I must have been. I was under some sort of living quarters—you could see the inlet pipes and so on—"

"If you're right about where the drain runs, it must have been the Italian huts," said Goyles. "It's just playing fields this side of the wire."

"Yes. Well, that's what made it so funny."

"What was funny?"

"I could hear voices—you can, sometimes, you know, quite a long way underground. They carry along the pipes—"

"What was funny about that?"

"One of them was speaking English."

"It might have been Benucci," suggested Goyles.

"Oh, no, it wasn't Benucci's sort of voice at all. You can always tell an Italian speaking English, however good he is. This was quite different."

"Might it have been Coutoules?"

"Well, that did occur to me, but I don't think so. As a matter of fact, although I couldn't hear the words, the sort of general rhythm of them and the accent was quite plain."

"Well," said Goyles.

Meynell looked unhappy.

"I thought," he said, "that it sounded like a Colonial. Either that or an American."

"I see," said Goyles thoughtfully. "Well, thanks for telling me."

Later that evening Baierlein found time for a word with him.

"I can't tell you much," he said, "about what actually happened on that night, because, as you know, I was in jail, with Grim and Tony, for my sins. But there's one thing which did strike me—I may be making a mountain out of a molehill—"

"Let's have it," said Goyles.

"It was the wireless. I've never heard it before that night, and I've never really heard it since, but that night it was terrific."

"What wireless?"

"The wireless in the carabinieri office block. Some band or other. It really was making a terrific shindy. It almost blew us out of our beds. Tony remarked on it, too. He found it very helpful when he was scrambling up onto the roof. About five minutes later it stopped altogether."

"What was your idea about that?" said Goyles. He had a considerable respect for Baierlein.

"It did occur to me to wonder whether it had been turned on loud to hide some other noise."

"I suppose it might," said Goyles. "But wasn't it a bit late? I mean the camp was all shut up by then. The Italians could hardly have got in and kidnapped Coutoules at that hour of the night without attracting some attention."

"I suppose not," said Baierlein. "It was just a thought."

Goyles hesitated for a moment. He very much wanted to discuss with someone what Meynell had told him. He supposed, however, that it was the duty of an investigator to listen to everybody and confide in nobody.

As soon as Baierlein had left, a further thought struck him.

Was it not highly probable that the two pieces of information which he had received, highly intriguing though each of them was, might cancel each other out? The more he thought about it the more likely it seemed. What Meynell had heard from underground had been a wireless set. One of the Italians had been secretly listening to an American station—that, of course, would account for the accent.

Goyles dismissed all thoughts of the problem from his mind and stomped off angrily down the passage to keep a bridge date. He was an enthusiastic if over-scientific player.

Next morning, after breakfast, he sought out the camp Quartermaster, Captain Porter, a wily old regular soldier, on the whole sympathetic to escapers, but inclined to stand on his dignity.

"You have most to do with the Italians of anyone here," said Goyles. "You see them every day about parcels and that sort of thing, don't you?"

"I suppose I do really," said Porter cautiously. "If it's Red Cross boxes you want you're out of luck. I gave the last lot to the sports committee."

"I don't really want anything," said Goyles. "Except information. I was wondering if you could find out for me which sentries were on certain posts on certain nights."

"I expect I might," said Captain Porter. He knew the power of a tin of Red Cross butter in fat-starved Italy. "Which one had you particularly in mind?"

"I wanted to know who was on duty on the northeast guard platform round about midnight on July first."

Captain Porter looked out of the corner of his eye at Goyles and said, "That would be the night—"

"Yes," said Goyles. "That was the night when Coutoules bought it."

"Funny thing that," said Captain Porter. "I'll see what I can do. Come back and see me after lunch."

After lunch, however, the Quartermaster's room was empty, and Goyles was lying on his bunk before tea when Porter came in. "It's a damn funny thing," he said, "I've never known them so sticky. Usually, a little thing like that you can get for the asking. Someone's been scaring the pants off them. I had to blow a whole Red Cross parcel and fifty cigarettes. I hope it was worth it. The two you want are Private Biancelli and the carib who was with him was called Marzotto."

Goyles wrote down both names, and said, "Do you think you could possibly get Biancelli into the camp?"

"I can't get him into the camp if he doesn't want to come. What I can do is give you the tip when he next shows up. There's a big fatigue coming in tomorrow after tea with new beds for Hut E. If he isn't actually on guard he might be on that."

Goyles thought for a moment.

"If he is on the fatigue," he said, "could you get him away from it for five minutes, to the cookhouse, say?"

"It'll be as much as my job's worth if I'm caught tampering with an Italian detail," said Captain Porter. "However, I'll do what I can. I suppose you know what you're up to."

"I hope so," said Goyles. "I'm not doing it just for my own amusement, if that's what you mean."

"So I understand," said Captain Porter. "I had the tip from Colonel Baird this morning. I'll do what I can."

A message at five o'clock the following afternoon told Goyles that the Quartermaster had been as good as his word. He accordingly made his way to the cookhouse and was waiting when Biancelli came in. He was escorting two British orderlies who were carrying rations. As soon as the door was closed the orderlies made themselves scarce and Goyles was left alone with his man. He recognized him as one of the sentries who had often stared down from the walls at him: a small, ducklike person with a sallow face and an ill-fitting uniform.

"Please sit down," said Goyles, in passable Italian. "Have a cigarette." He passed over a whole packet which Biancelli pocketed, unopened, and without comment.

Goyles tried one or two of the normal conversational openings—the hardness of the war: the shortness of food: the separation from family and children. None of these evoked any response at all and Goyles found this, in itself, curious. Always before when he had made the opportunity to talk alone with Italian soldiers he had found them sympathetic—almost childlike in their anxiety to please. Why, he wondered, was Biancelli suddenly acting the strong, silent man. Was he trying to put the price up? He did not look in the least naturally strong or silent.

He found the answer suddenly.

Faraway across the barrack square Captain Benucci's voice was raised in anger.

Biancelli shot to his feet, and scuttled toward the door.

Goyles got in front of him.

"Look here," he said urgently, "there's nothing to be frightened about. Do you want to earn a hundred pounds?"

"I cannot say anything," said Biancelli. Nevertheless he had stopped moving and his eyes looked interested.

"You know as well as I do," said Goyles, "that Italy will be out of the war before many months are passed. The carabinieri and all Fascists will be in hiding for their lives and honest people will come into their own."

"*Speriamo*," said Biancelli.

"It is not a hope. It is a certainty."

"You mentioned one hundred—"

"One hundred pounds in British gold"—he wondered as he said it where on earth he was going to get it from. "We cannot talk here and now, but I have an idea. Can you arrange it so that you are one of the guard on the walk tomorrow?"

"Yes. That could be done."

"I will get myself put on the walk. I will be in the last file. There should be plenty of opportunity to talk at the halts, if we are careful."

"It shall be arranged."

"Tomorrow then. And death to all Fascists."

"May they dine together for eternity on their grandmothers' tripes," said Biancelli.

Goyles was on his way back to his hut when he stopped because he noticed that something out of the ordinary was happening.

A large crowd of prisoners had gathered in the middle of the sports field, and all the hut windows looking onto the main gate were crowded with faces.

Goyles found Baierlein standing by himself.

"New prisoners," said Baierlein.

"What's the excitement?"

"I don't know," said Baierlein. "There's something up though. Have you ever seen prisoners arriving here in that state? This isn't a reception camp."

The little group of prisoners in the forecourt showed even at that distance a battered and disreputable look. Their clothes hung from them, they were carrying practically no kit, and they looked as if they had spent the last three nights in a coal truck.

"You're absolutely right," said Goyles. "They're straight from the front line."

The excitement in the crowd was growing. If new prisoners were being brought direct to a camp as far north as 127, the implications were obvious.

"Looks as if the guards are expecting trouble," said Baierlein.

A third man had appeared on each of the guard platforms and a line of carabinieri had stationed themselves by the inner wire between the forecourt and the main camp. In the forecourt Benucci and the Commandant were talking together, and eying the growing crowd of British officers on the playing field.

"I don't believe they're going to let those chaps in here at all," said Baierlein. "They're putting them in one of the Italian blocks."

As the little group of new prisoners started to move, an officer on the sports field cupped his hands to his mouth and shouted, "Where are you from?"

Benucci screamed out an order and two of the machine guns on the wall turned quietly in the direction of the crowd.

Goyles suddenly went hot and cold.

"I hope no one starts anything," he whispered to Baierlein.

"Get flat on your face if there's any shooting," said Baierlein. "Whatever else you do, don't run for it."

The little file of prisoners were moving off now. Then something rather exciting happened. There was a moment when the last of them, a small dark man, was out of sight of the guards at the head of the file. He jumped round toward the group in the camp, his back against the wall of the guard hut.

His arms rose and fell about a dozen times, quickly.

Goyles was unable to read it but more than one of the prisoners was expert enough in semaphore to take the message.

"Sicily Invaded."

Chapter 6

Colonel Lavery Makes a Speech and

Goyles Practices Ventriloquism

1

"I have called you together, gentlemen," said Colonel Lavery, "because, in my view, this may be the last opportunity we shall have to think matters over calmly, and to plan, so far as we are able to plan, our own future actions. Things should start moving fairly soon."

He looked down at his audience of four hundred officers gathered in the theater hut. He was well aware that they were four hundred individualists, and that his authority over them was tenuous. He sometimes thought that the only real reason that any of them obeyed his orders was that they came, most of them, from a people to whom order and discipline were as natural as breathing. A people, moreover, who had learned in the hard school of history that in a crisis it pays to hand over authority to one man and to follow his orders. As he looked at the faces in front of him Colonel Lavery felt all this, without perhaps precisely thinking it out; and he chose his words very carefully.

"It's no news to you that the Eighth Army is in Sicily. That fact, which was first passed across to us by one of the new prisoners, has been confirmed from other sources. I can't suppose that they intend to stop at Sicily. The Straits of Messina are no great obstacle. It is quite certain that they will land, rather sooner than later, in Italy. When that happens, so far as I can see, one of three things may happen—or perhaps a mixture of all of them.

"The Italians may go on with the fight. Or they may give it up, in a straightforward and orderly way, doing the best they can by their present allies: in which case one of the things they will be sure to do is to hand us over intact to the Germans. Or they may chuck in the sponge at a moment's notice, without consulting the Germans at all, in which case a pretty fair period of chaos is liable to ensue. I imagine a lot will depend on Mussolini. I understand, from guarded references which our intelligence people in camp here have deciphered from the daily press, that the two ends of the Axis may not be revolving at quite the same speed just now.

"However, please let no one deceive himself. Whichever of those three things happens our course is not going to be easy or straightforward.

"If there is chaos, then we will take what advantage of it we can. If, on the other hand, it seems that we are going to be moved further north, under Italian control, or handed over lock, stock and barrel to the Germans, then a very awkward decision may face us. I don't want to make too much of it, because it may never happen. But in such circumstances, we might have to face the fact that it would be our duty to rush these walls regardless of cost."

Colonel Lavery paused for a moment and looked round at his audience, which had fallen strangely silent. He himself was thinking of Benucci's words to him a week before—on the night, in fact, that Coutoules had disappeared.

He repeated, "Regardless of cost. If the British Army was in Italy and advancing toward us fast, through a friendly—or at any rate a neutral—countryside, then it might be our plain duty to go over those walls on the calculation that if sixty or seventy per cent of us got clear we should have taken a justifiable chance. As I said before, I am not stressing this, because we are working now on certain alternative methods which may be available when they are required.

"Meanwhile, I intend that the whole camp—I include the orderlies—they are not here at the moment but they will be told later—the whole camp will be organized on an infantry basis into companies and platoons, so that a proper chain of command will exist, and anything which has to be done can be done promptly and efficiently. Details will be given out later, by hut commanders. Two or three other things. I have noticed that

Army boots, of which a fair number have been issued lately, are being cut down and made into walking shoes. This will cease. All boots will be carefully preserved, also all Army clothing, particularly overcoats, raincoats and macintoshes. Everyone should see that he is equipped to the best of his ability for a long, hard, cross-country march. Secondly, the issue of additional Red Cross food parcels, which has been possible lately from our accumulated stocks, will stop. I have instructed the Quartermaster to save all possible food. Lastly, since it is particularly his province, I have asked Colonel Baird to have a word with you about security."

Colonel Baird was a less practiced speaker than Colonel Lavery, but he made up in directness what he lacked in flourish. He said, "Things have been happening in this camp in the last few days that we don't like, and that we can't explain. Most of you know, and if you don't it's time you did, that the body of Lieutenant Coutoules was found about ten days ago in very suspicious circumstances. Captain Byfold has been arrested by the Italians on suspicion of having had a hand in his death. We happen to know that this is nonsense. A lot of people thought Coutoules was an informer—I mean that he told the Italians about escape plans and so on. I don't suppose we shall ever know the truth of that now. But something else more unpleasant has grown out of it."

Colonel Baird paused here, not for oratorical effect, but simply because he wanted to be very careful about what he said next. The silence in the hut was painful.

"Certain facts have led us to believe that there may still be an informer among us. I can't say any more at the moment. I asked that the orderlies should not be here today. I don't want this information passed to them."

Colonel Baird paused again, almost as if he had finished. Then it seemed to occur to him that some explanation of his closing remarks might be required.

"I don't want you to think," he said, "that we suspect any particular orderly. We don't. It's just that their backgrounds are more difficult to check than yours are. Most of you chaps come from a very small number of regiments and schools, and businesses and families. We've done a certain amount of work on you already. I hope you won't take it the wrong way, but we're going through the whole business again to see if we haven't missed someone. It may mean asking you a lot of silly questions, but it can't be avoided."

He turned to Colonel Lavery to indicate that he had finished.

"Very well," said Colonel Lavery. "That's all."

2

"Just picture me," said Rupert Rolf-Callender, "trudging through the Italian countryside, dressed in some or all of these clothes." He had laid his spare wardrobe out on his bed. It consisted of two very thin Italian cotton shirts, a pair of bathing trunks, three pairs of sunglasses and a pair of sandals.

"You shouldn't have swapped all your issue stuff for cigarettes," said the Honorable Peter Perse. "Now you'll have to get it back again. It's going to be a buyers' market, too."

"It just shows you," said Tag Burchnall virtuously to his friends. "What did I say all along? Don't worry about footling escape schemes, just keep absolutely fit and let the Army think for you. Can anybody lend me some dubbin?"

Overstrand said to his friends in Room 10, "My God, that shook them. Were you looking at their faces when the S.B.O. talked about storming the walls?"

"They didn't look too happy," admitted Tony Long. "I'm not sure that I exactly welcome the prospect myself, not in broad daylight. It would be an awfully long way up that wall with a couple of machine guns firing at you."

"It was the first time that half of them have faced up to the fact that the war isn't finished," said Overstrand. His voice sounded bitter. "They've spent a year lying in their beds in winter and on them in summer, and physically and morally they're as hard as a school of baby jellyfish."

"I didn't quite get what Baird meant about security," said Baierlein. "What's the connection between security and Coutoules?"

This question was obviously aimed principally at Goyles, who weighed for a moment the claims of professional integrity against friendship and decided that a limited amount of indiscretion could do no harm.

"They think," he said, "that the Italians knew that Coutoules was going to be killed and dumped in a tunnel."

"In our tunnel?"

"No. In some tunnel; when we produced him in the Hut A tunnel they naturally assumed that that was where the interment had taken place."

"So they knew all along that it was a fake," said Baierlein. "I thought they got onto poor old Roger rather smartly."

"Yes, but look here," said Overstrand, his face getting red, as it usually did when he was excited, "that means there's another informer in the camp."

"That's Baird's idea," said Goyles patiently.

"But was it this other informer and his pals who killed Coutoules?"

"Not necessarily. They just told the Italians it was going to happen."

"Then who did kill him?"

"That's the thing we've got to find out. There are really two inquiries going on, you see. One's a sort of security check to spot the informer. The other's a criminal investigation—who was doing what, where and with whom on the evening of July first—that sort of thing."

"Well, Tony and you and I were all right," said Grimsdale a little tactlessly. "We were all in jug. What about you three?"

"It can't be Goyles," said Baierlein, "he's the detective in the story. And Byfold has been arrested for the crime by the Italians, so by all the canons of detective fiction he can't be guilty. It must have been Overstrand—"

"Plenty of motive," said Grimsdale, "we all know he hated Coutoules."

"I don't see," said Overstrand angrily. "Why has it necessarily got to be one of us six?"

"Don't be a goat," said Baierlein. "Grim was only pulling your leg."

"One good thing," said Goyles, adroitly changing the subject. "We've got the word to push on with the tunnel, double shifts. They want us to have it ready by the end of this month."

"All very well to talk about pushing on," said Baierlein. "It's true that we've cleared the fall, but we can't go ahead without putting a proper roof across that cavity. It's a bloody big hole. You can't do it with fiddling little pieces of bed board. I was down there yesterday to measure it. If you stay the four corners as close as possible to the fall, you're still going to need a huge sheet of plywood, or something of the sort. At least four foot by six."

"I doubt if there's such a thing in the camp," said Goyles.

"My God, but there is," said Overstrand. "And you shall have it."

3

"Good morning, *Tenente* Mordaci," said Tony Long affably, as he leaned from his window.

"Good morning," said Mordaci. He hitched his cloak over his shoulders and creased his face into an amiable smile. He was not averse to paternal conversations with blond young English lieutenants. Nevertheless, he was never quite certain that *Tenente* Long was really as respectful or as ingenuous as he liked to appear. Indeed, the respect of the prisoners for their jailers seemed to be getting distressingly smaller every day. There was an undercurrent of feeling. Even Mordaci, who was not the most sensitive of men, had noticed it.

"And how are '*i nostri*'?"

"Our gallant troops are everywhere in good heart."

"As at El Alamein?"

"At El Alamein we were grossly betrayed and deserted."

"And at Tripoli?"

"The greater part of our troops were safely evacuated from Tripoli."

"And at Pantelleria?"

"An unimportant outpost."

"And now in Sicilia?"

"In Sicilia great victories are daily being gained."

"And soon in Italia?"

"Italia—never." Mordaci waggled a fat forefinger reprovingly at his young interrogator. "Never shall foreigner defile the sacred soil of Italy."

He hitched his cloak once more round his massive shoulders and rolled off across the compound with the satisfied smile of one who has dealt firmly with a tiresome interrogator. It may be that had he known that Tony had spoken to him simply because it was part of his duty to detain him for as long as he could—or had he even guessed that, somewhere beneath his feet as he stood talking, the sacred soil of Italy was being excavated at the rate of more than a square yard a day—it is possible that had he known all this his smile might have been less complacent.

4

That afternoon the new prisoners were allowed to join the rest. Since the news of the invasion of Sicily was by now general and had in fact appeared, suitably garbled, in such Italian newspapers as were allowed into the camp, there seemed no point in keeping them in the already over-crowded Italian staff quarters.

Normally new prisoners were welcomed immediately into the living huts, where they found themselves the center of a gratifying amount of attention. They personified the outside world. They *were* the latest news. On this occasion, however, Colonel Baird's hand was over them from the moment they entered the camp, and they were taken immediately to the senior officers' quarters, where they were brought, one at a time, before the Escape Committee, in session in Colonel Baird's room. The interrogation was friendly, but thorough.

The first of them happened to be the little dark subaltern who had semaphored the news of the fall of Sicily. His name turned out to be Potter.

"Now, Potter, perhaps you could give us a few details. Regiment and division and so on. I see you were in the Signals."

"Yes, sir. I was Signals officer in the 15th R.H.A."

"What division was that?"

"Eighth Armored—that's their divisional flash I'm wearing."

"So it is, I hadn't spotted that. Who commands them now?"

"Colonel Williams."

"Is that Chubby Williams?"

"No, sir. It's his brother. Chubby commands the Ninth."

"Of course. By the way, where did you say you were at school?"

"Shelton."

"Oh, yes. Which house?"

"School House."

"Let me see. You're just twenty-two. I suppose you would have left there in thirty-nine."

"Thirty-eight actually, sir. I left early to start my articles."

And so on.

At the end of about fifteen minutes the officer concerned, feeling that he had been very carefully and skillfully taken to pieces and put together again, was allowed to join his hut.

Where, of course, the questions started all over again.

"You were in the Fifteenth, were you? Oh, Tag—here's a chap who was with the Fifteenth in Sicily. He says Mike has got a battery."

"If Mike's got a battery," said Burchnall, "all I can say is, it's a damn shame I was ever captured. I should have been a brigadier by now."

5

Next day Goyles' plans suffered a setback. He heard about it after breakfast from Long.

"I say," said Long, "have you heard the latest?"

"Nobody ever says that, in that particular tone of voice," said Goyles, "unless it's bad news, so out with it."

"I'm not sure whether it's bad news or not," said Long. "Rather a sign of the times really. Benucci has stopped all walks."

"Curse," said Goyles.

"If you ask me, it's not because he's worried about people escaping. It's simply that he's afraid that the populace will begin to show too much sympathy with us. They haven't been exactly hostile as it is. With the Eighth Army in Sicily they'll begin to pelt us with flowers."

"It isn't that," said Goyles. "I'm not all that keen on walks. It's just that—look here, you'll have to keep your mouth shut about this."

"This detection business is ruining your faith in human nature," said Tony coldly. "Of course I'll keep my mouth shut. What is it?"

Goyles explained about the arrangement he had made with Biancelli.

"I see," said Tony. "Yes. That is a bit awkward, isn't it? What exactly were you hoping to get out of him?"

"Coutoules had the end room in the S.B.O.'s hut. The northeast sentry platform is the only one that overlooked his window. If Coutoules was in his room at lockup, almost the only way he could have been got out was through the window."

"Why? They don't lock the hut door at night. It's the only hut that doesn't have its outer door locked at night."

"I know. But think of the risk. Even if Coutoules was dead when they got him out of his room, it would have meant carrying the body past half a dozen doors. Anyone might have looked out. If he'd still been alive and kicking the risk would have been greater still."

"I don't believe you could kidnap anybody out of one of these huts without everybody knowing about it," said Tony thoughtfully. "But that's not the point. I agree that if anything was to be seen Biancelli probably saw it. I don't imagine you could have got much out of him on a walk, though. The sentries nearly always walk in pairs. There's only one place in this camp that you can rely on an hour's undisturbed conversation with a sentry. Do you think you can get a message to Biancelli?"

"I expect so. The Quartermaster seems to be able to get hold of them."

"Then ask him when he's next going to be on guard in the cooler."

"Tony," said Goyles, "that's brilliant."

"It's the fish diet," said Long modestly.

6

"I say," said Baierlein, "have you heard what's happened?"

Goyles turned over on his bed and groaned. "Yes," he said, "they've stopped all walks."

"No doubt," said Baierlein, "but that wasn't what I meant. They've removed Potter."

"Which Potter?"

"He wasn't in the camp long enough for us to get on Christian-name terms," said Baierlein. "Young Potter—the chap in the Royal Corps of Signals who came in with the last bunch."

"The one who did the semaphoring?"

"That's the chap."

Goyles sat up slowly, to consider the new development. On the face of it, it didn't seem to make a great deal of sense.

"What actually happened?"

"They didn't make any palaver about it. Nothing like they did about Roger. Paoli came in after lunch, and told him to get packed, as he was going on somewhere else. Not that he'd got much to pack, poor chap. The people in his hut had a quick whip round for him and got together some food and a set of battledress."

"Did Paoli stay with him while he was packing?"

"Yes," said Baierlein. "Why?"

"I don't know," said Goyles, "it just occurred to me that they might have wanted to stop him talking. Supposing he had a bit of information they particularly didn't want him to pass on. If he suddenly heard he was going to be moved to another camp, his natural reaction would be to try to tell it to someone. If Paoli was standing over him, he couldn't. That's all."

"It's possible," said Baierlein. "But don't forget he'd been in the camp nearly twenty-four hours. The Escape Committee and the I people had already had a go at him. To say nothing of the people in the hut. The poor chap hardly stopped answering questions from the moment he got into the camp till he was removed. If there was anything, surely he'd have spilled it already."

"Always supposing," said Goyles thoughtfully, "that he knew exactly

what it was that he knew that the Italians didn't want us to know."
"This detecting business is going to your head," said Baierlein.

7

"It's all very well to talk about getting yourself arrested," said Goyles,
"but it isn't so damned easy, just at the moment."
"There's ingratitude for you," said Tony.
"I'm not ungrateful," said Goyles. "I still think it was a brilliant idea.
And I've been in touch with Biancelli. He says he will be on the cooler
guard tomorrow night. It's a twenty-four-hour guard—two hours on and
four off. All I want is a few days solitary, starting tomorrow, and every-
thing in the garden would be beautiful."
"Forget to salute the Commandant."
"He never comes into the camp nowadays."
"Be rude to Benucci."
"That's the trouble. Benucci's such a tricky customer. If you say some-
thing perfectly outrageous to him, he just grins like a cat, and you feel a
fool. I suppose you could go a step further and trip him up and kick him in
the stomach or something. Then he'd probably pull out his toy revolver
and shoot you."
"Hmph," said Long.
"The trouble is everybody's in such an awkward frame of mind at the
moment. It's going to be damned tricky—"
"You just leave it to me," said Long. "Everything shall be arranged.
You want the best prisons. We have them. Tactful insults a specialty."

8

"Well, I call the whole thing a lot of nonsense," said Rolf-Callender.
"Ever since the S.B.O.'s speech people have done nothing but form fours
and slope arms and talk the most ropy old nonsense about attack in depth
and where they're going to site the B Echelon. I suppose one can't prevent them making fools of themselves, but when it comes to suggesting
that we give up the play—"
"Has anyone actually suggested that we drop it?"
"Not in so many words, but I can tell from the way Uncle Percy looks
at me—" he referred to his hut commander, an elderly regular major in
Indian cavalry—"that he thinks we're just fiddling while Rome burns.
Personally I can't see it at all. Didn't the Duchess of Thingummy give a
ball on the eve of Waterloo?"
"If she hadn't," suggested Peter Perse, who never missed an opportu-
nity of provoking Rolf-Callender, "Wellington mightn't have come so
jolly near to losing the battle."
"I can't see it," said Bush. "It isn't as if we were using anything that

anyone else would want if we did have to escape—unless you suggest that Peter try to get to Rome dressed as Elizabeth Barrett Browning. I agree that the general getup is smashing, but I'm afraid the skirt would date him."

"Exactly," said Rolf-Callender. "Just because they want to play at soldiers, is that any reason to stop us playing at theatricals? When it comes to the big night, I expect our performance will be far more amusing than theirs. And I shall tell Uncle Percy so next time he wants me to join one of his TEWTS."

"If that's all agreed," said Bush, "what are we waiting for? On with the rehearsals."

"There's one thing," observed Captain Abercrowther, who was trying on a formidable pair of side whiskers. "I haven't haird yet how you propose to deal with that wee dug."

"Flush," said Rolf-Callender thoughtfully. "Yes. He is going to be a bit of a problem. I suppose that if the worst came to the worst we could cut—"

"Shame," said Bush. "The Barretts without Flush! It would be like Hamlet without the First Grave-digger."

"I know, but—"

"I had an idea about that," said Captain Abercrowther. "Has that fellow Paoli not got a wee dug—"

"But it's not a spaniel."

"Not precisely a spaniel, no. But it's a plain, white, podgy little creature and seems tolerably placid. Could not some of our makeup artists—"

"Liver and white markings," cried Rolf-Callender.

"A pair of false ears!" suggested Bush.

"And a nubby little tail!"

"Mac," said Peter Perse. "It's the idea of the century. I can plainly see that this performance is going to be a riot."

9

The next morning, making his rounds of the camp, *Tenente* Mordaci suddenly stopped.

He stopped because he fancied he heard his name.

Not only his surname, which would have been interesting, but his Christian name, too.

More interesting still.

He looked round him. He was standing in the open space between Hut B and Hut C and it was from a window in Hut C that the voices seemed to come.

He knew well that Hut C was notorious for containing a high percentage of evil characters, maniacs, who could not see that they were well off out of the war but must ever be plotting and scheming and disturbing the peace of mind of those lawfully placed in authority over them.

It was clearly his duty to investigate. His presence did not seem to be suspected. Hitching his cloak round his shoulders—a subconscious gesture, in moments of crisis—he tiptoed to the outer wall of the hut and sidled along toward the window.

What he saw transfixed him with astonishment.

Seated on a bed, surrounded by a grinning group of prisoners, was a most extraordinary figure. Padded into gross obesity with many pillows, the lips puffed and reddened with makeup, a doll on his knee, a blanket thrown cloak-wise round his shoulders, and an absurd travesty of a carabiniere's cocked hat on his head, it took Mordaci a few seconds to recognize the usually sedate Goyles.

It had never occurred to him that Goyles was an actor. It now appeared that he was a very competent ventriloquist also.

Mordaci peered closely at the doll.

It appeared from its dress to be a lady of doubtful taste and nonexistent virtue.

Since nobody was looking toward the window he was able to study this edifying scene for some minutes.

"But, Ercolo," said the doll, "your suggestions fill me with alarm and suspicion."

"Come, come now," said Goyles, in a revolting imitation of Mordaci's unctuous bass. "You are a woman of the world."

"It is because I am a woman of the world that I hesitate."

"Then hesitate no longer. It is I, Ercolo Mordaci of the Carabinieri Reali, who speaks—"

"It is I indeed who speak," said Mordaci.

All heads in the room swung toward the window in gratifying unison.

"It is I who speak, and I say that you will cease this imposture and accompany me to the office—"

"But, *Tenente*—"

"At once."

"It's only a play I was rehearsing."

"And its name?"

"Oh—we hadn't thought of a name."

"Beauty and the beast," suggested someone from the crowd.

"Enough," said Mordaci. "This vileness will bring its own reward. For seven days at least you shall not pollute the camp with your presence."

"There you are," said Tony Long five minutes later, "absolutely painless. I'll help you carry your kit as far as the guardhouse."

10

The punishment block, or the cooler, stood, as has been already explained, in the outer section of the camp. In this area, between the inner wire and the north wall, lay the guard quarters, the carabinieri offices, the

Italian administrative huts, and the prisoners' food and clothing store.

Surrounded as it was on all sides by Italians, the cooler itself was not particularly well or systematically guarded. It comprised a small brick block, divided by a central corridor, with two cells on either side. Those on the north (or outer) side were traditionally reserved for British prisoners, those on the other side for Italian soldiers who had been found guilty of derelictions of duty. On one side, at the end, was an ablution room. At this point the corridor turned through a right angle, so that the actual entrance door was out of sight of the cells themselves.

In this entrance door a sentry was posted. It was his duty to take a periodical turn up the passage and inspect such cells as were occupied, by glancing through the inspection slit in the door.

Since the sentry wore heavy, studded boots and the floor of the corridor was tiled, his arrival on a tour of inspection never really took anyone by surprise.

The possibilities of this arrangement had been quickly appreciated, and a succession of self-condemned prisoners, suitably equipped, had already rendered the barred windows of the two British cells rather more ornamental than useful. Long and Baierlein had also proved that a rough dummy in the bed was sufficient to satisfy a sentry, particularly one who was looking from a lighted passage into an unlighted cell.

The whole arrangement was so scandalously careless, Goyles reflected, as he sat on his bed that evening with his phrase book of modern Greek, that it would be criminal not to take some advantage of it. There seemed no reasonable doubt that four prisoners, if only they could get into prison suitably equipped, could get out of the window, onto the roof, and over the wall, with a minimum of difficulty.

The loose bar and brick could be replaced from the outside, as Tony Long had already demonstrated, and if dummies were left in the beds they would not be missed until reveille.

Suitably equipped—that was the snag. Even in Italy in summer, for a cross-country journey, you needed food and warm clothes and maps, and a host of other things; you could scarcely hope to smuggle them past the very thorough search which took place before you were jugged.

Even so, there might be a solution that—

At this moment the lights went out and Goyles glanced at his watch. It was ten o'clock.

Biancelli, he knew, was not due on guard until eleven.

He got up onto his bed, covered himself with a blanket, and prepared to wait. To prevent himself from nodding off altogether he forced himself to think about the death of Coutoules. In his mind he went over and over every fact that he knew, and then again, remorselessly.

He realized that he had very few facts to build on. But equally, as Colonel Shore had said, the whole problem was so crazy that any feasible solution must surely be the right one.

Might Biancelli be bringing him just that one little *extra fact* which would make all the difference—the twist which would unlock the whole puzzle?

It was very quiet in the cell.

There was no Italian wireless blaring tonight. In the silence Goyles could hear a murmur of voices from the carabinieri block next door. He could almost make out individuals—the unctuous bass of Mordaci, the thin pipe of Paoli, the incisive tones of Captain Benucci.

When he looked at his watch again, it was eleven o'clock. He swung his feet over the edge of the bed and sat up. His bed was alongside the door and on a level with the peephole, so that he had a clear view of the passage as far as the turn. He could hear the sentry, who had not stirred for the last hour, moving about, no doubt in preparation for his relief.

Suddenly there came a snap and a double stamp as the sentry sprang to attention.

There was a noise of feet, and a few words were spoken, which he could not catch.

Then the light threw a long shadow down the corridor and Captain Benucci appeared. He walked right up to the door and stood outside for a moment, looking at the darkened peephole. His face was not more than twenty inches from Goyles, who could smell the peculiar pomade which he used.

"Captain Goyles."

"Yes," said Goyles cautiously.

"Ah—you are awake. I wondered. I have a message for you. I have to tell you that Private Biancelli will *not* be on duty tonight. He shot himself this evening. He was cleaning his rifle. It was an accident."

Goyles had nothing to say. He saw Captain Benucci turn and he watched his back disappear down the passageway and heard the clock as the guard came to attention, and the sound of Benucci's feet clattering away down the path.

Chapter 7
Fracas

1

"I don't like this Potter business a bit," said Colonel Baird.

"Stinks," agreed Commander Oxey.

"Why do you think they did it? They can't have got on to that sema-phoring stunt—even if they did—"

"Even if they did," said Commander Oxey, "it would be stupid to take any notice of it days after the event, when everybody knew about Sicily anyway."

"Then why pick on him? They haven't tried to shift any of the other newcomers?"

"Not that I know of."

"He seemed a perfectly genuine and harmless little man. He knew a lot of the officers in 15 R.H.A.—"

"By name."

"Certainly. Why? What are you getting at?"

"Well," said Commander Oxey slowly, "I've been digging round among the gunner officers here—we've got one or two from that regiment, and others who were in the same division. They all agree that Potter seemed perfectly genuine. He knew the right answers. He'd heard of all the right people. He knew them by their names—even by their Army nicknames—only—"

"Only what?"

"Only they none of them remember meeting him."

"That's quite reasonable. He was a replacement signal officer. He was straight out from England and he only joined the regiment a few days before the actual Sicily show—"

"Quite," said Commander Oxey. "Then how did he come to know all those other people? He must have done some remarkably intensive visiting round the division in those few days, to pick up all that gossip. I'm not too well up in Army matters, but I should have thought that if he'd only been a few days with his regiment he might have known one or two of the officers—the ones he actually messed with and worked under—but he'd still be a bit vague about the rest of the regiment, wouldn't he? Let alone the division."

"There's something in that," said Baird. "What's your idea?"

"I haven't really got an idea yet—but I asked Lieutenant Long to come and have a few words. I think he might be able to help us."

"Tony Long," said Baird. "What makes you think that? He's not a gunner—and he was in Special Service most of his time."

"Not all his life," said Commander Oxey with a smile. "That sounds like him now. Come in, Long. I was just talking about you to Colonel Baird. So far as I can see from our records you're our only Sheltonian in the camp. At least the only one of the right age."

"The right age, sir?"

"Young enough, I mean. You were there in 1936, weren't you—in School House?"

"Yes. I went in winter thirty-three and left in thirty-seven."

"Then you'll remember Potter?"

"Potter," said Tony slowly. "Was Potter at Shelton?"

"That's what we're asking you," said Colonel Baird and he looked up sharply.

"I can't say I remember anyone called Potter. When was he supposed to have come?"

Colonel Baird referred to his notes—"New boy in 1935."

"Oh, well, that would make him two years younger than me. It's quite possible I wouldn't know him. After all there were six hundred boys there, in a dozen different houses. If he was in another house—"

"That's just it," said Commander Oxey. "He was in School House."

"Well, that settles it," said Long. "He wasn't. You're sure he said School House?"

"Certain."

"Then he's a liar."

"I thought he might be," said Commander Oxey. "I just wanted to be sure. Thank you very much."

When the door had closed behind him Colonel Baird said, "Well, what do you make of that?"

"It's obvious, isn't it?" said Commander Oxey. "Somebody killed off their former stool pigeon. They waste precious little time over installing a new one."

"No doubt. But why remove him before he's had a chance to do any stooling?"

"Perhaps," said Commander Oxey with a grin, "they heard of the precautions we were taking. They wouldn't want him to go the same way as the first one, would they?"

2

"We're to go ahead with the tunnel at full speed," said Hugo Baierlein. "I saw Baird this morning and he approved most of my suggestions. It's a pity that both Roger and Cuckoo should be out of circulation just now, because they both know the ropes. We're going to work three shifts instead of two—the first from nine to one, the afternoon shift from two to six, and a short evening shift from six till just before lockup. We're going to take some steps to speed things up. First, we're only going to half-shore the tunnel. We'll put in complete box sections of wood every other foot, and only have a few thin pieces across the interval to form a ceiling—"

"That's all right as far as it goes," said Overstrand, "but it doesn't solve the main problem. It's the disposal of the sand that's holding us up. Even using the A tunnel—which is very nearly full now—we're getting out more than we can dispose of."

"I was coming to that," said Baierlein. "The order there is—anything goes. You can put it on flower beds, paths, the playing fields, underneath huts. You can store it in boxes round the cookhouse. The Escape Committee have come to the conclusion that the Italians know very well that there's a tunnel being dug. They just don't know where it starts from. If they find fresh sand it won't tell them anything they don't know already."

"Provided people aren't spotted coming away from this hut with it."

"Yes. That's vital. Well then—" Baierlein turned to Duncan and Anderson—"I take it you're on."

"You may take it so," said Duncan—"and we can probably raise a complete working shift from our hut. Tunneling stock has gone up a point or two after the S.B.O.'s speech."

"Right," said Baierlein. "Will you collect your people now and dribble them across? We'll have the tunnel mouth open and show you the way around. You can start proper work this evening."

"By the way," said Duncan, "have you roofed over the fall yet?"

"Surely," said Overstrand. There was a degree of malice in his smile. "We've found a perfect roof for it."

When their visitors had gone Baierlein and Overstrand walked along to the kitchen.

"No hurry," said Baierlein. "We shall have to wait for them anyway, to help us up with the lid."

"As a matter of fact," said Overstrand, "it's perfectly possible for two people to do it if you take it slowly. Grim and I did it the other day."

"Did you now?" said Baierlein. "Well, I'm not Grim. We'll wait till the others turn up if you don't mind, and do it properly."

3

"Come in," said Colonel Lavery. "The Adjutant tells me you want a word with me."

"If I could," said Rolf-Callender. He was looking pink but determined and his rather girlish mouth had tighter lines round it than usual.

"It's about some property of ours, sir, that's been stolen."

"Stolen. That's a horrible word to hear in a prisoner-of-war camp. Are you certain?"

"Absolutely, sir. In fact I don't think the thief is even troubling to deny it."

"I see." A wary look came into Colonel Lavery's eye. "You said 'our' property. It's not just your private stuff?"

"No sir. It's a roulette board. It belongs to Captain Perse and Lieutenant Bush and myself. We bought some of the stuff from the Italians, and got the rest from the Quartermaster. We made it ourselves."

"I see. You're quite sure you haven't just lost it?"

"I don't think that's really possible, sir. It was a huge thing. It was hinged in the middle, but when it was flat it was about six foot by three."

"Yes—"

"Besides, we all know who's got it. They've practically boasted about it. It's Overstrand and his friends—we know—at least we're practically certain—" Rolf-Callender almost gobbled over this final indignity—

"they're using it to roof a tunnel."

"I see."

"And that's not all, sir. They—or some of the other escaping people— stole the rugger posts. I don't know if it was a tunnel—it was something to do with escaping—and people are getting pretty fed up about it."

"Yes," said Colonel Lavery.

"It's not only me—you could ask anyone in our hut. We're all for live and let live, and when it comes to the point—I mean, what you said in your speech—I hope we'd do our bit like anyone else, but it's these cloak- and-dagger types—why *should* they go round pinching other people's stuff and behaving as if they owned the place? Why should they have special privileges?"

"What do you want me to do?"

Rolf-Callender became aware that he might have been saying a little more than he had started to do. He pulled himself up and said, "We'd like our board back, sir."

"There's one practical difficulty to that," said Colonel Lavery with a smile. "I don't even know where their tunnel is—"

"Well—I expect Colonel Baird does."

"Do you want me to ask him?"

This suggestion made even Rolf-Callender hesitate. He was as con- scious as anyone of Colonel Baird's personality. He therefore hedged.

"Am I to take it, sir, that escaping activities have official priority over any other form of activity?"

Colonel Lavery felt tempted to tell the petulant young man that he could take what he liked and do what he liked with it, but he restrained himself in time. Though badly put, the grievance was, he knew, a real one in the minds of many people.

"I can't give any general ruling," he said. "You know that it's your military duty to take every reasonable chance of escape."

"Every reasonable chance, yes, sir."

"Quite. Well, all that means is that every case must be judged on its merits. In this case, since you put it to me, I do think that particu- lar piece of wood is serving a better purpose where it is now. I know enough about this tunnel to know that it's a good and careful one, and has a very fair chance of success. And if it does come through it may be very useful. I think that the people concerned should have asked you openly for the board—you might even have felt it your duty to give it to them."

"Hmph!" said Rolf-Callender.

"But now that it's been done, I don't think I can possibly order it to be given back again."

"I see, sir."

Rolf-Callender saluted insubordinately and withdrew.

Colonel Lavery sighed.

4

It was certainly unfortunate that on his return to Hut A the first person that Rolf-Callender met should have been Overstrand.

Overstrand had come across to the hut to work out with Anderson and Brandy Duncan the last details of the new digging teams. For various reasons they were anxious, if possible, that one complete shift should come from Hut A. They wanted eight men at least and had been finding last choices a bit difficult despite the fact that, as Duncan said, digging stock was temporarily on the rise. For the truth of the matter was that digging tunnels was a very specialized pursuit, in which experience counted for a good deal more than enthusiasm.

The three of them were standing in the passage when Rolf-Callender arrived.

Rolf-Callender pushed past the little group, trod on Overstrand's foot, apologized unconvincingly, and made for the door of his room.

"Been playing much roulette lately?" inquired Overstrand genially.

Rolf-Callender stopped in his tracks, turned round slowly, and said, "Just because you stole some of our property and got away with it doesn't give you any right to be funny about it."

"Sorry if I've said something to amuse you," said Overstrand. "Now, perhaps, if you told me what on earth you are talking about—"

"You know damned well what I'm talking about."

"And what exactly do you mean by 'got away with it'?"

Rolf-Callender said nothing. His face was white and he was breathing heavily.

"So that's why you wanted to see the S.B.O."—continued Overstrand, suddenly enlightened. "Sneaking again! And the S.B.O. told you to go and chase yourself, did he? Good for him."

"Half the trouble in this camp," said Rolf-Calender, "is that you escaping people think you're a race apart. You're above the law." His mouth was working so that he found it hard to shape the words. "Some of the things you do would get you kicked out of any decent regiment—"

"I'll take your word for it," said Overstrand, who was as red as Rolf-Callender was white. "I can never remember whether that flash on your battledress represents the R.A.S.C. or the Army Pay Corps—"

"Acting as cowboys and Indians all over the camp. If you didn't interfere so much with everyone else's comfort you'd just be a joke—"

"If I'm as funny as all that, possibly you could find a part for me in your forthcoming production—"

"But when it comes to stealing property and murdering a harmless little creature like Coutoules—"

"Why, you little twerp," said Overstrand.

"You thought you'd got away with it, didn't you—"

Overstrand slapped Rolf-Callender hard, with his open hand, on the side of the face.

Rolf-Callender hit out, and caught Overstrand without any force on the point of the nose.

Overstrand took two paces forward and hit Rolf-Callender under the heart. The three blows were as quick and as pat as in some well-rehearsed music-hall turn, only there was nothing funny about their intentions or their effect. Rolf-Callender fell forward onto his knees, stayed there for a moment, fighting for breath, then, with sudden energy, seized Overstrand round the knees, heaved with his shoulders, and toppled him to the ground. Then he threw himself onto him and started to claw. As the two of them rolled round in a threshing, dusty cloud, doors began to open along the passage.

Overstrand was a great deal bigger and heavier than Rolf-Callender and about three times as strong. As soon as he was on top the fight was over. He had Rolf-Callender's throat in his hands and was banging his head on the floor.

"This has got to stop," said Duncan. He was well aware that what was happening was one of the things which simply must not be allowed to happen—anyway not in a prisoner-of-war camp, where nerves were constantly frayed by proximity and boredom. It was the ultimate indecency.

He and Anderson got hold of Overstrand and dragged him off his opponent, and somebody helped Rolf-Callender into a sitting position, with his back against the passage wall.

"Look here," said Duncan. "You'd both better apologize and call it a day. I think there were faults on both sides."

"All right," said Overstrand. He was still red and breathing hard: but it is easier for the victor in these affairs to be magnanimous. "Let's forget it."

"I expect you hope so," said Rolf-Callender. His face was covered with blood and dirt, and his mouth looked like a mean little slit in a disheveled mask. "I suppose, if all these people hadn't been here, I should have been finished off the same way as Coutoules."

Overstrand looked down at him for a moment. Then Duncan touched him on the arms and the two of them walked out of the hut, which had suddenly grown silent.

5

"How on earth did it start?" said Baierlein.

"Why get angry with a little blot like that?" said Grimsdale. "He's not worth powder and shot."

"I suppose he wanted his roulette board back," said Long.

"Yes, that's what started it."

"How did he know we'd got it?"

"I don't know—I think it must have been something I said." Overstrand sounded uncomfortable. "Anyway, he went to the S.B.O. and complained. I gather he didn't get much change out of him, though."

"Serves him right," said Long, "but in that case what was all the fuss about? Was it just his usual anti-escape moan?"

"Yes, that sort of thing."

"Why—did—we—go—on—trying—when—no one—had—ever—got—out—of—the—country?"

"No—he didn't get as far as that. He said that pinching property was one of the things that wasn't done in the best regiments."

"What does he know about the best regiments?"

"When I was in the Sixtieth," said Grimsdale, "we hardly ever stopped pinching things—"

"Doesn't seem much to fight about," said Long.

"He also as good as accused me of murdering Coutoules."

"Well, you didn't, did you?" said Baierlein, "so why worry?"

6

"Have we got time to dress tonight?" inquired Captain the McInstalker.

"'Fraid not," said Captain Abercrowther. "I've got a rehearsal later on."

"Pity." The McInstalker looked at his watch. "Now that we've got our clean shirts we never have a chance to use them. What are you doing in this play, by the way?"

"I'm Barrett."

"Who's he?"

"A chap who bullied his children."

"Good idea, really," said the McInstalker. "I was always bullied when I was a child. Look at me now."

"I see what you mean."

"Talking of dress shirts, do you know, I always thought it was rather odd."

"What was odd?"

"You remember that night what's-his-name was killed—that Greek."

"The one they found in a tunnel."

"Yes. You remember we were waiting for our clean shirts then. When I saw the laundry van come in I reckoned we should get them."

"We didn't though, did we?"

"No. The van didn't actually come to any of our huts at all. I didn't see it delivering any laundry. I don't believe it collected any either."

"Come to think of it, I believe you're right. What do you think it was up to?"

"I think you ought to tell Goyles about it."

"He's in the cooler at the moment. I must remember to tell him when he comes out."

7

"I love you," said Rolf-Callender.

"I should have refused to see you again after our first meeting," said Peter Perse. "For I loved you then, though I would have denied it—even to myself. ... Oh, Robert, I think Eve must have felt as I did when her first dawn broke over Paradise—the terror, the wonder, the glory of it—"

"No, no," said Rolf-Callender. "You mustn't look at me like that, Peter, really you mustn't. The book says 'with restrained *spiritual* passion.' 'Spiritual,' please. You're looking at me like a greedy little parlormaid with her first date."

"It's all very well," said Perse, stretching his legs as comfortably as he could on a couch made up of two packing cases, "but how can you expect me to be spiritual about someone with a big black eye and a plummy nose."

"If you were really concentrating on your part," said Rolf-Callender stiffly, "you wouldn't notice my appearance."

"How can I help noticing it when you drop blood over me?"

"Come, come," said Captain Abercrowther—he had on an excellent pair of side whiskers and contrived to sound, despite a Scots accent, every inch the Victorian parent. "We'll never get anywhere at this rate. I suggest we take the scene again from 'Forgive me, I won't be silent any longer,' and will you boys please remember that you're in love."

8

"I told you I'd give you the word when we were ready," said Overstrand to Desmond Foster. "I think we can make it in about two days' time."

"You and Hugo and Grim?"

"Yes. We've been quite lucky with our kits. We haven't lost anything in the last searches. Either the Italians are losing their touch or their minds are not on the job."

"All right. I'll tell Tim. I hope he can cut the underground cable without killing himself."

"He's a Sapper—he ought to know what he's doing."

"Rather him than me. However, if you're sure you want to try it. I think everything's set."

"Certainly we want to try it," said Overstrand. "You're not backing out, are you?"

"I'm not backing out," said Foster. "I just thought that as your tunnel was so far on—"

"I don't think," said Overstrand slowly, "that the tunnel is ever going to come to anything."

"What makes you so certain?"

The two of them were walking round the perimeter path, and they had gone almost a hundred yards before Overstrand replied.

Then he said, "You mustn't repeat this to anyone, Desmond, because I can't prove it—at least not in a way that anyone would believe—but I think the Italians know all about that tunnel."

9

"Come in, Pat," said Colonel Lavery to his Adjutant. "Shut the door. Take a seat on the bed. It's more comfortable than the chair. Have a fig?"

"Thank you very much, sir."

"Now, what's all this about Overstrand and Rolf-Callender?"

"They had a scrap, sir, this afternoon, in Hut A."

"Not a very level fight, I should have thought."

"No, sir. More of a massacre."

"Any idea what it was about?"

"I thought at first it was just an ordinary escaper versus non-escaper row. They've been spoiling for it for a long time—"

"Yes. I had Rolf-Callender in here after lunch. He seemed to think that Overstrand had pinched some of his property. I suppose he went straight back to his hut and happened to run into Overstrand and—"

"Yes, sir. I thought it was that at first. But I was having a word with Terence Bush, who didn't see the fight but came out after it was over and heard what was being said, and he got the impression that Rolf-Callender had accused Overstrand of murdering Coutoules."

"He said that, did he?" Colonel Lavery looked more interested than surprised. "Any reasons given?"

"No. Just a general accusation."

"I wonder," said Colonel Lavery. "He couldn't have done it alone—I think that's pretty well established. It takes four people to open the trap."

"I'm not so sure about that either," said the Adjutant. "I've been talking to one or two people about it myself, and Grimsdale apparently told someone that *if* you understood the trap, and if you were strong enough, two of you could manage it. He said that he and Overstrand had done it once or twice when the regular team wasn't available."

"Did he now?" said Colonel Lavery. He sat for a few moments, picking the fig seeds out of his teeth and considering the possibilities opened up by this new information. "I take it that it's not just *any* two people who could do it. You've got to have the knack of the thing, and you've both got to be hefty sort of chaps."

"Yes, sir. And I don't imagine that one person could do it, however strong he was. To start with, it would be impossible for one man to pull his weight on all four ropes at the same time."

"Yes. Even so I don't quite see—I suppose the idea is that Overstrand and—well—let's say one other person in Hut C—might have come to the conclusion that Coutoules was overdue for dispatch, might have taken him apart somewhere, finished him off, and hidden him—then dropped him down the tunnel later that night."

"Yes, sir—but, of course—"

"There are a million difficulties," said Colonel Lavery. "Where did they kill him? Where did they hide him? How could two people do all that without being seen a dozen times over?"

"Quite so, sir."

"I've come to the regretful conclusion that there's only one body of men in this camp with the means and the space and the organization to pull off a job like that—"

"Who's that, sir?"

"The Escape Committee," said Colonel Lavery.

Evening had been drawing in as they were talking and in the uncertain light Captain Armstrong found it very difficult to decide whether Colonel Lavery was smiling or not.

Chapter 8

Viewed from Off Stage

1

There was one thing to be said for solitary confinement: it gave you plenty of time to think. Goyles, who had never been so fond of the company of his fellows that he felt lost without it, lay in his favorite position on his bunk with the pillow under his shoulders. It was three hours since the orderly had brought him his breakfast. In another hour he would doubtless bring in his lunch. He let his thoughts drift.

First he considered the disappointment of the night before last. He could find no explanation for it at all. Or rather, the obvious explanation did not seem to lead anywhere.

Clearly the unfortunate Biancelli had been indiscreet. He must have revealed to one of his fellow guards that he had a secret to sell: he might even have been rash enough to explain the arrangements he had made with Goyles. The person to whom he had spoken had reported him to Benucci. That was the sort of rotten thing that people did in Fascist countries. Whether Biancelli had actually been shot seemed doubtful. Such a step would have been drastic, even for Benucci. No doubt, however, he had been removed to another camp.

That Benucci should have taken the trouble to come along himself that night at exactly the time when Biancelli was due to come on guard was, thought Goyles, entirely in character.

There was no doubt about it: Captain Benucci was a four-letter man.

So far his real, inner beastliness had been cloaked to a certain extent by the necessary minimum civilities of an officers' prisoner-of-war camp, regulated technically by the General Protocol and watched over by the Protecting Power. Goyles wondered how long all that was going to last. When the pinch came, which of the two Benuccis was going to take charge? The suave, capable, formal Latin, or the German-trained sadist? Goyles had met many Italians, both of the old and of the new regime: but he had never met anyone quite like Benucci. He hardly seemed of the native stock at all, or if of native origin, warped from it by alien forces.

The strange thing was that out of these rambling thoughts an idea began to grow.

It had no definite beginning and no very logical thesis, but it centered around an expression which he had heard Hugo Baierlein use some weeks before.

"War criminals."

At the time the idea had been quite new to him. If he had considered the matter at all he had thought of war as a sort of football match—when the final whistle blew you went back into the pavilion and changed into your ordinary clothes and became friends again.

Now it seemed that this was not the invariable rule: that there were people whose crimes were so full-blown that they would be tried for them after the war: tried in a court of law, and duly punished with death or lesser penalties.

If there were going to be any war criminals in Italy, thought Goyles, Benucci must be well up on the short list. Consider the cases which he knew about himself. There had been Lieutenant Colley. Goyles had not been in the camp at the time but he had heard all about it. Colley, who was an excellent linguist and a professional actor, had disguised himself as an Italian officer, and with two friends dressed as Italian soldiers had bluffed his way out of the main gate. The security precautions in those early days had not been so strict. The trio were actually passing through the outer of the two gates when Benucci had happened to come out of the office building. He had recognized them as imposters at once. What happened next was not entirely clear, but all eye witnesses were agreed that Colley and his friends had from that moment no chance of escaping. There were groups of Italian soldiers in the road itself and in the square at the end of the road. Benucci had, without hesitation, ordered the sentries to shoot. All three escapers had been shot down at point-blank range.

The case of Major McFadden had been a good deal worse. There had been a faint cloak of military necessity about the killing of Colley and his friends. The McFadden case, if what was suspected was true, was unvarnished murder.

Major McFadden of the Ulster Rifles, an intemperate but likable Irish-man and a declared enemy of Benucci, had been Colonel Baird's prede-cessor as head of the Escape Committee. In this capacity he had been a constant thorn in Benucci's flesh. After a number of undignified brushes with authority he had been dispatched to Campo 5—the punishment camp, in the fortress of Gavi, in North Italy. Benucci and one sergeant of cara-binieri had gone with him as escort.

The party, however, did not arrive at Gavi.

McFadden, as Benucci had reported on his return, had been shot while trying to escape. The carabinieri sergeant had been posted elsewhere. At all events, no one had seen him again.

Very well, then, thought Goyles, assume for a moment that all these suspicions were correct. Assume that Benucci might be a man with a dirty past and a sticky future. How did that tie in with Coutoules?

He began to see how it might very well tie in.

Coutoules, it seemed certain, had been a creature of Benucci's. He had been introduced into the camp by him, for his own purposes. They must have been, to a limited extent, in each other's confidence.

With the immediate approach of the Allied Armies, and, over the hori-zon, the ending of the war itself, two things might have happened. First, and most probably, Coutoules might have tried a little gentle blackmail. He was well placed for it. With a foot in both camps, the chances were that he not only knew about Benucci's war crimes, but might be in a position to prove them to a disinterested authority.

As he lay on his bunk in the sunlight, and thought of these things, Goyles experienced that faint electric current, the water diviner's touch, which every investigator feels when, for the first time, he forces his way down from the surface of things as they seem, into the opaque depths of things as they might be.

It was at least a solution which put motives and actors in their proper perspective. He had felt all along, when he was considering the matter generally, that the killing of Coutoules had been an affair of organization. It was no sketchy improvisation. He was far from seeing how it had been done—how the body had been spirited from a room in one hut to a tunnel under a different one—but if the Italians had done it themselves it did, at least, open up certain fields of possibility.

It also produced the distasteful corollary, that the Italians—or Benucci at least—must know all about the Hut C tunnel.

There was, however, a second and, in a way, an even less pleasant line of thought. The Escape Committee, as the intelligence authorities of the camp, would certainly have questioned Coutoules once his position was known. Supposing their questioning had been—well, a little more rigor-ous than they had intended—and Coutoules had collapsed. Would they not have been well equipped to dispose of him in a tunnel? On the other hand there was a good deal against this idea. Had not the Committee themselves been the prime objectors to disclosing the body to the Italians? Had they not, in fact, organized its removal to the other tunnel, and thus unwittingly implicated Roger Byfold in the design? Had they not, lastly and by no means least, employed him, Goyles, to investigate the matter for them? And yet—the beginnings of a third and perfectly horrible theory came into Goyles' mind.

He was so overcome by its nightmare possibilities that he did not hear the footsteps in the passage outside, and he nearly fell off his bed when the key grated in the lock and the door swung open.

He glimpsed a figure in British orderly's uniform.

"Oh, it's lunch already, is it?" he said. Then he looked more closely and saw that it was Tony Long. "What the devil are you doing in that rig? Glad to see you, anyway."

Tony put the lunch tray carefully down on the table, and walked back to the cell door, took a quick look down the passage, and pulled the door shut. Then he turned to Goyles and said, "Cuckoo, you've got to do something."

Goyles was shaken by the unmistakable note of panic in his voice.

"What is it?" he said. "What's up?"

"It's that ass Overstrand. If it was only his blood on his own head, I wouldn't mind so much, but he's dragging in Hugo and Grim as well."

"Just start at the beginning," said Goyles.

"They've been pretty hush-hush about it—and I only heard today, rather by accident, from Hugo. They've been working on a wall-jumping scheme. It's Desmond Foster's scheme really. They've made ladders—there was rather a rumpus about that"—Long managed to smile in spite of his anxieties—"they pinched the rugger posts. They're going to fuse the overhead lights at half past twelve tonight and get over the east wall between the theater block and the showers."

"They'll never catch them napping twice," said Goyles. "You remember what we all said after the last show—they'd be bound to put in an alternative system of wiring—probably underground."

"That's just it. They think they have." He told Goyles about Tim Meynell and his discoveries.

"Sounds just feasible," agreed Goyles. "What's worrying you particularly?"

"I don't know," said Long. He looked sick. "I've got a feeling about it, that's all. I don't believe that they can be certain of fusing all the lights—it seems too easy to be true—and if they *don't* succeed in fusing them—well—in the present state of nerves it's going to be an execution."

"Why is Alec so set on this scheme anyway? If he sits tight for a week or so the tunnel will be through, or the Italians will have packed up and let us out."

"That's what I said to Hugo. Apparently they don't think it's going to work out like that. To start with, they've got an idea—it's Alec's idea really—that the Italians know about the Hut C tunnel—"

Goyles looked up sharply, but said nothing.

"Then, again, they don't believe that the Italians are going to let us out if there is an armistice. They think that this is the best time there's ever going to be for a break. I'm not at all sure there mightn't be some truth in this part. They say that all one has got to do is to get out and go south and sit tight. The theory is that when the British do land in Italy, the Germans are going to form a line somewhere—but obviously it won't be right at the toe of Italy—probably somewhere about Naples—or even further north—"

Goyles nodded. It was what he thought himself.

"If you can get out now, and get south of this line and lie up, you're safe as houses. When the landing comes, you'll be picked up by your own side. On the other hand, if you're north of the defense line it's going to be a very different proposition—to say nothing of the fact that you may never get started at all. The Italians may simply bundle us up and hand us over to the Germans. It's all very well for the S.B.O. to talk about making a rush. Supposing one morning Benucci lines the walls with soldiers and says, 'Pack up your kit, gentlemen. There's a German column waiting outside to escort you'—do you think anyone's going to commit suicide?"

"Something in that," said Goyles. "Was that their only reason—"

"No," said Long slowly. "There's something else too. Something you haven't heard about. It happened yesterday, and I haven't quite sorted it out yet, but Alec had a scrap with Rolf-Callender. It started over something quite silly, but the upshot of it was that Rolf-Callender accused Alec of murdering Coutoules—"

"He did *what?*"

"Just that. And what's more, Alec didn't deny it. Not directly, anyway. He just went very pink and haughty, and intimated to Hugo and Grim that if that was the sort of thing people were saying about him, the sooner he got out of this camp the better—"

"That's crazy."

"The whole thing's crazy. Look here, Cuckoo. If Alec really is sure that the Italians know about this tunnel, he must have some information that we haven't got. He must tell us what it is."

"Ten to one it's nothing at all, or he's just imagining things."

"Then if he's wrong, he ought to call the stunt off tonight. It isn't just himself. If he wants to earn a V.C. and clear his good name one wouldn't mind him doing a crazy stunt like this—but he's dragging Grim and Hugo into it too. I got the impression Desmond himself would have called it off, if Alec hadn't been so keen."

"What do you want me to do about it?" said Goyles.

"I thought—look here, you've got more influence with Alec than either of us—couldn't you have a word with him?"

"From here?"

"I thought—it might work—couldn't you change into this kit and walk out with the tray? We're about the same height and shape. Even if they noticed in the end, you'd have time for a word with Alec."

"There's one very good reason against that," said Goyles. "And that is that the sentry, who's not such a fool as you took him for, has been standing outside the door looking through the spy hole for the last two minutes."

2

The afternoon light had gone out of the sky. At seven o'clock Goyles' evening meal had arrived. It was a genuine orderly this time—Corporal Pearce, a young, black-haired Irishman who worked in Hut C. He had nothing to report. He said that the camp seemed very quiet.

At eight o'clock the lights in the cell had been turned on, and at ten they had gone off again.

Goyles lay on his bed. There was no chance of sleep. His own thoughts, mingled with what Tony Long had told him, had thrown a long shadow of foreboding over his mind. He wondered if it would, in fact, have made any difference if he had been able to have a word with Overstrand. He had managed to talk sense to him on previous occasions. Could there be anything behind this idea that Overstrand had killed Coutoules?

It seemed, on the face of it, the most arrant nonsense. Where had Overstrand been between nine o'clock and lockup that evening? He himself had been taking his regular evening walk around the perimeter with Roger Byfold. Their room had been empty when they got back to it. Alec had come in at half past ten. He hadn't told them where he had been—why should he? You didn't go round explaining to people where you'd come from last and whom you'd seen.

Looking at his watch Goyles saw that the time was near.

He pulled the table up to the window, put a chair on it, and climbed up.

Without shifting the center bar he could look out far enough to see the northwest sentry platform and the line of overhead lights. The searchlight on the platform, which came on every few minutes, was almost blue, so intense that it paled the overhead lights to a dull yellow.

Everything remained quiet.

Goyles looked at his watch again. It was almost a quarter to one. A tiny flicker of hope sprang up, that the attempt might have been abandoned.

As he was in the act of looking up again, all the lights went out. First the overhead lights flickered and disappeared: then, in mid-sweep, the searchlights dimmed and faded.

They've done it, said Goyles.

Then something happened which made his stomach turn right over. The searchlights glowed and came on again.

A second later he heard the machine guns start. They went on and on.

Chapter 9

Captain Benucci Removes the Mask

1

Goyles slept very little and woke early.

He was lying on his bed, fully dressed, when Corporal Pearce brought in the breakfast coffee and bread.

"You know what happened last night, sir?" said Pearce.

"I heard it happening," said Goyles. "Put down the tray on the table, would you?" It took a momentary courage even to frame the question. "What was the result?"

"Major Grimsdale and Captain Overstrand, sir—killed. Captain Foster and Captain Baierlein were wounded. They don't think Captain Foster has got much chance."

"What about Baierlein?"

"They don't think he's too bad. He fell right up against the wall, and they couldn't get a machine gun onto him. He got some in the legs."

"I see," said Goyles. It was a tiny bit better than he had dared to hope. In his own mind he had written them all off. Poor old Grim—

"—all over the camp, sir," said Corporal Pearce.

"I'm sorry," said Goyles. "I didn't hear what you were saying."

"I was just saying, sir, that there's a funny sort of feeling in the camp this morning, if you know what I mean."

"Yes, I do," said Goyles. He had seen it, and noted it before: the after effects of successful violence. He remembered a train journey before he had come to that camp. One of the prisoners, a young Air Force officer, had tried to jump from the train in broad daylight and had been filled full of buckshot by an excited sentry. The other guards on the train, who up to that moment had been behaving quite reasonably, had become hysterical and arrogant. The prisoners had gone sullen. It had not been a pleasant journey and but for the tact of a senior officer might have ended in a massacre in the station waiting room at their destination.

"Does anyone know how it happened?" he asked.

"They say that the searchlights have all got spare power units now, sir. They run on the mains for most of the time, but if anything happens to the mains, they can run on their own juice for a bit."

It seemed a likely enough explanation.

"Would you like me to wait and carry your things out for you?"

Goyles looked surprised.

"You've miscounted," he said. "I've got about three more days to do."

"I was having a word with the sentry when I was coming in," said Corporal Pearce. "So far as I could make out they're clearing you out this morning. I reckon they think they're going to need all the cells they've got before long."

"I see," said Goyles. "As bad as all that, is it?"

"All the chaps are talking about stringing up Benucci next time he shows his face in the camp, and the Eyeties have put double lots of sentries on the walls and they're all talking monkey talk and cleaning up their guns."

"If they're as trigger happy as that," said Goyles, "I'd better wait for a formal order of release. Thank you very much all the same."

After Corporal Pearce had gone he went over to the window and stood looking out of it. He stayed there for a long time while his coffee grew cold and his bread lay untasted.

He was getting used to the thought that two people he had known so well should be dead.

2

"I'm very sorry," said Colonel Baird flatly. "It was a feasible scheme—a good deal more feasible than many—and it failed, because we were without one piece of information."

"I'm not quite clear about that," said Colonel Lavery.

He and his Adjutant were seated at one side of his table; the three members of the Escape Committee were on the other side. The atmosphere was formal.

"On the previous occasion," said Colonel Baird, "it was established that a single set of overhead power lines carried the current for the perimeter lights and the searchlights on the sentry platforms, and, as you knew, we succeeded in fusing these with secateurs mounted on poles. We had always anticipated that the Italians would guard against this by putting in alternative, underground, wiring. Well, we found this underground line and we arranged to have it cut, too. What we didn't know was that there was a *third* source of supply, a self-contained emergency power-unit for each searchlight. The sort of thing they have in operating theaters."

"I see," said Colonel Lavery. "You were satisfied that if the lights had been put out properly there was a fair chance of success."

"Certainly. Once the four of them were up on the wall in a direct line between sentry platforms, the sentries daren't fire in the dark for fear of hitting each other. All the escapers had to do then was to drop from the wall and disappear down the hillside."

"On the face of it, then," said Colonel Lavery, "it doesn't seem to have been anyone's fault." He paused. "It does bring me to my next point though. Up to now I've agreed—and I've been very happy to agree—that all escaping activities shall be run by your committee. I haven't asked to be told about them. I felt that knowing nothing about them has strengthened my hand in dealing with the Italians. I'm afraid that's got to stop."

"Stop?" said Colonel Baird.

"I mean," said Colonel Lavery, "that from now on I want to know about any attempted escape before it takes place."

"Know about it, or approve of it?"

"Know about it and approve of it."

The line of Colonel Baird's jaw had become a fraction more prominent. Commander Oxey was unsmiling but neutral. Colonel Shore seemed to be secretly amused.

"It worked very well before," said Baird. "I'd like to understand why it's got to be changed."

"It worked in normal times," said Colonel Lavery patiently, "but these times aren't normal. We're sitting on the edge of a land mine which is going to go up at any moment. The whole situation is all of a piece. Anything one party does affects everyone else. If I'd known about last night's attempt—however much chance of success I thought it had—I'd have stopped it."

"Could you tell us why you would have done that, sir?" asked Commander Oxey formally.

"Have you looked at the sentries this morning? Have you ever watched a cat the first time it tastes blood? Sooner or later—it may be weeks, it may only be days—we're going to have to deal with these gentry. I'm going to have to deal with their commanding officer. I'm sure you won't misunderstand me if I say that all our lives may depend on the sort of attitude we have toward them and they have toward us. Well, last night wasn't helpful."

"I can't see how us stopping trying to escape is going to make the Italians any more respectful," said Colonel Baird.

"This morning," said Colonel Lavery, ignoring this, "I had a message that I was to go and see Captain Benucci at his office at midday. I was to go and see *him*. Formerly, when he has had anything to say he has come to see me. It's a small thing, but it's an example of what I mean."

"Do I take it," said Colonel Baird, "that you want to know all the details of escape activities—or do you just reserve the right to veto them?"

"I want full cooperation," said Colonel Lavery.

There was an awkward silence which was broken from an unexpected quarter. Colonel Shore said, "If I might be allowed to say so, I think you're right. This isn't a situation where it's going to help to have people pulling in two directions."

"Oh, quite," said Commander Oxey hastily.

"I'm not disagreeing," said Colonel Baird. "I'll do what I'm told, of course. It's only that—well, just because we got a poke in the eye last night it doesn't seem logical to suspend all escaping activity."

"Far from it," said Colonel Lavery. If he breathed a sigh of relief he was too experienced a tactician to do so openly. "If there's one thing that stands out above everything else it is that the tunnel's got to be finished. I believe that it doesn't even matter now if they guess what's going on— provided, of course, they just don't know where the tunnel starts. Suppose they do catch people dumping sand? What does it prove that they didn't know already?"

"It might be helpful," said Colonel Shore. "You know what you were saying about moral ascendancy. It's a thing I've noticed about these Italians myself. If you shout at them and insult them, it just raises their morale. They're like a troop of monkeys. They're bucked to think you're taking so much notice of them. But if you laugh at them they're lost."

"All foreigners are like that," agreed Commander Oxey.

3

Tenente Mordaci had been in two minds about coming into the camp at all that morning.

In the end, being in receipt of a direct order from his superior officer, he had belted on a large Biretta pistol under his cloak, and had started out cautiously on his morning round.

The routine of the camp seemed to be proceeding normally. A dusty game of basketball was in progress on the sports ground. The Dry Fly Club was holding a casting competition behind Hut B. A row of builders-of-the-body-beautiful were busy adding another layer of tan to their already overcooked torsos.

None of these groups made any hostile demonstrations as *Tenente* Mordaci walked past them, clutching his Biretta moistly beneath his cloak. Nobody spoke to him at all.

The whole camp seemed unnaturally quiet.

Between huts E and F he came upon Lieutenant Long. Lieutenant Long was raking thoughtfully over a rose bed. It was, in many ways, rather a curious rose bed. When it had first been dug, many months before, its surface had been level with, or even sunk below, the surrounding soil. Now, with successive loads of sand from the Hut C tunnel, it had grown upwards in an ever more and more voluptuous curve until it threatened with extinction the row of struggling rose bushes which were by now barely managing to keep their heads above the surrounding surge.

"A lovely morning, *Tenente*," said Long as Mordaci came up.

"I am surprised you can say so," said Mordaci solemnly.

"Why, what's wrong with it?"

"Can it be that you have not heard of the events of last night? Two killed, two wounded. Useless stupidity—"

Tony suspended his raking and looked up at him. "Good gracious me," he said, "surely you don't believe that stuff—"

"Believe! I myself have seen."

"I thought everybody knew by now that it was a fake. Surely those dummies didn't deceive you?"

"Deceive me! What fantasy is this?"

"The truth of the matter is that the only people who got hurt were the two sentries who shot each other in the confusion."

"Is that so?" said Mordaci. "Then perhaps you will explain how—"

"The trouble with you Fascists," said Long, "is that you've been propagandizing people for so long that you can no longer recognize the difference between truth and untruth—I'm sorry I can't stop and gossip. I've got a date with a girl—"

4

At five minutes to twelve Colonel Lavery, accompanied by his Adjutant, walked across to the main gate and asked to be taken to Captain Benucci.

There were two sentries on the inner gate, and one of them pointed his short rifle in the direction of the S.B.O. while the other went to the telephone.

Colonel Lavery was aware that this was only a gesture, but he felt happier when the second man returned and started opening the gate.

"You only," said the sentry who had telephoned, "not the other officer."

Captain Armstrong hesitated for a moment.

"That's all right, Pat," said Colonel Lavery, "don't let's start an argument. I expect it's only something about the rations."

The Adjutant saluted, and walked back to the camp. Colonel Lavery, followed by the second sentry, made his way to the carabinieri quarters, which lay beyond the punishment block. This was arranged, like the punishment block, with an L-shaped passage, only it contained more and smaller rooms: three on each side, and one at the end. Benucci's office was at the far end, on the left, and Colonel Lavery had taken two steps toward it when he was stopped by a soft whistle. He looked round, and saw, at a slit in the nearest door, the anxious eyes of Roger Byfold.

"Nice to see a friendly face, sir," said Roger.

"Good heavens, Roger. How are they treating you?"

"E vietato—" began the sentry in an anxious squeak.

"A bit short on exercise," said Byfold. "Otherwise all right."

"Anything I can do for you?"

"E assolutamente vietato—" said the sentry.

"You go and broil yourself," said Byfold.

The sentry, despite the fact that he was still holding his rifle, contrived the childlike outward-turning gesture with both hands which an Italian makes when a situation is beyond him. Then he said "Eh—ma—" and bolted down the passage toward Benucci's office.

"We've got a second before they turn the dogs loose," said Colonel Lavery. "Are you sure you're all right? They haven't been—"

"Not a single rubber truncheon," said Byfold. His face was white but his grin was unimpaired.

"Has there been any sort of court proceeding?"

"If anything's been done," said Byfold, "it's been done behind my back. Nor have I yet been induced to sign the traditional confession. Ah—here comes Torquemada."

"I regret," said Benucci, "that talking to the prisoner is forbidden." His voice was polite but his eyes had a cold, inquiring look in them. "Will you come to my office please."

In the office there was a silence which Colonel Lavery was determined not to be the first to break. In the end Benucci said, "I expect you are wondering why I have sent for you."

"Since, in the past, you have always come into the camp to see me, I imagined it must be something out of the ordinary."

"Yes," said Benucci. "I think you will think so. I sent for you to tell you that Captain Byfold is to be shot."

The satisfaction was so apparent, the animal was so near the surface, that the spectacle turned Colonel Lavery's stomach. Also, it steadied him.

Without taking his eyes off the Italian's, and keeping his voice at a careful, conversational level, he said, "Oh. When?"

"The execution will take place at dawn the day after tomorrow."

"On what authority?"

"The sentence has been confirmed by the headquarters of this district."

"No doubt," said Colonel Lavery, "but whose sentence?"

"The sentence of the military tribunal convened by the Commandant of this camp."

"Is it customary in Italy for a prisoner to be tried on a capital charge in his absence?"

"Depositions were read from all witnesses including the prisoner himself. All possible evidence was considered by the tribunal."

"Yes," said Colonel Lavery. "Did you give evidence?"

"My deposition was read also."

"And no doubt you stated in it that you knew perfectly well that Captain Byfold had nothing to do with the death of Coutoules."

There was a sudden gleam of white as Benucci showed his teeth. Then he got up from his chair, came to the front of his desk, within a few feet of Colonel Lavery, sat on the edge of it and crossed one neatly booted leg over the other.

"I answered the questions that were put to me," he said.

"I see."

"If you consider that an injustice is being done, you must comfort yourself with the consideration that, in war, injustices are common. Particularly in prison camps. Both in ours, and, no doubt, also in yours."

Colonel Lavery considered this for a moment and then said, "Were you thinking of any particular instance of injustice?"

"No. Not of any particular instance. I was speaking generally."

"And is that all you had to tell me?"

"That is all."

Colonel Lavery hesitated. He knew quite well that he only had one possible card in his hand, and it was a matter of life and death that it be played carefully. Not too soon, and not too late.

He turned, as though to leave the room, then, over his shoulder, he said, "I suppose you realize that you will be held responsible for this, when the British Army takes over."

"When they do," agreed Benucci.

"Personally responsible, I mean. You can't hide behind a tribunal which hasn't even been given a chance of hearing the prisoner."

Benucci stifled a yawn.

"There is an English saying," he observed, "about crossing a bridge when you come to it. No doubt you are right. *If* this camp was taken over by the British military authorities and *if* I was still in the camp at the time, some form of reprisal could no doubt be exacted."

Colonel Lavery left the room without another word. In fact he had nothing left to say.

When he got back to his room he found the Escape Committee waiting for him.

"They're out for blood, all right," he reported.

"You don't think it's possible that Benucci was trying to frighten you?" asked Baird. "It would be well in character."

"No, I don't. He'd thought it all out and he means to do it. At one time, something he said gave me the impression that he might even be getting a sort of personal satisfaction out of it all. It occurred to me to wonder— still, that doesn't matter now. The thing is, what do we do?"

"I can't understand it," said Commander Oxey. "He must know that his German pals are taking a beating in Sicily and he must guess that the British Army will be in Italy soon. He can't hope to shut all our mouths."

"I put the point to him," said Colonel Lavery. "But it didn't ring the bell at all."

"That's not healthy," said Baird.

"So I thought. To my mind it can only mean that the Fascists are going to make a fight for it. Italy's a damned, long, prickly country, full of defensive positions, and we're about four hundred miles up it as the crow flies. If the Italians stick by the Germans and keep their heads it's going to take the Army months to reach us. By the time they get here, we'll all be in Germany,

Benucci included. Or that's what he's reckoning on anyway."

"Might be a seaborne landing," suggested Commander Oxey. He didn't say it very hopefully. All four men were thinking the same thing.

"There could be," said Colonel Lavery. "Hardly as far north as this I should have thought."

There was another silence.

"If we told them everything," said Baird, "where we found Coutoules and how and everything. Made a clean breast of it. Do you think it would be any use?"

"I think they'd laugh in our faces," said Colonel Lavery. "They'd appropriate the tunnel, say thank you very much, and carry on with Byfold's execution, as planned."

"Then what do we do?" said Baird. "Sit and wait for it, and hope for a miracle?"

"If I might make a suggestion," said Colonel Shore. "Stop me if I say anything you don't agree with, but isn't there one possible solution we've been overlooking? It's a golden rule, when you've got two dangers, to see if you can't set them to canceling each other out. The Italians have taken Byfold, and they're forcing our hands by threatening to shoot him—with just enough color of legality to make them feel good about it. The only possible way we can save him, and it isn't a very certain way at that, is by giving up our last trump card—the Hut C tunnel. All right. Now we know where Byfold is. Colonel Lavery saw him this morning. He's in the carabinieri block, next to the cooler. That's right, isn't it?"

"Yes," said Colonel Lavery.

"And the cooler's empty at the moment, waiting for an expected influx of prisoners. And the cooler is next door to the carabinieri block. Do you see?"

"Not at the moment," said Colonel Lavery, "but please go on."

"Why don't we stage a nice little riot this evening, and get half a dozen of the right types put in the cooler? There are officers in this camp who can pick a lock with their eyes shut. They break out some time tonight, quietly remove the sentry in the doorway of the cooler, move across to the carabinieri block, let out Byfold, and then—"

"Yes. Then what?" said Baird.

"And then," said Colonel Shore, "they simply *come back into the camp*. That part shouldn't be difficult. There's only one gate sentry at night—and he's in his box on the outer gate. Provided the guards on the platform don't spot what's happening—and remember, they are concentrating on the camp, not on the Italian quarters—then the whole gang should be back in the huts before the alarm is raised."

"They might," said Baird. "I agree. It's so mad, and so unexpected, that it might work. But how are we any better off? We can't keep Byfold if they want him. That would simply lead to a pitched battle that we should be bound to lose."

"Surely," said Colonel Shore. "That wasn't my idea at all. I suggest that once Byfold is safely in the camp, *we put him down the Hut C tunnel.*"

It was Colonel Lavery who eventually broke the respectful silence which greeted this suggestion.

"Pure genius," he said. "No other word for it. It puts them in a cleft stick of course. Once they've searched the camp and failed to find Byfold, they must guess that he's in the tunnel, because that's the only considerable hiding place they have so far failed to discover. If they *do* know about it, they'll have to show their hand. If they don't they've got to give up Byfold."

"What about the other six?" said Baird. "They'll know who they are and they'll be certain to take it out of them—or do you suggest we put them down the tunnel too?"

"I should hardly say that was necessary," said Shore. "I don't think even Benucci could shoot them out of hand—they'd need some form of hearing if only to protect themselves—and that's all going to take time—"

"Provided they don't kill the sentry, I don't see that there could be any question of shooting them. The most they would get would be a term of imprisonment—"

"All right," said Baird. "The first thing is, who's going to do it? We haven't got much time. Goyles and Long are obvious choices. If they're willing, we'd better let them pick the rest of the team. I'll have a word with Goyles now. What do you say, sir?"

Colonel Lavery took his time over answering. Before he did so he looked at the calendar on his wall. July 19th.

"I wish it was a week later," he said. "Yes, I agree. It's almost the only thing to do. It may come off. It's better than sitting back and waiting."

5

"I wonder if I could have a word with you," said Tag Burchnall.

"Of course," said Goyles. "Come in. If it's about those rugger posts," he added, "I can only say how sorry—"

"No, nothing like that. It's just that we heard—it may be quite wrong, but you know how things get about in this camp—we heard there was some scheme on foot for getting Byfold out of clink—"

"That's right."

"From what I heard, it sounded rather a sporting thing altogether. I wondered if you wanted any help—Jerry Parsons is quite useful if it comes to a roughhouse, and Rollo isn't such a fool as he looks—"

Goyles made very little effort to conceal his surprise or his pleasure.

"You'd be very welcome," he said. "We've got four already. Anderson and Duncan are helping, but we needed two more. Come for a stroll round the camp and I'll give you the details—"

6

Goyles was on the final tunneling shift, and after tea he changed slowly into his digging kit, and made his way to the kitchen. He had done it all so many times before that most of his actions were mechanical, and only a quarter of his mind was on his job.

He had a lot to think about at that moment. It was as if two enormous kaleidoscopes were being shaken before his eyes, forming and reforming their incomprehensible patterns; or two wheels rotating and two films unrolling simultaneously. Sometimes the pictures coincided, but more often they were different. On the one side was Captain Benucci and the Fascist machinery of their captors and beyond him the ranked Fascist hegemony of Italy itself, with the toadlike *Duce* at the summit, all revolving, in some inexplicable way, around the person of Roger Byfold, who was sitting in his cell, waiting for whatever the day after tomorrow might bring. On the other side was the microcosm, the little world of the camp itself, the cell-like organization through which its four hundred inhabitants crawled and swarmed. Those who knew you and those who didn't. Your friends and your enemies—and it was becoming difficult after his surprising conversation with Burchnall that morning to be quite sure which was which. And just as the one pattern seemed to center itself round the figure of Roger Byfold, so was the other concentrated on the awkward, unlikable, unforgettable figure of Cyriakos Coutoules who, in that very tunnel, only eighteen days before—

"Wake up, Cuckoo," said Long. "You're number one tonight."

"All right," said Goyles. "Let's go. Who's doing number two?"

"Andy's two, I'm three. I'll start the pump going when you reach the bend."

Goyles lowered himself onto the truck and started, with the expertness of long practice, to propel himself forward up the tunnel. Anderson crawled more slowly behind him, holding in his hand a rope attached to the truck. It was Goyles' job, as number one, to do the actual excavation. The sand which he dug was placed in cardboard boxes, six of which fitted onto the trolley. Anderson, from an excavation at the halfway mark, would pull the trolley back, and load the boxes into two sacks. Long, at number three, would then make two journeys to fetch the sacks back to the shaft. It was also his job to keep the pump going. Now that the tunnel was more than a hundred and fifty feet long this system saved time and meant that the man at the face could dig almost uninterruptedly.

The tunnel was no longer quite the comfortable, all-enclosed affair that it had been. The effect of the half-timbering which the Escape Committee had ordered in the interests of speed was already apparent. To move at all in the last thirty feet was an agonizing performance. It was all right as long as you were on the truck itself, but moving on hands and knees was like making your way across a series of diabolical railway sleepers, and the sides of the tunnel, which were naked in every alternate revetment, dribbled a small but increasing shower of sand onto you as you moved.

Goyles hardly noticed any of this. He scooped and dug mechanically, filling all six boxes once, and then again. The end of his forty minutes' turn at the face was nearly up. While he waited for the jerk on the cord attached to his foot which would indicate that the truck was ready for hauling back from the halfway house, his mind reverted once again to its pressing problems.

The cord jerked.

Goyles half turned on his elbow, his leg caught the woodwork of the last revetment, and the next moment he was lying, flat on his face, in pitch darkness. He was pinned to the ground, like a slug under a lawn roller, by the weight of the sand which had fallen on him.

It was a few seconds before he actually realized that he was unable to breathe.

But even in that agonizing moment, as he arched his back and strained his muscles in a futile effort to raise himself, as the red lights started to flare and wheel behind his eyes, and his heart came bursting outward from his lungs, even at that moment, in his mind, curiously detached from the agony of his body, a tiny but decisive piece of the puzzle fell into place.

Chapter 10

The Put-up Job

1

Goyles owed his life to the fact that Long and Anderson were both old hands at tunneling; to the fluke that they happened to be together, at the halfway post, unloading the last lot of sand when the fall occurred; and to the fortunate chance that the lights did not fail.

If any of these things had fallen differently he would certainly have died.

"Start the pump," said Long. "I'll dig him out. You'd better use the trolley to get you back to the shaft." Almost before he had finished speaking he was himself moving at reckless speed, toward the face of the tunnel.

As he moved he calculated the chances.

The air line of the pump was a series of jointed tins, and it ran in a shallow trench, on one side of the tunnel. It was the first rule of tunneling that you extended this line scrupulously, tin by tin, as you went, and he prayed that Goyles had not forgotten to do so. Even in a heavy fall the digger's body might come down across the end of the air line and protect the outlet from the sand, and in such cases experience had shown that enough air could be pumped into the fall to keep the victim alive during the period of his unearthing. The chief danger was that, so long as he was conscious, his struggles to assist might block the air line altogether.

It was a big fall, and it was obvious to Long as soon as he saw it why it had occurred. The tunnel had run into the footing of the outer wall; the soil having already been disturbed from above would be the more likely to collapse when excavated from below.

Long lay on one side, his head almost on Goyles' stockinged feet, and started to shovel the sand past his own body like a fox terrier at a rabbit hole. He could hear the wheeze of air under pressure coming out somewhere in the mass ahead of him. He hoped that all the sand which was going to come down had done so already.

Goyles was showing no signs of life.

"Probably better if he stays that way for the moment," thought Long. He himself was sweating all over and the tips of his fingers were already raw. There was no time for finesse. He simply worked his way in until he could get his hands hooked into Goyles' belt. Then he braced his knees against the last intact frame of the tunnel, humped his back and heaved with all the unexpected strength that was in his slight body.

The frame shifted ominously.

The sweat on Long's body seemed to turn cold all at once. He stopped pulling and resettled himself. Then he took a deep breath, and pulled again, less violently, but as strongly. Under this pressure, Goyles' body started to move. Tony pulled him back steadily, shifted his own position again, and pulled again. Now he had him clear. He disengaged one hand, felt down to the side of the tunnel, and tore open one of the joints in the air pipe.

The fresh air poured out over both of them, cool and sweet.

He was lying there, trying to think coherently, and aware that he had gone dangerously near the limit, both mentally and physically, when he felt a hand on his heel.

Help had arrived in the form of Brandy Duncan.

"I've brought the trolley up with me," said Duncan. "Better get him on it. We can't try any first aid here. There isn't room. Are you all right?"

Long was almost as white as the unconscious Goyles.

"I shall be O.K.," he said. "Let's get him moving."

Back in the Hut C kitchen they found Dr. Simmonds, who, like the stormy petrel, could smell trouble from afar. Under his direction they laid Goyles on the floor and started to work. His glasses had been broken in the fall and in the rescue operations a splinter of lens had dug a long furrow down the side of his nose. This was now bleeding.

"Very healthy sign," said Dr. Simmonds. "He'll be round in a minute."

"We'd better clear up," said Duncan. "Give us a hand and we'll get the trap down. And we'd better get some of this sand swept up."

At this moment Goyles opened his eyes. He lay for a moment looking at the ceiling and then said, in a conversational tone of voice, "You can't move your hands, you know."

"That's all right," said Dr. Simmonds, "take it easy. You'd better carry him along to his room."

"But you can't move them," repeated Goyles. "It's not true. You can't move them at all."

"Get him under the legs," said Duncan. "You take his head, Tony."

"I'll be along in a minute," said Dr. Simmonds. "I'll mix him a sedative. He'd better stay in bed for twenty-four hours."

After they had gone the doctor stood for a moment, a puzzled look on his face. He had just realized what Goyles was talking about.

2

Hands. Dozens of hands. Singly and in pairs. A hand, larger than life, dragging itself, like a maimed octopus across the sand.

Curious, thought Goyles, that he had never before realized how significant was the human hand. It was in its *shape* that its true secret lay. The broad river of the palm, flowing out to the delta of the fingers. Four fingers, each one with a life and a character of its own, four tapering, aristocratic fingers and a gross plebeian thumb, a bastard connection, sprung from its own root back in the wrist. A distant and disowned collateral to the four beautiful sister fingers: each one with its sensitive tip and its sheath of horn.

A man could live with his hands, by his hands and through his hands, thought Goyles. And, conversely, he could be more truly hurt in them, than in any other part of his body. The stout Elizabethan, John Stubbs, punning at the scaffold when his hand was to be struck off: "Pray for me, now my calamity is at hand." Gestapo torturers, with delicate precision, plucking off nail after nail from the living flesh, like shells off a ripe filbert.

It was in the hands of Cyriakos Coutoules that the answer to all the mystery was contained. With the clarity that sometimes comes in a nightmare and disappears within a few seconds of awakening, so that it must be caught instantly or lost forever, Goyles glimpsed the naked logic behind the mysteries that had puzzled him and it shocked him, so that he cried out, and woke up to find an anxious Tony Long shaking him by the arm.

"It's all right," he said, "just a nightmare."

"You've been talking to yourself for hours," said Long. "I could put up with that, but when you started screaming—"

"I shall be all right now," said Goyles.

When he next opened his eyes, it was late morning, and his head was clear. There was no one in the room.

He groped for his spare pair of glasses and put them on. They rested awkwardly on the thick strip of sticking plaster down the side of his nose. They were a pair which had been issued to him, many years before, in England, for use inside a respirator, and this was the first time he had ever worn them. He took them off, bent them into a more comfortable shape, and put them on again, as the door opened and Corporal Pearce came in with a cup of coffee.

"Thanks very much," said Goyles. "I'm afraid I'm a fraud, really."

"Doctor's orders," said Corporal Pearce. "I hear you were in a bit of a turn-up yesterday evening."

"Roughly speaking, yes. Very good coffee, this. By the way who told you about it?"

"These things get round," said Corporal Pearce. He started to brush diligently under the beds.

Goyles watched him for a bit. Then he said, "Stop that for a moment, would you, and come and talk. There's something I wanted to ask you."

Corporal Pearce obediently propped the broom against the bed post and sat down on the end of the bed. He was a good-looking boy of about twenty, with the dark black hair and deep blue eyes that sometimes come together in the Celt or the Spaniard.

"How many orderlies are there in this camp?"

"There's about forty of us now, sir. Used to be more."

"They sent a lot of you off about a fortnight ago, didn't they—to do farm work?"

"That's right, sir."

"How did they choose the party?"

"There wasn't any choosing, sir. They just took the first twenty in the queue."

"Everybody wanted to go, did they?"

"Almost everybody. It was more food, you see, and more freedom, and the chance of seeing a few *signorinas*—"

"Did you volunteer?"

"No, sir, I didn't."

"Why not? Aren't you fond of food and freedom and *signorinas?*"

Corporal Pearce grinned and said, "Well—you had to give your parole—I didn't fancy that—particularly not just now."

"Are you hoping to escape, then?"

"You never know, sir. There's sure to be a chance—when things pack up—"

"I'm not arguing with you," said Goyles. "I just wanted to know. Would that be the general view among the orderlies—or is it just your own idea?"

"One or two of the lads think like I do. It's difficult to say, really."

Goyles pondered for a moment.

"Look here," he said. "This is something that perhaps I oughtn't to ask—and you mustn't pass it on. You say that some of you—you and a few of your friends—are keen to escape. The others, I take it, don't mind one way or the other. They're glad the fighting's over—and as long as they get enough to eat and don't get pushed around, then they're happy enough—"

"That's about it, sir."

"All right. But does it go any further than that? Would any of them actually help the Italians—if a suitable reward was pushed in their direction?"

Corporal Pearce looked unhappy.

"They're a mixed crowd," he said. "Some of those South Africans are very rough characters—don't even speak English, some of them—jabber, jabber, jabber, in a lingo of their own, sounds just like German to me—"

"But you don't know of anyone in particular—"

"Oh, no, sir. It's just that you can't answer for them, not knowing them."

"If any of you wanted to get a word to the Italians it wouldn't be difficult for you—"

"Easy as falling down. We're in and out all day—fatigues, Red Cross carrying parties, odd jobs—like that time I was bringing you your meals in the punishment block, remember—?"

"Yes," said Goyles. "That's rather what I thought. Well, forget all this, will you?"

An hour later he had another visitor. Colonel Baird came to see him.

"I thought you'd like to know," he said, "that the tunnel is all right. We had an inspection party down this morning. What fell on you was practically all the sand under the foundations of the outer wall."

"It felt like quite a lot of sand," agreed Goyles.

"We're not even going to roof it over. There's no need. In fact we'll probably develop it into a sort of second 'halfway house.' I reckon it pays to have a few sitting-out places in a tunnel of that length. You can get some traffic control installed when the time comes—"

Goyles agreed, but absentmindedly. His interest in the tunnel, at that moment, came second to more urgent problems.

"Any news of Roger, sir?"

"Nothing reliable."

"Do you think they mean business—or are they only bluffing? It would be just like Benucci—"

"Very like," agreed Baird. "I don't know. One can't rely on it, being one thing or the other. We're going ahead with this evening's show, anyway. That was one of the things I wanted to talk about. I don't think, in your present state, you could quite pull your weight in a show of that sor—"

"But I'm as fit as a fiddle, sir—really—"

"Well, there are plenty of others who can do it. Besides, we needed one more lock expert, so that both cell doors could be opened at once—"

"But really, sir—I'm not—"

"Look," said Baird, kindly but firmly, "this is just one of those rare cases in this goddamned camp where an order is an order. You're not going. Now relax."

Which was all very well, thought Goyles, as he lay on his bed at six o'clock that evening, and looked out of the window.

He knew that, as originally organized, the riot was due to take place somewhere on the playing field and at about that time. It might, of course, have been changed. No one would have told him anything.

He could see the usual evening sports program getting under way. There were games on both of the basketball pitches and a small group of experts were pitching a baseball in one corner, but the chief attraction that evening was the rugger game. The Old Hibernians appeared to be playing a Scottish team. Goyles could see nothing out of the ordinary, except that Tony Long (neither a Scotsman nor, incidentally, a rugby enthusiast) had apparently been co-opted into the Scottish scrum in which Anderson and Duncan were also performing. He noticed both Burchnall and Parsons in the Hibernian scrum.

The Italians as usual were suspicious of the whole performance. Ever since an enterprising escaper, under cover of a reconstruction of the rugger pitch, had caused himself to be buried in a shallow trench from which he hoped to emerge after dark, the orders had been that sentries were to exercise an active vigilance during all such games. When it did happen, everything happened very quickly.

At one moment a small sentry, his rifle slung over his shoulder, was pacing importantly across the halfway line. The next moment the ball had appeared from nowhere and struck him on the chest. He had barely time to utter a single, indignant bleat before the scrum had caught him, and he disappeared under a cataract of arms and legs.

The sentries on the walls were plainly in two minds. Outrages were being committed in front of their eyes, but they were unable to shoot. They relieved their feelings by screaming. The gates opened and a file of carabinieri doubled on, headed by Paoli. The scrimmage subsided and the sentry reappeared. He had lost his rifle and bayonet and, as became horribly apparent when he tried to stand up, his braces as well.

Goyles held his breath.

It was always touch and go at moments like this whether the Italian sense of humor or sense of dignity was going to come to the top. It was with mixed feelings that he saw that Captain Benucci had arrived and appeared to be taking command of the situation.

The groups separated and the dust settled.

To his surprise it became apparent that most of Captain Benucci's wrath was concentrated against the sentry. His admonitory remarks practically reached the hut. The sentry, holding his rifle in reverse in one hand, and the top of his trousers with the other, scuttled off.

The game restarted.

Half an hour later a disheveled and despondent Tony Long arrived and perched on Goyles' bed.

"You saw it?" he said. "Seemed to go pretty well, didn't it? Well, it was an absolute flop." He sat for a moment swinging his legs, and then said, "Wouldn't you have thought it a safe bet that they'd have arrested the lot of us? We were all there, all six of us, as arranged, holding little bits of that sentry's clothes and gear. All unutterably arrestable. I had his hat and bayonet scabbard. If ever you could have bet you were onto a safe thing, I should have thought that was it. I was only scared they were going to machine gun the lot of us. Then Benucci arrived—"

"I saw him," said Goyles. "What happened?"

"What happened?" said Long. "He laughed."

"I see."

"I'll do him this much justice," said Long. "He behaved exactly as an English officer would have behaved in the same circumstances. He tore the sentry off an awful strip—so far as I could follow what he was saying—for getting in the way of the game. He then told him to get back to barracks and get dressed. Then he gave everybody a sort of paternal tick-off. 'Boys will be boys—don't get carried away'—that sort of thing, and sauntered off."

"With the honors of war—"

"Oh, Lord, yes," said Long. "With every honor that was going. I've never seen a bluff called more competently."

"You don't have to be a good poker player," said Goyles, "to call a bluff when you know exactly what cards all your opponents are holding."

"Say that again."

"Look here," said Goyles, "either I'm mad or everyone else in this camp is blind. But isn't it perfectly obvious that everything we do and say *goes straight back to Benucci?*"

Long suspended his undressing and stood for a moment, with his head on one side, looking anxiously at Goyles.

"You're not still delirious, are you?" he said.

"I've never been clearer-headed in my life. You remember that first morning—when the Italians found Coutoules' body in the Hut A tunnel. All that fingerprinting and photographing and measuring marks in the roof of the tunnel. It stuck out a mile that they knew perfectly well that they were being offered a put-up job. I don't go so far as to say that they knew where or how Coutoules was killed, but they knew that he had been put in that tunnel for them to find. That stuck out so far that even the Escape Committee noticed it."

"All right," said Long. "When else?"

"Well, you remember my fiasco in the cooler. I thought at the time that poor little Biancelli might have blown his mouth off and got nabbed for indiscretion. Now I'm not so sure. And this business tonight makes me even less sure. You said yourself that it was unnatural. It was more than unnatural. It was plain bloody incredible."

"You realize what you're saying, I suppose," said Long slowly. "Take those three cases alone. If Benucci got hold of them as quickly as you say he did, he's got to have an informer who's well in the swim. Not just anybody. I don't suppose that more than a dozen people knew about any of them."

"I agree," said Goyles. "And it means a good deal more than that, too. Benucci's not a fool. He must know we're capable of working this out. Why should he practically go out of his way to give us the information? Why should he come and rub my nose in it, as he did over that Biancelli job—?"

"You tell me," said Long.

"I'll tell you what I think," said Goyles. "I don't think he cares a brass farthing for the safety and well-being of his informer in this camp. Any more than he did for his other stooge, Coutoules. And I'm beginning to think—and hope—that the reason for this is simply that he realizes, better than we do, that time is running out. We can't see the rope running off the end of the reel, but he can."

"Hang onto that," said Long soberly. "It's almost the only hope left for Roger that I can see."

3

Very late that night Colonel Baird was sitting in Colonel Lavery's room. They had been talking for a long time. Neither of them felt much desire for bed.

Breaking the silence, Baird said, "I don't believe he'll do it. I don't believe anyone in his position would risk it."

Colonel Lavery had no need to ask him whom he was talking about. "Anyone but Benucci, no."

"He's a tough character," agreed Baird.

Another silence.

"Do you remember once telling me," said Colonel Lavery, "about the time when you had a German prison camp under your command in the Delta? About the Nazis who ganged up on one of the prisoners and tried him and executed him. You had the ringleaders shot—very properly, in my opinion—you can't allow mob law like that in a prison camp—or anywhere else."

"Certainly I remember it," said Baird.

"Did it ever occur to you that Benucci—who's a pure Nazi, if I'm any judge—might be taking a sort of backhanded swipe at you for that incident? It's got all the usual Nazi trimmings. You manacle ten of our prisoners, we manacle twenty of yours. That sort of thing."

"You mean," said Baird slowly, "that because I have three men shot who *are* murderers, self-confessed murderers—he's going to shoot an innocent man?"

"That's about it. With all suitable display of justice and washing of hands, but that's about what it boils down to. I got the idea from something Benucci said when he broke the news to me about Byfold. 'Injustices are apt to happen in prison camps. They happen in your camps and in ours.' "

"If you're right about that," said Baird, "we shouldn't kid ourselves that there's much hope, should we?"

"The only glimmer I can see is in a report I had this evening from our I people. I can't make very much of it, but apparently the Fascist Supreme Council had an emergency meeting yesterday afternoon. It seems to have lasted until after midnight."

"Another of Musso's gags?"

"I suppose so. The only thing is that one usually reliable source says that the meeting wasn't called by Mussolini at all. Some people think it was Roatta. There's another school of thought that it was Graziano."

"One Wop's very like another to me," said Baird. He sat for a few minutes puffing at his empty pipe. "I'm inclined to fall back on the old infantry motto 'When in doubt, dig.' It may be a waste of time, but we've got so far with that tunnel, I think we ought to bring it through."

"I hear you had some trouble."

"Yes. Some sand came away under the outer wall. It's always apt to fall if it's been disturbed from above. We've got it all under control again now."

"How far are you going?"

"That may depend on the time element. I want to go at least another fifty feet. We're twenty foot below the surface now. If we go straight on for fifty feet we shall hit the slope of the hill over the crest and out of sight of the wall. It should make a very snug exit."

"Provided it doesn't collapse again," said Colonel Lavery. "I take it you'd thought of that. It'll be more vulnerable as it comes nearer the surface."

"It will be, and we had thought about it. From now on every inch of that tunnel's going to be revetted, if it means using every last bed board in the camp. Let 'em sleep on the floor. It'll harden them up for what's ahead of them."

Colonel Baird got to his feet, and added, apropos of nothing at all that had gone before:

"I'm sorry if we haven't seen eye to eye in the past. That's all over now. I'm on your side."

He was gone before Colonel Lavery could frame any suitable reply.

Chapter 11

Colonel Lavery Takes Over

1

Goyles was lying propped up on one elbow, on his bunk. He was looking out of the window. It was six o'clock in the morning and it was as quiet and as peaceful as the beginning of time.

The sun had come up from behind the eastern wall and was sucking the dregs of the early morning mist. Everything in camp was silent. Only faintly from outside came the sounds of the little village at the foot of the hill as it woke. An occasional car went past on the lower road. A woman could be heard shouting something in a high-pitched voice. The bells of two churches were wrangling for an early service.

Goyles sensed that Tony Long was awake, too.

"They can't do it," he said, without turning his head. "Not on a morning like this."

Tony said nothing.

There was a shuffle of steps in the passage and the door opened. It was Dr. Simmonds. He was fully dressed.

"Would you come along here," he said, "and see what you make of this?"

"Make of what?"

"I may be imagining things. Come and see."

Goyles and Long both pulled on some clothes and followed the doctor along the passage to the small room at the other end of the hut which he shared with the padre.

From this room you could see most of the northern wall of the camp.

"What's up?" said Goyles. "The sentries seem very pleased with themselves."

"That's not all of it," said Dr. Simmonds. "Where are the caribs?"

"You're right," said Long. "There's not one in sight."

The sentry on the platform nearest to them caught sight of the faces at the window, and a grin split his face. He put down his rifle, extended his left arm, and executed that indescribable Italian gesture which is made by chopping the forearm with the palm of the right hand.

"What does he mean?" said Long.

"It's usually a sign that someone's bought it," said Goyles grimly. "You don't think the little bastard means—"

"He's pointing at the camp gate—what the devil's up?"

"We can see the gate from our room," said Goyles. "Come on."

The three of them raced back.

When they got to the window of their own room they saw that something unusual was, indeed, happening. Normally no Italian ever came near the camp before eight o'clock. Now there was a small crowd in the compound and the inner gate was being thrown open.

"My God," said Goyles. "My God, it's Roger."

A small procession had entered the camp. There were two figures in front, one of whom was undoubtedly Roger Byfold. The other looked like Colonel Aletti.

"I'm going out," said Goyles suddenly.

Before anyone could stop him he opened the top of the window level with his bunk, pushed his long legs through and slid to the ground.

The sentry on the near platform must have seen him but he made no move.

Trying to look as if it was the most natural thing in the world to break out of your hut in broad daylight, Goyles strolled across to the next line of huts, walked along the side of Hut D, and peered round.

The deputation had passed him and had reached the senior officers' hut. Colonel Baird, Colonel Lavery and the Adjutant had all come out to meet it.

Goyles, realizing that nobody was worrying about him at all, sidled up and attached himself to the group. Everybody was talking at once. Roger Byfold caught Goyles' eye and grinned and at that moment Colonel Lavery turned round and saw him.

"Please, sir," said Goyles, "what's happened?"

"What's happened?" said Colonel Lavery. "Mussolini's fallen. Graziano's taken over. The Fascists are out."

2

"It doesn't mean that they're going to open the gates, you know, and let us all go," said Colonel Baird.

"I suppose not," said Byfold. He had eaten an enormous breakfast and, apart from a tendency to grin at everyone who spoke to him, was showing little outward signs of what had passed. "I suppose," he added, "that life should be a bit easier."

"In a way," said Colonel Baird.

"All the really top-line thugs have gone, sir. They melted last night. Benucci and Mordaci and that horrible little Mariescalo Butsi—the one we called the Butcher."

"When did you hear about it?"

"Late yesterday evening. I was lying on my bunk practically composing my own funeral oration—"

"You knew what was going to happen to you?"

"Oh, yes. Benucci told me yesterday morning. In detail."

"I see," said Colonel Baird. "Please go on."

"Well, about nine o'clock last night I think it must have been, there was a lot of coming and going. I take it that was Benucci and Company packing up. About an hour later, the Commandant arrived and after a good deal of huffing and blowing said that the dawn firing party had been postponed. I said, that was all right so far as I was concerned—"

"He didn't tell you about Mussolini?"

"No. But a bit later I noticed that I'd got a new sentry—an ordinary Eyetie—not a carib. He was bursting with the news. Didn't need any prompting. He told me the whole thing. I gathered from him, incidentally, that he wasn't really a Fascist at heart. Just an ordinary citizen who did what the brutal Fascisti told him to."

"I expect we shall meet a lot of those," said Baird dryly. "When you said that all the top-line thugs had gone, what exactly did you mean? Have all the carabinieri cleared out?"

"Oh, no, sir. At least, I don't think so. Paoli's still here—he was looking a bit seasick last time I saw him—and the ordinary carib is just running round looking for someone to give him orders."

"I see," said Baird. "As I said before, this doesn't mean that we're all going to be set loose. It's bound to make a difference though. Everybody must know, now, that Italy's going to pack up their piece of the war. That's bound to affect their attitude toward us."

"They'll be ever so tenderhearted," agreed Byfold.

"Another thing. You realize that the gentry who cleared out last night were all the real anti-escape experts. That's going to make life a bit easier."

"There's something I meant to say about that," said Byfold. "I got the impression that Benucci knew about the Hut C tunnel—"

"You're not the first person who's thought that," said Baird. "How did you get the idea?"

"Something he said—I can't remember exactly what it was—not in so many words. But I remember thinking that he did know about the tunnel, and that it was just like him to tell me that he knew, when he imagined I was going to be—well, when he thought I couldn't do anything about it."

"I see."

"Then, when I was thinking it over last night, I couldn't help thinking what a joke it would be if Benucci and his own particular buddies *did* know about the tunnel, but in the general excitement they had pulled out, and had forgotten to pass the information on to anyone else."

"Either forgotten, or not bothered," said Baird. "I don't suppose there was much love lost between the two gangs. Was there anything else you picked up that might be useful?"

"Well—no. Nothing in particular." For a moment Byfold looked almost embarrassed.

"Certain?"

"Yes. Quite certain. If I do think of anything I'll let you know."

"All right. The S.B.O. wants a word with you before you go back to your hut. You might go and see him now. I think he's in his room." Colonel Baird paused. He felt that the occasion demanded something. "I'm glad they didn't shoot you," he said.

3

"All I really wanted to see you about," said Colonel Lavery—"do sit on the bed—it's much more comfortable than the chair—is to get your ideas on the present setup on the other side of the wire. You're probably in a better position than any of us to judge it. In particular I'd like to know what you make of our Commandant. He's going to be the important factor now that Benucci's gone."

"I didn't see a great deal of Colonel Aletti," said Byfold. "I was kept to the carib quarters. He presided at both of my official examinations—if you can call them that, they were hardly trials—more like a court of inquiry in the Army. He never said much and left most of the talking to Benucci. I don't know whether he knew what was in the offing, but I think he was quite glad to put most of the responsibility onto Benucci's shoulders."

"I expect he feels that now," agreed Colonel Lavery. "What I was really getting at was, what sort of person you thought he was—"

Byfold considered this. He realized that a considerable compliment was being paid to his judgment and he did his best. "I think," he said, "that he's like any weak man when he's forced into a position of responsibility. He'll be pleasant as far as he can, so long as it doesn't put *him* on the spot. But if any higher authority threatens him, he'll go back on us without any compunction."

"And if the Germans say one thing and his Italian bosses say something different—?"

"It would depend which was in a position to kick him hardest."

"That's much as I thought," said Colonel Lavery. "But I'm glad to have your confirmation. Did you pick up anything else that might be useful while you were over the other side?"

"No, sir. Nothing startling."

If there was, once again, a certain hesitancy in Byfold's manner, Colonel Lavery apparently did not notice it.

4

"Come in," said Colonel Lavery. "Who is it? Oh, it's you, John. Sit on the bed—it's more comfortable than the chair. What's up? You look as if you've had some bad news."

"Not bad news, just news," said Major Gibb—he was the tall major in the I Corps who had been coordinating security arrangements for Hut C tunnel—"I'm trying to make out what it means."

"How did it come?"

"The usual way," said Major Gibb. "I think there's no doubt it's a War Office instruction all right." He produced a sheet of paper on which he had himself transcribed the following message:

> In the event of an Allied Invasion of Italy, officers command-ing prison camps will ensure that prisoners of war remain within camp. Authority is granted to all officers commanding to take necessary disciplinary action to prevent individual prisoners attempting to rejoin their own units.

Colonel Lavery read it thoroughly carefully once, and then again. He seemed to be weighing the value of every word.

"How long do these messages take to come in?" he asked.

"It's difficult to say, sir. It's not a quick system, you know. That mes-sage might have originated two or three months ago."

"That's rather what I thought. I take it that no one else knows about this?"

"Actually two of my chaps got it independently. I've shut both their mouths, I hope. I'm the only other person in camp who knows about it."

"It had better stay that way for a bit," said Colonel Lavery. His eyes again sought the calendar on his wall.

July 21st.

5

"Come in," said Colonel Lavery. "Oh, yes. The Adjutant told me you wanted to see me. Do you think you could make it after lunch, I'm a bit rushed—"

"It won't take a minute, sir," said Rolf-Callender.

"All right, then." Colonel Lavery repressed an inner sigh. It was soon apparent, however, that Rolf-Callender was not in an aggressive mood. On the contrary he appeared to find it difficult to start.

In the end he said, rather abruptly, "I wanted to clear up a bit of a misunderstanding."

"Yes."

"It's about Overstrand, sir. Some time ago—you may have heard—we had a bit of a row. It wasn't anything much—just one of those things that happen."

"I did hear something about it," admitted Colonel Lavery.

"Well, I lost my temper, and—among a lot of other nonsense I hinted that he knew something—that he had something to do with killing Coutoules."

Colonel Lavery looked up sharply, but said nothing.

"I thought I ought to tell you, sir, that it was nonsense. It was just one of the stupid things people say when they're in a temper. There was nothing to it at all. In view of what happened—"

"If it's any comfort to you," said Colonel Lavery, arriving with some skill at the real heart of Rolf-Callender's discomfort, "I can assure you that Overstrand's attempt to escape had nothing to do with your accusation. We're pretty sure now that he could have had nothing to do with Coutoules' death and presumably he knew that he himself was innocent."

"Thank you, sir."

"In fact," said Colonel Lavery, "if anyone was to blame for his death, in the last analysis it was probably me."

6

"Come in, all of you," said Colonel Lavery. "There's one chair, but I expect some of you can get on the bed—it's a bit of a squash but I won't keep you long."

Besides the Colonel there were seven men in the room: the five hut commanders, Colonel Baird and the Adjutant.

"I expect," he went on, "that you've all heard what's happened. It's a bit difficult to straighten out, but I gather that Mussolini's out of office, and his personal gang are on the run. General Graziano has taken over, nominally still under orders from the Fascist Grand Council. I imagine, however, that there's no doubt about his real position. He's only got one brief—and that is to get Italy out of the war, by hook or by crook."

"How soon, do you think, sir?"

"As soon as he can—but I don't imagine it's a thing that can be done in a matter of days. Getting out of a war is a two-sided business. They've got to get in touch with our military headquarters, and fix up some sort of terms, and I don't imagine that the Germans are going to sit by and watch that happening—it'll all have to be done very carefully under cover."

"How long do you think, sir?"

"I give it a month. But that may be two weeks wrong in either direction. It's that interval we've got to use to the best advantage. We've got to get on with the tricky business of ousting the Italians and taking the real control into our own hands. We can't go the whole hog yet—" Colonel Lavery grinned—"but it will be instructive to see how far they *do* let us go. First of all, I intend to make the evening parade for roll call a British parade rather than an Italian one. You all know how it's run at the moment—people slope onto parade just in time to have their names called and get away as soon as they are allowed to. As from tomorrow that's going to be changed. Huts will parade, as companies, under their company commanders, five minutes *before* the time fixed by the Italians for the roll call. Moreover, no one will dismiss until I give the word."

Of the five hut commanders, four made no attempt to conceal their satisfaction at these rather startling orders. The fifth, a small major from a heavy antiaircraft regiment, looked so upset that Colonel Lavery made a mental note that he would have to be replaced immediately.

"We don't want to run before we can walk," he went on, "so I'm not going to risk a full-dress inspection at once. I'll give you ample warning when it is going to come off, and by that time"—he allowed himself another fleeting smile—"I don't want to see *any beards*. That's as far as I've got at the moment. Has anyone else got any suggestion?"

"Are we going to adopt any sort of uniform dress?"

"I think not—not yet, anyway. It would attract attention, and would be asking for trouble. You might make sure that everybody has one serviceable outfit for an emergency."

"Can't we introduce some proper system for requests and complaints? At the moment anyone who wants anything comes straight up and starts blowing his head off—"

"I entirely agree," said Colonel Lavery, remembering his encounters with Rolf-Callender. "We'll have the Army system put into force—complaints to be put forward through the usual channels."

"Security," suggested Baird.

"I was coming to that," said Colonel Lavery. "I think that for the next few days you can chance your arm to almost any extent—I mean, over sand disposal and that sort of thing. They're bound to be disorganized, with Benucci and his trained thugs gone, and it's going to take them time to sort themselves out."

"I was thinking the same thing myself," said Baird.

7

"It is my destiny," said Roger Byfold, "to do the right thing at the wrong time. I am told that I grinned fatuously while I was being christened, and I broke into loud howls during my wedding ceremony. No doubt at my funeral—"

"What's all this about?" said Goyles.

"I was referring to my recent incarceration. Normally a period in the condemned cell will set a man up for life. He can sell his life story to the *Daily Yell* and his love story to the *Daily Smell*. Serial rights alone should be enough to keep him in modest comfort for the rest of his life—or his widow, should his appeal fail—but look at me!"

"If you insist," said Long agreeably.

"What sort of rake-off have I got from my harrowing ordeal? When I was coming back to the hut this morning I met Dopey Gibbon. He had almost got past me when he stopped, came back, and said, 'Weren't you going to be shot this morning, or something?' 'They've postponed it,' I said. 'Oh, good,' he said. 'It just occurred to me to wonder if you had any spare *vino* tickets. You won't have been able to use yours lately, I suppose.' "

"Never mind," said Goyles. "Tony and I are glad to see you back."

"Did you pick up any ideas about what's going to happen to us—all of us, I mean?"

"I've no doubt in my own mind at all," said Byfold, speaking, for him, fairly solemnly. "This country's heading for one great big typical Italian shambles, with everybody screaming and waving their hands and shooting their best friends, and it's going to be up to us to take the best advantage of it. As from tomorrow morning I propose to do P.T. twice a day and to spend the rest of the time brushing up my Italian."

The other two looked at him.

"Are you serious," said Long, "or is that just a line?"

"Dead serious," said Byfold. "I got a good many chances to talk to those characters who were guarding me, and they all said the same thing, carabinieri and all. Once Italy gives up the war you can go anywhere you like in this blessed countryside and count on help. Now that the Fascists are gone, that's doubly true. If you were outside these walls now, you could walk the length and breadth of Italy, and count on a meal and a bed every night."

"And when do they think the shambles is going to occur?"

"As soon as Allied troops land in Italy. And I reckon that that's going to be the time when we all have to prove whether we're mice or men. It's going to be the sort of chance no prisoner of war is ever going to get again."

"If he can get started."

"Yes," said Byfold. "*If* he can get started."

"You don't sound too happy about that," said Goyles. "Any special reason? The tunnel's five-sixths done. It's well past the outer wall. We three are almost first on the roster to go out of it. It ought to be money for old rope."

"I suppose so," said Byfold.

"What's on your mind?" said Long.

"I—look here, you've got to keep quiet about this, because I may be quite wrong—although they both asked me—but something *did* happen while I was in the carabinieri hut. It was the first morning I was there. I wasn't in the end cell, where they put me later, but in a room next to Benucci's office. It hadn't got a spy hole, so I couldn't see who went past, but there was a good deal of coming and going, and I couldn't help thinking that some of it was probably on my account, so I listened as carefully as I could to see if I could pick up anything that was being said next door. It wasn't at all easy, and you couldn't hear anything very distinctly, but I suddenly realized that something rather odd was going on. At least one of the voices was English."

Goyles remembered Meynell's story.

"Could it have been the wireless?" he suggested.

"It didn't sound a bit like the wireless. You could hear that all right, when it was on. Dance music and announcements and so on. This sounded quite different."

"Educated or uneducated?" said Long.

"Educated, I thought. You could only pick up the general tone of it, but there were occasional words—I heard 'roll call' more than once. No Italian says 'roll call' in just that way."

"Could it have been the S.B.O.?"

"I don't think so," said Byfold. "According to Pat the only time he's ever gone over there to talk to them was when I saw him on the morning after the shooting. Before that, Benucci always used to come in here."

"Was it distinct enough," said Goyles, "for you to pick up any sort of intonation?"

"Yes," said Byfold, "that's just it. There was. I'm prepared to swear it was either an American or a Colonial speaking."

He paused, and added unhappily, "That's what makes me wonder about our tunnel."

8

That afternoon, as he had half been expecting, Colonel Lavery was summoned to a conference by the camp Commandant.

"No doubt," said Colonel Aletti, after the preliminary courtesies had been exchanged, "you will have been thinking about the somewhat startling news which was received this morning."

Colonel Lavery agreed that he had been thinking about it. Conversation was not easy. Colonel Aletti spoke slow grammatical English, but he had nothing like Benucci's smooth competence. Nevertheless he seemed to understand Colonel Lavery fairly enough.

"I am not a man who interests himself in politics," went on Colonel Aletti. "I am a simple soldier. I receive orders from my superiors. I carry them out to the best of my ability."

Colonel Lavery indicated that this was roughly the system in the British Army, too. As he spoke, he was weighing up the man in front of him. He thought that Byfold's diagnosis might prove to be reasonably accurate. Colonel Aletti did not look to him like a strong man. He had the long, sad, aloof, slightly petulant face which many Englishmen imagine to be typical of the Italian upper class because it is the face they most often see, in the good clubs in Rome, the villas above Firenze, and the *salles privées* in casinos up and down the Corniche. With his well-pomaded gray hair, his correct carriage, his bemedaled uniform and his thin, neatly booted legs, he looked, thought Colonel Lavery, quite strikingly like the late Sir Henry Lytton in his role of the Duke of Plaza-Toro. He also reminded himself that this was the man whose decision, or lack of it, might mean the difference for all of them between a chance of liberty and an unthinkable prolongation of their imprisonment, and chose his next words carefully.

"I take it," he said, "that the case against Captain Byfold may be assumed to be at an end."

"Certainly," said Colonel Aletti. "The process was conducted, at the instigation of Captain Benucci, under the orders of the Fascist hierarchy: such orders are no longer effective."

"I am glad to hear it. Now with regard to the camp. Have you any idea what will happen to us?"

"My orders, at the moment, are to carry on as before. Marshal Graziano has published a communiqué, proclaiming Italy's unalterable intention of fighting on until victory is won."

"Yes," said Colonel Lavery, "I read it in the *Corriere*. Might I suggest, however, as men of the world, that we are entitled to look beyond the words and consider the realities behind them."

"Certainly," said Colonel Aletti cautiously. "What particular reality had you in mind?"

"When the English land in Italy, what will the Italians do?"

"Since you ask the question frankly, I will answer it frankly. Much depends on where they land."

"Yes," said Colonel Lavery. There was plain sense in that. He shifted his ground slightly. "I take it that pending this happy outcome, it should now be possible for us to cooperate more than we have done in the past."

"Nothing will give me more pleasure. It has often pained me in the past that we could not conduct affairs with more amiability."

"I agree," said Colonel Lavery, rather grimly.

"Such trouble as there has been, you must realize, has not been of my making. I was under the necessity, in many respects, of taking orders from Captain Benucci. Nominally, he was my subordinate. But being of the Party, he had authority exceeding mine in many matters. Many of his actions I did not approve of, but I could not prevent."

"I quite appreciate that."

"I doubt it," said Colonel Aletti frankly, "for it is a system which would be inconceivable in any but a Fascist country. I was responsible for all matters of routine administration, but where there were questions of policy, I had to accept the Party decision—as announced by Captain Benucci. All security matters, too, were controlled by him, through his senior carabinieri officers. I was left almost entirely in the dark. They had their own methods. You may know, for instance, that they employed spies in the camp."

"I had heard it suggested," said Colonel Lavery, "that Coutoules—"

"Was Coutoules in the pay of Benucci, then?" Colonel Aletti sounded genuinely surprised. "I did not know that. I was told nothing. The identity of the other was also kept from me—"

"Of the other?" Colonel Lavery hoped that his voice did not sound too eager.

"You did not know, then," said Colonel Aletti, "that there was a German Intelligence officer in the camp?"

Chapter 12

The Barretts of Wimpole Street

1

"He said *what?*" said Colonel Baird.

Colonel Lavery repeated the information.

"He must have been pulling your leg," said Colonel Baird. "The idea's fantastic. Did he give you any idea who it was?"

"He couldn't. He didn't know himself."

"Then how did he know about it?"

"I asked him about that. Apparently Benucci was rather tight one evening and was boasting that nothing went on in this camp without him knowing about it. The Commandant, who hadn't got much use for Benucci said, far from it. The English were so stupid that they didn't even realize that they'd got a full-fledged member of the German Intelligence Service planted among them."

"He might have meant Coutoules."

Colonel Lavery considered this. "He might have," he agreed. "Coutoules didn't look much like a German."

"Did he say whether he was posing as an officer or as one of the orderlies?"

"He didn't say."

"If it's one of the officers," said Colonel Baird, "I'll eat my desert boots, in public."

2

When he thought about it afterward Colonel Lavery came to the conclusion that the most remarkable feature of this period was the slow, almost imperceptible, but very steady rise in the morale of the camp. There was no lack of grumblers when his orders were first made known, but the majority opinion was so solidly behind him that he felt strong enough to ignore them.

Through that boiling month of August—and it was hot even by Italian standards—organization and discipline improved and the camp ceased very gradually to be a collection of individuals and became a community, inspired by an object. What that object was—what precise hand fate and the Italian Government were going to deal—nobody knew. It was sufficient, at the moment, if they put themselves in the best position to play the cards as they fell.

Hut commanders instructed their assistants and cursed their black sheep. Colonel Baird drove his digging teams to more and more furious endeavor and Colonel Lavery found every morning on arising one new gray hair on his head.

Some of the most surprising converts to military enthusiasm were the Old Hibernians.

"I must confess, I never saw much sense in that escaping nonsense," said Tag Burchnall, "but give me a decent, limited, military objective and I'm for it. It might be an idea if we green-blancoed our webbing, don't you think, before parade tonight. It'll wipe the eye of B Section, if it does nothing else."

It was about this time also that Roger Byfold began his keep-fit campaign. Like everything else that he undertook he went into it with a rational and compelling enthusiasm.

"I've given the matter a good deal of thought," he said to Goyles and Long. "As I told you, it's quite clear that the time is coming when some special effort will be demanded of everyone. I am not sure what form this effort will take. It may demand a rapid gymnastic feat, such as the scaling of these walls, or jumping from a moving lorry or train—we must therefore maintain bodily suppleness and agility by means of Muller's exercises before breakfast and a regular physical-training class at least once a day. Further, since the initial break will undoubtedly be followed by a long period of marching, we will harden our feet by making first ten, then twenty and later thirty circuits of the compound every evening, in our heaviest boots. Finally, since we shall be traversing a friendly or neutral countryside we had better brush up our Italian. Tony is the best linguist— he shall give us both an hour of colloquial Italian each day before lunch. Thus when the moment comes, we shall be armed at all points—"

"*Speriamo,*" said Long, in his best colloquial Italian.

It was during this period, too, that Goyles realized the truth about the death of Coutoules. He did not reach his conclusions by any blinding flash of intuition. Like all problems long and seriously thought over, the answer arrived in installments. New, apparently irrelevant, facts came to light, and old facts, long sifted and half forgotten, assumed a new significance, until finally, as to one who stares into the red heart of the fire, the shapeless began to assume a shape and the formless to take form.

One such odd fact came out of a conversation with the padre, a tall Etonian, who had done good work all the previous winter in one of the "other-ranks" camps; had nearly died of enteritis; and had been moved to Campo 127 direct from hospital.

He and Goyles attended the same Greek class, and it was coming away from a morning session that the conversation turned to the remarkable difference between the ancient and the modern inhabitants of Greece, and so, by easy stages to the late Cyriakos Coutoules.

The padre said, "I suppose I was the only person who met Coutoules before he came to this camp."

"How's that?" said Goyles, surprised. "I thought this was his first camp."

"Indeed not. He was in the Modena other-ranks camp with me last autumn. I believe there was some doubt at that time about his officer status. Then he got himself shifted to Cremona."

"Was that the camp at Modena where they nearly had a mutiny?"

"That was the one."

"What exactly happened?"

"The prisoners found out that the Italian staff were appropriating Red Cross parcels for their private use and lodged a complaint. The authorities then stopped *all* Red Cross issues and halved the ration—"

"And a lot of the prisoners nearly starved."

"It wasn't a question of 'nearly,' " said the padre shortly.

"I see," said Goyles. He turned this over for a moment in his mind. "Is it known who was responsible?"

"I think so," said the padre. "Yes, I think we know all right. Nominally it was the Commandant who gave the orders, but I think the real villain of the piece was his second-in-command, Captain Bernadi—"

"A carib?"

"Yes."

"Well, I hope someone's got a note of it," said Goyles.

At the time the information made no further impression on him.

It was some days later that he heard the word Cremona mentioned in conversation and linked it up by an effort of memory with what the padre had told him.

The speaker was a submariner, a naval lieutenant who contrived (it is a secret known only to the Navy) to combine a look of youthful innocence with a huge red beard.

"Were you at Cremona?" said Goyles.

"For my sins, yes," said the submariner.

"Was it a strafe camp?"

"Not really. We called it the 'sorting house.' I think it was the sort of camp you got sent to if the Italians weren't certain about you. If they came to the conclusion that you were a hard case you probably went to

Campo 5 at Gavi. They evidently decided that I was innocuous and sent me on here."

"Do you remember Coutoules at Cremona?"

"Yes, more or less. His last week there was about my first. We weren't chums. Anyway, there wasn't much time for beautiful friendships at Cremona. Life was grim and life was earnest and the end, in a number of cases, was the grave."

"I heard it wasn't very pleasant," said Goyles. "Who was the cause of it all?"

"The real villain was the Italian Intelligence officer, a deep blot called Marchese. He had one eye and no morals."

"He was a bit of a terror, was he?"

"He was a swine," said the submariner.

"He can't have been much worse than Benucci."

"Put them in the same cage in the zoo," said the submariner, "and there wouldn't have been a cloven hoof's difference between them."

"Hmph," said Goyles.

He picked up the next thread in the theater hut. He had strolled in one morning and was sitting quietly at the back watching one of the final rehearsals of *The Barretts of Wimpole Street*.

He could not help thinking that Rolf-Callender for all his faults was an extremely accomplished actor. On the stage, even without makeup or broadcloth, he opened out, somehow, into the flamboyant personality of Robert Browning. Offstage he was insignificant. Behind the footlights he was a person.

As the rehearsal was breaking up Captain Abercrowther caught sight of Goyles and came across to talk to him.

"Good show, Angus," said Goyles. "You looked as if you really enjoyed bullying all those children."

"It answers a deep-felt want in my nature," agreed Captain Abercrowther. "But that wasn't what I had to say to you. There's something I've been meaning to tell you for some time."

Whereupon he repeated to Goyles the observations which Captain the McInstalker had already made to him about the strange movements of the Italian laundry van.

"Look here," said Goyles, "are you absolutely certain that was the night that Coutoules—"

"July first?"

"Yes."

Captain Abercrowther took out a small diary and consulted it. "There's no doubt about it," he said; "we were both going to dinner that night with Lady Pat Keyne—Basingstoke's youngest, you know—and that was why we particularly wanted our shirts."

"Did you see where the van stopped on its way round the camp?"

"It only stopped in front of the senior officers' hut. We were hoping it would come on here, but it didn't. When it went it went straight out."

"What time would that have been?"

"Between half past nine and ten. It was getting a bit dark."

Goyles mentioned this conversation to Tony Long that evening, and Tony was able to confirm it.

"I saw the van going out," he said. "I was at the cooler window. I should have said that it was nearer ten than half-past nine. What's it all about?"

"I'm not quite sure," said Goyles.

Nevertheless, the pieces were beginning to join together.

3

"I'm afraid," said Colonel Lavery to his Adjutant, "that the Commandant is no longer quite the old friend that he used to be."

"I thought it was too good to last," agreed the Adjutant. "I expect yesterday's fiasco upset him a bit."

He referred to an unfortunate moment at roll call on the previous evening. Evening roll call, under the new regime, was now a smart, reasonably well-turned-out parade. It was also becoming apparent to the Italians that it was a parade which was conducted almost wholly by and for the benefit of the prisoners themselves.

Companies fell in under their company commanders, were inspected, and stood at ease. When the Italian orderly officer was signaled, Colonel Lavery appeared, and the parade was called to attention and handed over to him. At the end of the roll call—which took about a fifth of the time it had done in the old, disorderly days—the parade was again called up and properly dismissed.

On the evening referred to, Colonel Aletti had elected to come and watch proceedings for himself.

At the conclusion of them, when the last name had been called, he had given the order, "You may fall out." No one had moved an inch. Thinking that he might have been misunderstood, he had repeated the order. Upon which Colonel Lavery had given the order, "Parade dismiss."

It was not perhaps the most tactful way of demonstrating to Colonel Aletti that the control of his camp was changing hands.

"We shall have to butter him up a bit," said Colonel Lavery. "We can't afford to get at cross purposes just now."

"The Italians will have to make their minds up soon which way to jump," said the Adjutant. "It's more than a month since Sicily was finished. We must land in Italy before long."

"I wish we weren't quite so far north," said Colonel Lavery. "With the best will in the world it's going to be tricky, and if the Italians turn sour— Yes, who is it? Oh, come in, Baird."

"I thought you'd like to hear this," said Colonel Baird. It was difficult to say whether he was amused or annoyed. "We've just suffered our first security search since the fall of Mussolini."

"Was it a thorough one?" said Colonel Lavery. "Did you lose much?"

"I should have described it as concentrated rather than thorough," said Baird. "Paoli brought in a dozen soldiers and caribs and a few workmen. They went straight to the kitchen and took up the whole of the floor, including the stove which they removed bodily and the slab it stands on—they seemed mighty suspicious of that stove."

There was a moment of horrified silence.

"Then they've found the Hut C tunnel," said Colonel Lavery.

"Fortunately no," said Baird. "Indeed, they had very little chance of doing so, since the kitchen they elected to demolish so thoroughly was the one in Hut A."

"But—" said Colonel Lavery.

"What—?" said the Adjutant.

"By the time they had finished operations," went on Colonel Baird smoothly, "and had discovered absolutely nothing for their pains except the undisturbed subsoil of the hut, I had caused to be gathered a large and sympathetic crowd of onlookers who gave them very generous applause as they came out empty-handed. They didn't look pleased—"

"So I should imagine," said Colonel Lavery. "What's your idea of it?"

"Unless we're being made the victims of a gigantic and rather pointless double bluff, the answer seems to me to be plain. Benucci and his immediate circle knew about the Hut C tunnel. When they quitted the camp in such a hurry they either forgot to tell—or didn't bother to tell—anyone else."

"The latter, I should think," said Colonel Lavery. "It would suit their book much better if the opposition made fools of themselves."

"Well, I should imagine that Paoli—who was about twenty-five per cent in Benucci's confidence—may have had an idea that the tunnel started from one of the hut kitchens—or he may have been deliberately misinformed, and told that it started from Hut A. Hence this afternoon's demonstration."

"It's possible," said Colonel Lavery. "How is the tunnel going?"

"Much too well to want to lose it now. We've taken it straight on, without raising the level at all. That means that it is going to run out into the slope of the hill, over the crest from the camp wall."

"How long will it be before you're out?"

"We could break any day. We're going slowly and tidying it all up as we go. It's a beautiful job."

"I hope you're right about Paoli," said Colonel Lavery thoughtfully.

4

"Tony," said Goyles, "will you cast your mind back to that evening you were in the cooler?"

"The night Coutoules was killed?"

"Yes. What I really want to establish is some definite timings."

Long cocked an eyebrow at him.

"The great detective?"

"Yes," said Goyles. "The great detective at work. And I'll tell you something about this detecting business which you may find it hard to believe. Once you pick it up you can't put it down even if you want to."

"Like a dog with a piece of stinking rabbit," suggested Long helpfully.

"Perfectly," said Goyles. "If you want the truth, I don't believe anyone ever will be able to say exactly what happened to Coutoules that night—not so as to prove it. A lot of the people who know about it are scattered already, and when the British land in Italy the rest of the cast will be dispersed too. All the same, I can't stop. The fascination of fiddling round and filling in the gaps is too strong. It's like trying to finish a crossword puzzle—in a train going headlong toward a crash."

"All right," said Long. "What do you want to know?"

"I want to establish the times," said Goyles—he sounded quite serious—"when the wireless set in the carabinieri quarters was playing jazz that evening."

"You mean when they had the set full on?"

"Yes."

"It was rather odd, now you come to mention it," said Long. "It wasn't just loud, it was fortissimo—almost as if someone had turned the control knob full on and forgotten about it. We heard it from time to time afterward, but nothing like that evening."

"When did it start?"

"Now you're asking something," said Long. He reflected. "I was standing looking out of the window—I think it was about ten o'clock when the laundry van went out—I was noticing all the absurd precautions they took at the two gates. I stood there for quite a long time, waiting for it to get dark enough for me to start up onto the roof. I guess it was about eleven before I was able to get going. I should have said that the wireless came on at about half time."

"That would be about half past ten."

"Yes. I remember hoping that it would keep going long enough for me to get up onto the roof under cover of the row it was making."

"And it did?"

"Yes—just. It was switched off or turned down about five minutes after I got up."

"Fine," said Goyles. He made a methodical note in his book.

"Glad to be of assistance," said Long. "Don't get carried away by it, though. Remember you're due on P.T. in ten minutes' time. After that, colloquial Italian till lunch."

That afternoon Goyles sought an interview with Colonel Lavery and put a question to him which seemed to puzzle the S.B.O. considerably.

"Yes," he said. "I'd forgotten about it. But as a matter of fact it's quite true. Coutoules came to see me that afternoon. In fact, it was the last time I spoke to him—and the last time but one that I saw him—"

"The last time but one, sir?"

"Yes. I saw him, of course, on roll call that evening. Not being attached to any hut he was one of the last to have his name called. He walked off just ahead of me, toward our hut. As far as I know he was making for his room."

"That afternoon," said Goyles. "Can you remember anything—did anything strike you as out of the ordinary?"

"The whole thing was extraordinary. He was easily the most unpopular person in the camp. I'd arranged for him to have a room by himself, partly to stop stories that he was spying on people, but chiefly because I didn't want to see him lynched."

"And then he asked you to have him moved back."

"Asked," said Colonel Lavery, "is an understatement. He begged me to put him back. He practically went down on his knees."

"Did he say why?"

"Nothing that I could really get hold of. You know he spoke English quite well, but he was liable to get a bit incomprehensible when he was excited. He repeated two or three times that he didn't want the room and he was sure there were many people who deserved it more than he did—which was true enough in a way. Right at the end, when he saw that I wasn't going to change my mind, he did say something which I thought rather odd—"

"Yes," said Goyles.

"He shrugged his shoulders, in a sort of resigned way, and said, 'To think that I had only myself to blame for coming here.' I said, 'I suppose we might all of us say that.' He said, 'Ah, but I'm the only one of you who actually prayed for my move.' Then he went out."

"Are you sure he said 'prayed'?" said Goyles.

"It was either 'prayed' or 'paid,' " said Colonel Lavery. "It didn't seem to make a lot of sense either way."

5

Monday, September 6th at 8:30 in the evening

Positively the first performance in Campo 127
(And probably the last)

THE BARRETTS of WIMPOLE STREET
(A Comedy in Five Acts by Rudolf Besier)

With the following distinguished cast

As Elizabeth Moulton-Barrett—your favorite star, Captain the Honorable Peter Perse.

As Robert Browning—Lieutenant Rupert Rolf-Callender.

As Edward Moulton-Barrett—that accomplished character actor (remember *The Man Who Came to Dinner!*), Captain Angus Abercrowther.

And full supporting cast.

"Roll up in your thousands."

There was no need for the last exhortation. The theater hut had a maximum seating capacity of two hundred and tickets were strictly rationed. A seat in the front row was reserved for the camp Commandant (he liked to attend all such functions, though in view of the nature of some of the jokes in the previous Christmas pantomime it was perhaps fortunate that his knowledge of colloquial English was limited).

The Old Hibernian Rugby Football Club occupied a block at the back of the hall, and, in the interval before the curtain went up, seemed to be continuing an argument from some earlier occasion.

"Anyone with an elementary knowledge of tactics," said Tag Burchnall, "would see at once that no general would land his forces at the toe of Italy when he could just as easily land them halfway up."

"It isn't only a question of landing them," said Jerry Parsons. "You must remember that you've got to supply them, too. From a logistical point of view the further south the better."

"All you've got to do is land a force halfway up the peninsula on both sides, and you'll cut off most of the German Army."

"Then why not land at the top of the peninsula and cut it all off?" said Rollo Betts-Hanger.

"Logistics—"

"The obvious place to land a large force is Ancona. There's practically no tide in the Adriatic—"

"Lines of supply—"

"On the other hand, if they establish their forward base in Northern Corsica and land between Livorno and La Spezia that gives them a straight run to the Po Valley at Modena—"

"Certainly no further north than Naples."

"Here comes old Aletti," said Burchnall. "I suppose it would be a civil gesture if we all stood up."

6

"Why the devil didn't someone think of it before?" said Rolf-Callender. "What's wrong?"

"It's the window at the back. You know Mr. Barrett has to throw it open just before the final curtain. Now it seems it can't be opened."

"What's wrong with it?"

"When we put the set in we put it too far back. It jams on that side beam."

"Has anyone got a saw?"

"What are you going to do? For God's sake don't bring the whole thing down."

"It's all right," said Captain Abercrowther, who had removed his morning coat and rolled up his sleeves. "I'll just take a bit out of the end of that cross beam, knock it along a trifle, and then the window will open fine."

He was far too old a hand at amateur theatricals to let a contretemps of that sort worry him. In his experience it would only have been surprising if nothing had stuck at the last moment.

"Astounding," said Colonel Aletti, as the curtain fell for the first interval, "such acting, such decor. And that young lady on the ottoman, is she in reality one of your officers?"

"Indeed, yes," said Colonel Lavery. "I'm glad you are enjoying it."

"It seems unbelievable," said the Commandant. "The voice—the gestures—so anatomically correct. Will there be rapine?"

Colonel Lavery cast his mind over the plot. "So far as I can remember," he said, "the ardors in this play are more poetical than physical."

"Incredible," said Colonel Aletti "Incredible. And the enthusiasm when the name of Italy is mentioned!"

"Incredible," agreed Colonel Lavery.

"Damned good," said Goyles, as the curtain came down for the second interval.

"It really is extraordinary," said Byfold, "what a complete twerp a chap can be off the stage and how damned entertaining when he's on it."

"I can't take my eyes off that dog," said Long. "Every time he wags his tail I'm sure it's going to fall off. And it beats me how they keep him from licking off his makeup. Are we going out for a quick breather?"

Though all the windows were open the packed hut was as hot as an oven.

"We'd better stick it out," said Goyles. "We'll never get in again if we move."

The play had come to its tremendous last minute. The lovers had stolen away. The empty room at Wimpole Street had filled with members of the Barrett family. Last of all had come Edward Moulton-Barrett—Papa in person.

Captain Abercrowther, who really was an actor of considerable parts, had his hand by now on the pulse of the audience. For those few minutes belief was suspended, and the hatred, fear and pity of two hundred souls was following him as he walked to the window at the back.

In a moment the curtain would fall, illusion would depart and the present would rush back.

As he laid his hand on the casement window he sensed that it was going to prove difficult to open. He thought for a moment of abandoning the gesture. It would be almost as effective if he simply stood with his back to the audience, staring out of the closed window. Then he took a grip of himself, seized the bottom of the window, and threw it up. It resisted; then, when he applied his strength to it, it came with a rush.

At this moment, unperceived by anyone in the theater but himself, the amazing thing happened.

As the window came up, a small square of boards, at the very back of the stage, behind the backcloth, hinged downward. A beam from the overhead spotlight shone straight through this cavity and lit up the shaft beneath it. It lit up also what lay at the foot of the shaft, and with incredulous eyes Captain Abercrowther picked out the word IMPAIR in red on a green background.

He realized that he was looking directly down at a roulette board.

Behind him the curtain fell to a solid roar of applause.

Chapter 13

The Wheels of Circumstance

1

"If I hadn't seen it with my own eyes," said Colonel Baird, "I should never have believed it."

It was nine o'clock on the following morning and the Escape Committee, with Goyles and Abercrowther in attendance, were examining, behind carefully locked and guarded doors, the stage in the theater hut.

"It was some finale," agreed Colonel Shore. "I thought you seemed a little anxious to head off the Commandant—otherwise I didn't spot anything particularly wrong."

He referred to a difficult moment on the previous evening when Colonel Aletti, who had evidently planned to congratulate Elizabeth Browning personally, had been kept with some difficulty from the stage.

"How does it work?" said Colonel Baird.

"What actually happened, I think," said Captain Abercrowther, "was that, when we were originally fixing in part of the set, we put it too close to the framework at the back of the stage, and the window wouldn't open. At the last moment I had to shorten and lower one of the side stays. I was cutting the end off with a saw about five minutes before the curtain went up. You may have heard me. Even then we couldn't lower the window until I'd knocked this bit of bottom studding along about six inches—" he demonstrated. "You see what happens. It looks like studding but it's really the bolt which keeps this little trap door shut."

"Then from the moment you did that there was nothing keeping it up at all."

"No, except that it was a tight fit. The jerk I gave to the window was the thing which finally loosened it. It just fell open."

"Yes," said Colonel Baird. He was standing on the stage, straddling the trap door, staring down into the shaft. What had looked, in the dark and from below, like a partial collapse of the tunnel roof, was now only too obviously man-made. The trap door was skillful enough, but apart from that there had been no attempt at concealment. The excavated sand lay in heaps under the back of the stage.

"Who do you imagine—?" began Captain Abercrowther, and caught Goyles' eye and stopped.

"Look here," said Baird. "You're a bit of a carpenter, Abercrowther. If I get a small party in here to shovel back the sand into the shaft, could you fix this trap door so that it can neither be opened nor spotted?"

Captain Abercrowther nodded.

"And if you gentlemen would come with me for a moment, I think I'd like a word with you about this."

Goyles waited to see if he was being included in the invitation. When he saw that he was not he had to make a very quick decision.

What he did was to move across, catch Colonel Baird as he was about to leave the hut, and say something to him.

Colonel Baird looked startled.

"I take it you know what you're talking about," he said.

"I'll explain as soon as I can, sir," said Goyles.

Colonel Baird hurried after the other members of the Committee and Goyles walked slowly back to his own hut. Although his body moved with deliberation his mind was at stretch.

The first person he looked for was Dr. Simmonds, whom he found in his room turning over the pages of a six-months-old copy of the *Lancet*.

He came straight to the point.

"You examined Coutoules' body, didn't you?" he said. "Did you have the opportunity to do it thoroughly?"

"Reasonably so," said Dr. Simmonds cautiously. "I had one quick look at him when you first discovered the body. Then the Italians gave me a further opportunity of examining him when he was brought up for the second time—largely, I surmise, to make certain that I should agree with their own diagnosis."

"What was the exact cause of death?"

Like most doctors who are asked this question directly, Dr. Simmonds took a few moments off for thought. Then he said, "Asphyxiation caused by sand. There was sand in the stomach and in the trachea—a little in the lungs—not very much. You wouldn't expect much. The reflex would have kept it out until the moment he lost consciousness."

"It wouldn't have been possible to fake that effect after he had died from some other cause—shock or heart failure?"

"You mean by pouring sand into his mouth?"

"Yes."

Dr. Simmonds considered the suggestion carefully and shook his head. "Quite impossible. You wouldn't get any sand into the stomach at all, if he was already dead. Or it would be very difficult. You'd need a force pump to get it down, and that would leave obvious signs."

"Was there *anything*," said Goyles, "anything out of the ordinary at all? Anything that shouldn't have been there if he died simply under a fall of sand? Was there anything to suggest—I don't want to put ideas into your head, you know—but was there anything at all to suggest that he might have been killed by being *held* face downward in sand?"

"How exactly do you visualize it being done?"

"If I am right the operation would have been carried out by two or three men—men who wouldn't make any obvious mistakes—I mean they would know about post-mortem bruising and that sort of thing. I thought that one of them might perhaps have got hold of each of his arms *by the sleeve of his coat* and twisted his arms behind his back to force his head down and prevent him moving while the other would press his head down into the sand—"

"Hold it a moment," said the doctor. "That rings a bell. I'll just have a look at the notes I made at the time." He took a notebook out of the drawer of his desk and turned the pages—"Yes, I thought so. There was slight but distinct marking on the nape of his neck. I discussed it with that professor and we rather assumed that it was done by a stone in the sand which fell on him—"

"But it might equally have been a hand holding him?"

"More probably, I should say."

His next visit was to the Quartermaster.

"You remember," he said, "some weeks ago, getting hold of one of the Italians for me—a chap called Biancelli—"

"The one that shot himself—"

"The one that was said to have shot himself," amended Goyles. "But that's not the point at the moment. It's the other man."

"The other man—?"

"When you found out about Biancelli for me, you told me the name of the carib who was with him—I think it was Marzotto. Could you fix it for me to have a word with him?"

Captain Porter looked doubtful.

"I wouldn't ask you," said Goyles, "only it's hideously important."

"Of course I'll do it for you if I can," said Captain Porter. "It isn't that—but I've got a sort of feeling—wait here a moment, would you."

He was back inside five minutes.

"You're out of luck," he said. "Marzotto left with the other bunch of thugs when Mussolini fell. I fancied I remembered the name. He was the only ordinary carib who went with them."

"Thank you," said Goyles.

Although he was well aware that time was running against him he hesitated before taking the next step. He stood for quite ten minutes watching a basketball match which was being contested with more venom than science, on the dust pitch between A and B Huts. Outwardly the microcosm was unchanged. It was underneath the surface that the sands were shifting and the currents running.

Not so far under the surface, either, thought Goyles. He walked across to the infirmary hut. Its only occupant was Hugo Baierlein. The health as well as the morale of the camp was evidently on the up grade. The beds, which were usually all occupied, were now empty. Even Baierlein was out of bed. He was hobbling very slowly across the floor, both legs swaddled in plaster.

"I've been across the room four times," he announced. "I feel like a very old, very depraved man with the gout which his forefathers have visited upon him."

He left the hut and went back to his own room, where he found Tim Meynell and a fellow Sapper officer. "I heard you wanted to see me," said Meynell. "I brought Punch along with me. He knows more about these gadgets than I do."

Punch Garland grinned down his enormous nose. "I'm a bit out of date now," he said, "but I'll do what I can. Where do you think the instrument is?"

"In Colonel Baird's room," said Goyles. "Come on."

They found Colonel Baird waiting for them.

He said, "When you asked me not to hold another committee meeting in my own room I guessed what was in your mind. In fact we were fools not to have thought about it before. I've had a rough search but I can't find anything obvious."

"The microphone they make nowadays," said Garland, "is a tiny little thing. I saw one the Americans were using in their interrogation center at Tozeur. I knew the man in charge. He showed me the corner of the room it was in and bet me five dollars I couldn't find it in half an hour. I lost."

"What about following the wire?" said Meynell.

"That's almost the only way to do it. It shouldn't be too difficult here. The hut's raised on brick piles. Let's dig round outside."

The two experts disappeared and Colonel Baird said to Goyles, "What put you onto this?"

"It was the very first real clue I was given," said Goyles. "And I threw it away. Tim Meynell told me how he'd been under the carabinieri office in one of his sewer crawls, and heard what he thought was an American or a Colonial voice. Roger heard the same thing later, when he was shut up in one of the rooms in the block."

"And they were listening to a relayed session of the Escape Committee."

"That's about it," said Goyles.

"Got her," said Garland, his great beak appearing at the window. "She comes in under the lintel—run the top of your knife in, Tim."

"I fancy the whole thing comes out," said Meynell. "It's only held by a couple of screws." He was busy unscrewing them as he spoke. Then he drove in the end of his jackknife and, levering outward, brought away the whole of the piece of wood which formed the sill of the window.

Colonel Baird looked into the cavity. "I can see the end of the wire," he said. "Nothing else."

"It's inside the wood," said Garland. He pointed to a knothole in the underside of the sill. He put the point of his knife into the hole and moved it, and they could hear that there was something metallic inside. He turned the piece of wood over.

"No join at all," he said. "They make the whole thing out of plastic wood, and paint it to match the surrounding woodwork. Neat, isn't it? Practically a standard fitting in all the best prison cells."

"Do you think that the other rooms in this hut—?"

"I shouldn't imagine so," said Garland. "However cleverly they hide the mike, the wire's always the weak point. They wouldn't want wires trailing all over the place. So far as I can see this is the only lead in, and it stops here." He was screwing the window sill back into position. "It's quite harmless now—"

"But look here," said Baird. "Why pick this room? They didn't know I was going to use it. The chap who ran the Escape Committee before I got here had a room on the other side of the passage."

"That's what I meant when I said it was a standard fitting," said Garland. "An experienced workman could install the whole thing in about an hour—provided the approach line had been laid—"

"And I think I know when it was done," said Goyles. "Do you remember that 'strafe' search we had—after the first wall break—just after you arrived, sir? They kept us all out on the courtyard from morning roll call till after lunch. That would have given them time to install half a dozen microphones."

"If there's nothing else we can do—" said Meynell.

"No, that's all right," said Colonel Baird. "I don't think I should say anything about this, just yet. Thank you very much."

When they had gone he stood looking at Goyles, who could see that he had worked out all the first implications of the discovery and was beginning to feel his way toward a second installment.

"Goyles," he said, "I think it's time you came out into the open."

"I was thinking the same myself, sir," said Goyles. "I've got one or two ends still to tie up. I'd like to say my piece this evening. Could you ask Colonel Lavery if that will suit him?"

"Colonel Lavery—?" said Baird. It was difficult to say whether he was surprised or annoyed. "Yes—I suppose so. After tea, then—in his room."

2

"Colonel Baird says you have something to tell us, Goyles," said Colonel Lavery.

The three members of the Committee were seated on the bed: Colonel Lavery and Goyles had chairs. The Adjutant was perched on the table. It was past four o'clock, but the heat was still intense. All of them were in their shirt sleeves.

"What I'm going to say," said Goyles, mastering the feeling that he was facing a board of viva-voce examiners, "is every bit as much surmise as anything else you've heard. But I think, if you'll bear me out, you'll come round to my way of thinking in the end. I'd like to start by reminding you of a remark made by Colonel Shore—to the effect that when you have a situation which is starkly impossible, then *any* logical explanation stands a good chance of being the right one. So I'm going to start with what I might call my basic supposition. At all events it's the key which seems to unlock the door. And that is that we have all of us greatly misjudged a very courageous and very loyal little man—Cyriakos Coutoules."

Goyles paused, but the only person who broke the silence was Colonel Shore. He said something under his breath that sounded like "Check."

"I've done what I can to confirm this," went on Goyles. "We shan't know for certain until we can get in touch with one of the high-ups in our own M.I., but it seems the likeliest explanation. It's common knowledge, I think, that there are a few 'phony' prisoners on both sides. The Germans use them, and so do we. I think Coutoules was a British agent. I don't think his job was strictly military intelligence. I think that he was put in to keep track of potential war criminals so that they could be dealt with promptly and effectively after the war. At each of the camps he was in before coming here there was at least one Italian whose conduct would be likely to bring him before an Allied tribunal. Here, of course, he was angling for the biggest fish of the lot."

"Captain Benucci," said Colonel Baird softly.

"It's an attractive theory," said Colonel Shore, "but can you explain one thing? How does any prisoner get moved round as he wants to?"

"I'm no expert on these things, but if you sent me into Italy with a million lire carefully concealed about me and a few contacts I reckon I'd manage it," said Goyles.

"So that's what he meant when he said he'd paid to get here," said Colonel Lavery.

"Yes. That remark was one of the things which confirmed my suspicion."

"And you're saying that Benucci spotted him and had him put away."

"Benucci had him put away," said Goyles. "Whether it was he who spotted him I don't know. I should say not. I should think it was more probably Benucci's assistant who spotted him—"

"Assistant?"

"I'm afraid there's little doubt about it. Colonel Aletti, though indiscreet, was being perfectly truthful. There is, in this camp, a German Intelligence officer. He worked under Benucci—or it may even have been that Benucci was subordinate to him. He was—and still is—close to everything we do. He is an excellent actor and, I need hardly say, a brave and ruthless man. He escaped suspicion because it never occurred to anyone to suspect him."

"Do you know who he is?" said Colonel Baird.

"I think so," said Goyles. "In fact, it's so perfectly plain that anyone who reasoned the thing out must come to the same conclusion as I have. For the purpose of what follows, once his existence is accepted, his identity is not of any great importance. If you don't mind I'll take the traditional line for the moment and refer to him as X. X had at least one accomplice, among the orderlies. I can't prove who that orderly is, and unless X himself tells us I doubt if we shall ever know for certain. They are a mixed bag. When I put the point, in a roundabout way, to Corporal Pearce, he said it was probably one of the South Africans. The South Africans no doubt equally suspect the Poles. And the Poles the English. The point is that they are not a homogeneous body, and it would be very simple for a traitor to exist among them. Also, in the peculiar way in which things are run in a prisoner-of-war camp, while the officers are segregated, the orderlies have every chance of talking to the guards. Among the orderlies was X's assistant. He sent information direct to Benucci, or possibly through Benucci's familiar, Mariescallo. But apart from the orderly, I fancy that Benucci was the only person who knew who X was. Just once, in a fit of bravado, he revealed the fact of X's existence to Colonel Aletti. He must have been kicking himself ever since."

"What was X's job?" said Colonel Lavery.

"Military Intelligence, sir. Or so I think. He and Benucci weren't really interested in camp security. Benucci had to pretend to be—that was his job. But in my view he was a genuine, Nazi-trained, case-hardened Intelligence man. One of Himmler's own. Anything which X could tell him—it might be of Intelligence value, or it might more often be of propaganda value—would go straight to the top. We may not have any high-ranking officers here, but remember we've got a Cabinet Minister's nephew, two prewar M.P.'s and one of the staff officers who helped to plan the battle of Alamein—to say nothing of representatives of almost every arm in the service. A prisoner of war is taught to keep his mouth buttoned when he is first captured, but once he gets into a permanent camp, among his own friends—what subjects under the sun are *not* discussed in the long nights? It must have been rather like having an enemy microphone in the lobby of the House of Commons—"

"More like the smoking room of the Guards Club," said Colonel Lavery. "Please go on."

"Well, the next thing is that Coutoules realized he had been spotted. He was nervous about it—but he didn't say anything because he probably reckoned that he could hardly be kidnapped from the heart of the camp. Here he underestimated his enemies. That is exactly what they did do. But before they did it, they had certain preparations to make. Benucci could have had Coutoules arrested and shot any time he liked. He wanted something more out of it. As has already been suggested he wanted revenge. And he thought out an idea which appealed profoundly to his peculiar sense of humor. He and his own band of cronies *started a little counter-sapping*. At night they would climb the east wall of the camp— seen by the sentries, but of course not challenged—and would disappear into the theater hut. That, by the way, is no doubt why they were so keen to stop 'visiting' between the huts after dark. If they had been seen by one of the prisoners it would have blown the gaff. They cut a trap door in the stage of the theater hut and sank a vertical shaft to meet the head of the Hut C tunnel. With plenty of time, all the tools they wanted, a good space under the stage for sand disposal, and no fear of interruption, they probably completed the job very quickly. It doesn't take long to sink a shaft under those conditions—"

"But, good God," said Commander Oxey. "If they knew enough to be as accurate as that—"

"Yes—" said Goyles. "I see that you take the point. I did warn you that once you examined the evidence the identity of X would not be in any great doubt."

"Go on," said Colonel Lavery sharply.

"When they were ready—that is to say, when their shaft was just about to break into the Hut C tunnel—they carried off Coutoules. Two carabinieri came in with the laundry van. I fancy Benucci was actually talking to you, sir, while it was being done. Two caribs knocked Coutoules on the head, tied him up, gagged him and rolled him in a bundle of washing, and drove him out of the camp. There was one typical little incident at the gate. The sentry—who wasn't in the know—spiked two of the bundles with his bayonet. I don't know whether one of them was Coutoules or not. Possibly so. The caribs thought it was a tremendous joke. Their sense of humor was pretty well in evidence all that evening. Later that night they took Coutoules into the carabinieri office and questioned him. That was when his fingernails came off."

"Not under the sand."

"No," said Goyles, "not under the sand. There was a lot of loose thinking about that and it needed a ton or so of sand on my own head before I saw the truth of it. If ever you have been in a tunneling collapse you will realize the fallacy of the suggestion. You are knocked flat and pinned. All your energies are spent in trying to breathe—and that doesn't last long. Even if you did have your hands free you couldn't pull your nails off—not in sand. It's a pretty toughly rooted growth, a nail. You might bruise the tips of your fingers or even scrape them raw. But you wouldn't pull a nail off. It was Benucci and his fellow humorists who did that. Incidentally that was why they had to have the wireless on so loud."

"Poor devil," said Colonel Lavery. "When they'd got what they wanted out of him, I suppose they finished him off by holding him face downward in a box of sand."

"That's about it, sir," said Goyles. "The medical evidence suggests that. Then they carried him over the wall, by ladder—Biancelli and Marzotto were the only sentries close enough to see what they were doing. Marzotto was safe, but Biancelli wanted to talk later. That's why he was removed. Then they dropped Coutoules down the shaft, and tumbled enough sand in on top of him to partly fill the hole and make it look like a fall."

"Benucci must have had a good laugh when we served up Coutoules in the Hut A tunnel," said Colonel Shore.

"He had us on toast," said Commander Oxey. "And was he loving it."

"To say nothing of the fact," said Colonel Baird, "that with his microphone in our committee room he could forestall any move almost before we made it—"

"There's one thing I can't understand," said Colonel Lavery. "Why are we still being allowed to use the Hut C tunnel?"

"I think that's quite easy, sir," said Goyles. "The whole Coutoules business was a Benucci affair. It was him and his particular stable companions who plotted and carried out the whole thing. *They* knew about the tunnel—everything there was to know about it—to the nearest inch and the nearest degree. But neither they nor X cared much about escaping. If Benucci had stayed in power I have no doubt he would have stepped in at the last moment and staged a pretty little massacre at the tunnel mouth. The moment he went into opposition his feelings naturally altered. I don't suppose he minds now if the whole camp escapes—I don't mean that he's become Anglophile, but anything that upsets the existing regime would naturally be in his favor. As for X, now that all his contacts at the top have gone, I don't quite know *what* his plans are. I expect he aims to escape with everybody else when the armistice comes, and carry on the good work from somewhere else—possibly from a German prison camp."

"I see," said Colonel Lavery.

"Yes—" said Colonel Baird.

"Yes, but—" said Commander Oxey.

"Look here, Goyles," said Colonel Shore, "who is this chap X?"

Goyles said, "I'm afraid there's no doubt at all—about it being Long, I mean."

As soon as the words were out of his mouth, Goyles realized that something irretrievable had been done. The change was physical. It was like a drop in temperature.

Up till that moment he had been dealing with the past, the fairly recent past, but nevertheless the past. It was history. It was something which touched nobody emotionally. His explanations had been accepted because they were an ingenious, and even a probable solution of a problem which people had found puzzling.

Now, with one word, he had stepped into the present. He saw all that, even before Colonel Baird spoke.

"You'll have to make that good, you know," he said. "It's a very serious—"

"Do you imagine I enjoyed saying it?" said Goyles.

"No," said Colonel Lavery. "He was a friend of yours, wasn't he?"

"I've shared a room with him ever since he came into camp," said Goyles shortly. "But you asked for the truth—and I think, for a good many reasons, it's time that you had it."

"When did you start suspecting this?" said Colonel Shore.

"And why—and how?" said Colonel Baird. He seemed put out about something.

"It all started," said Goyles, "on the night that Coutoules was killed. Long, remember, was in the cooler. He had arranged to have himself put there. There was no secret about that. It was part of an escape plan. It was also very necessary for Long's own schemes. Did it never occur to you, sir, that the Italians were being a little clueless about those cell windows? They probed and peered into everything so carefully—and yet—not just for a week or so, but month after month—they overlooked the fact that one of the bars in each cell window could be removed at will. Of course it suited Long's book. All he had to do was to get himself jugged, get out onto the roof, slide down the other side, and he could have a couple of hours' quiet talk with Benucci—exactly as he did that night—"

"Then he was there when Coutoules was being tortured?" said Colonel Shore slowly.

"I don't think so," said Goyles. "I checked—"

"Need we go into that just now?" said Colonel Baird. "I don't know about all of you, but the first thing I want is a lot of convincing that it was Long who was doing all these things."

"All right," said Goyles. "The first hint was given next morning. By-fold went down to rebury Coutoules in the Hut A tunnel. As soon as he had finished, he went back to his room, where he found Long, who had been let out of the cooler that moment. Of course he told him all about it. Now think back to what the Italians did. At first—the usual routine. They roped off the area of the tunnel and started breaking down the roof. As soon as Long got the word back to them all that stopped. Instead, they got *inside* the tunnel and started taking photographs and measuring marks in the roof and picking up fingerprints—all that scientific sort of stuff. It was a small pointer—and I didn't make a lot of it at the time. But I re-membered it afterward. The next thing was my own effort to see Bian-celli. I reported it to the Escape Committee as a matter of routine, but Long was the only other person who knew about it. I had to be stopped, of course. Give me five minutes' free conversation with Biancelli and I'd have known everything. He and Marzotto had the only post that was near enough to where Benucci and company used to climb over the wall—and where they took the body of Coutoules over, that night—to be certain what was happening. No doubt one or two of the other posts could see that something was up, but they'd each had a carib put alongside them, remember, to keep their eyes exclusively on the job. Well—you all know what happened when I got into the cooler. Benucci marched up and prac-tically announced that he knew all about my plans. There could have been other explanations of his knowledge—I thought up one or two my-self—but it stayed in my memory. Even then I was far from suspecting the truth. After that came the plot to rescue Byfold. Benucci went so far out of his way to make it plain that the plot had been betrayed to him that I suggested to Long—rather maliciously—that he had done it on pur-pose. That he had no further use for his stool pigeon and was deliberately trying to give him away. I hoped to raise some reaction, but Long was too good to make silly mistakes like that—"

"Look here," said Baird, "take those three cases. I admit they were all known to Long, and I admit that the other side got hold of them pretty fast. But they were also all known to the Committee."

"The coincidence," said Goyles with a dry smile, "did not escape me."

"Furthermore," said Baird, in his most uncompromising voice, "we were none of us very easy people to check up on. I'm the only New Zealander in this camp. Oxey's one of our very few Navy representa-tives. And Shore is the only Air Force man here."

"Also the only American," said Colonel Shore with a smile, "and a German-American, one generation back."

"Yes," said Goyles, "but you none of you went to the School House at Shelton in the thirties."

"We none of us—"

"What—?"

"Why, of course," said Colonel Baird. "Potter."

"Potter was the final proof," said Goyles. "He was the ultimate, obvious clinching argument. He was quite harmless and insignificant in himself—but he had been to Shelton. That was the chink in Long's armor. His background was perfect, and his accent faultless. His Army career was Special Service—a small cliquey set where you worked on your own and your identity was purposely kept rather secret. No regimental connections. But the one thing he couldn't entirely fake was a public school background. He had to take a certain degree of risk. He knew when he came to the camp that there was no Sheltonian here—"

"How did he know that?" said Baird.

"He knew," said Goyles gently, "because everyone in the camp had been interrogated in your room, and the details went straight over the microphone to Benucci. When Potter arrived his cross examination was also recorded—and as soon as it was realized where he had been to school it became imperative to remove him. Which was done forthwith."

"We were fools about that microphone," said Colonel Baird.

"In a way," said Goyles, "its discovery was a blessing for Long. It might have postponed the evil hour a good deal. What with the obvious way Benucci was behaving—as I said, I don't know whether deliberate or merely careless—one or two people were beginning, I fancy, to think along the same lines as myself—"

He looked at Colonel Shore, who nodded, but said nothing.

"Now immediately the microphone was discovered there was a tendency for everybody to say 'Oh, that explains it. That's how all that stuff's been getting back to the authorities.' But as a matter of fact, if you thought about it carefully, it didn't explain it at all. Of the three occasions I mentioned, two of the discussions took place in our room in Hut C and the Byfold rescue plot was hatched in your room, sir." He turned to Colonel Lavery.

Instead of answering, Colonel Lavery turned to Colonel Shore. "I'd like your view," he said.

"I think the case is proved," said Colonel Shore. "I hadn't succeeded in thinking it out quite so lucidly, but I've had my doubts of Long since that school incident."

"And yours?"

"Well," said Commander Oxey, "there's an awful lot for Long to explain—"

"And yours?"

"It's ingenious," said Colonel Baird. "But I wouldn't hang a dog on it."

Colonel Lavery got up and looked out of the window: at the groups of prisoners already starting to form up for roll call, at the sentries on the walls, and then at the lengthening shadows.

"I look at it this way," he said at last. "We're not a court-martial—at the moment. We're a court of inquiry. A suggestion has been made to us.

I'd go further than that. I'm inclined to think a case has been made out. If it's true we've got a very ugly decision ahead of us."

He paused, and added, "It just couldn't have happened at a worse time."

Nobody seemed inclined to comment on this.

"Obviously the fairest thing to do," he went on, "is to have Long in and hear what he's got to say. We'll do that immediately after roll call this evening. I want three men detailed—they'd better be from Hut C—useful types who can use their hands. Will you see to that, Pat?"

The Adjutant nodded.

"There's no need to tell them what it's about. Just say that a certain amount of force may be necessary and we want them standing by. Also I'd like Baierlein brought over here, if he can be moved—"

"Yes, sir. He's out of bed," said Goyles.

"Very well. Also Byfold, and, of course, you, Goyles. Is there anyone else who may be able to tell us anything?"

"Dr. Simmonds?"

"Yes, tell him to stand by—"

The bugle sounded for roll call.

Chapter 14
Court-martial

1

"We're all three wanted in the S.B.O.'s room after roll call," said Goyles.

"What's up?" said Byfold.

"I've no idea," said Goyles.

"I saw the Adjutant giving some orders to Tag and Jerry Parsons and Rollo," said Long. "They're coming over as well. It looks as if something's up."

"It looks like it," agreed Byfold. "Quiet now—here comes the Commandant. He's getting thinner every day."

2

What made everything so difficult, Goyles realized, was that they were all sitting too close together. Some extra chairs had been put in the S.B.O.'s room, but even so it was much too small to contain the company assembled in it. Apart from Colonel Lavery and the Adjutant there were the three members of the Escape Committee, with Goyles, Byfold, Long and Baierlein. There was none of the space and order and dignity which seems to make judicial proceedings tolerable. The whole process suddenly seemed to Goyles to be sordid and furtive. It was like having to accuse your wife of murder when you were lying beside her in bed. He wished that he could somehow avoid touching Long, but he was pressed too closely against him.

When everybody was settled Colonel Lavery said in his cold, clear voice:

"Lieutenant Long."

"Yes, sir," said Long.

"Would you mind standing up?"

Long got up.

"An accusation has been made against you," said Colonel Lavery, "which is so serious that the very least I can do is to let you hear it, and to see what you have to say about it."

Long's head came back a little but otherwise he made no move. The crowded room was absolutely still.

"The accusation is this. That you are in the employment of the German Secret Service—that you are, in fact, yourself a German."

Long said abruptly, *"Mir scheint das als Anklage nicht zu schlimm."*

In common with everyone else in the room, Goyles lifted his eyes to Long's face as he spoke. Then he dropped them. He saw something in that moment which he was never likely to forget. A shutter had lifted, and the cold light of fanaticism had peeped out. He saw Baird's face flush scarlet as if someone had slapped him across the cheek.

"In case no one else speaks the language," said Colonel Shore—and he, at least, had his voice under easy control—"I'd better translate. Lieutenant Long remarked that the accusation of being a German didn't seem to him to be a very terrible or serious one."

"It might simplify matters if you would speak in English," said Colonel Lavery.

"Ausgeschlossen!"

"As you wish. What we have just heard sounds like an admission. The only thing that remains is for us to make up our minds what we are going to do about you."

Long spoke again. Colonel Shore said, "The Lieutenant says that you have no jurisdiction to try him. This is Allied territory—his own allies, I guess he means—and he is doing a legitimate job."

"Was it part of his job—" began Colonel Baird angrily.

"Please," said Colonel Lavery sharply. "I think the more formal we keep these proceedings the better. If you've a question to ask, please put it to me."

Colonel Baird swallowed hard, and said, "Ask him whether it was part of his job to torture Coutoules."

Long spoke again at some length. "The Lieutenant says," said Colonel Shore, "that he was not present when Coutoules was tortured. He says that he arrived in time to put a stop to it. The torturing was done by Benucci and his friends."

"Has he got any proof of that?"

"I think, sir," said Goyles, "that he's speaking the truth there. That's one of the things Baierlein should be able to help us about. Right at the beginning he told me about the wireless."

"The wireless?"

"Between about ten and eleven that night, sir. The wireless in the carabinieri hut."

"Yes, I remember you suggested that they had it turned up to drown any—any noise that Coutoules may have made."

"I think that's a fair assumption, sir."

"I see. And it had stopped before Long left his cell?"

"Not before, sir. It was going on while he was getting up onto the roof. But it stopped within five minutes of his leaving."

"About five minutes," Baierlein agreed.

"Very well." Colonel Lavery turned again to Long. "How was Coutoules killed?"

Colonel Shore translated throughout the following.

"He was held face downward in a bucket of sand."

"Were you there when this took place?"

"Yes. But it was nothing to do with me."

"Did you make any effort to stop it?"

"Certainly not. Why should I? Anyway, nothing I could have done would have stopped it."

"That's a matter of opinion," said Colonel Lavery. "How many people were present at this scene, besides yourself?"

"Benucci, Mariescallo Butsi and two senior carabinieri. I do not know their names."

"But they are all among the people who left when Mussolini fell?"

"Certainly. They were the first to go."

Colonel Lavery then put to Long the account given by Goyles of what he supposed had happened later that evening.

Long smiled slightly for the first time when answering this.

"He says," said Colonel Shore, "that he congratulates Goyles on his perception and has very little to add."

"Would you ask him," said Colonel Baird suddenly, "whether he has had any communication with his superiors since Mussolini fell."

"He says, none at all. There has been no one to communicate with. He is responsible to the German General Staff."

"What did he propose to do then?"

"He says that he proposed to wait and see what happened. If the whole camp was moved to Germany he had no objection to being moved with them."

"Ask him," said Colonel Baird again, "what the name of this orderly is who's been carrying messages for him."

Long's answer to this was perfectly comprehensible even to those who spoke no German.

"Tell him," said Colonel Baird, "that it won't be easy to treat him leniently unless he is perfectly frank with us."

Long said nothing.

Colonel Baird said, "Ask him if it was part of his job to give away escape attempts."

To this Long answered something abruptly.

"The Lieutenant says," said Colonel Shore impassively, "that since he has been threatened by him, he does not propose to answer any further questions by Colonel Baird."

Colonel Lavery intervened.

"I think," he said, "that such decisions as we have to make can more easily be made in Lieutenant Long's absence. I should just like to ask him before he goes if he has any statement he would like to make."

After a moment's hesitation Long spoke two or three sentences.

Colonel Shore said, "He points out that it is customary and lawful for dummy prisoners to be placed in prison camps. He says that it has always been done in the past and that it is a ruse which the English certainly employ in their own camps. He says that he has never stepped outside this role."

"Very well," said Colonel Lavery. "Pat, will you get the three men I asked for? They're next door. That's right. They needn't come in—there's too much crowd already. I'd like Long to hear what I say to them." He spoke to Tag Burchnall. "You three are a guard. You are to guard Lieutenant Long. You will take him with you into the next room. If he tries to escape, or to make a noise, or to attract the attention of the guards, you are to use any degree of force necessary to stop him. If an Italian comes into the hut, you will knock Long out, and hide him under the bed. Is that understood?"

"Yes, sir," said Tag stoically. He turned to Long and said, "Er—come along," as if it was the most natural thing in the world to have to stun a fellow prisoner and hide him under the bed.

After they had gone a heavy silence fell on the room; no one seemed disposed to break it. In the end Colonel Baird raised his eyes from the floor and said, "It's about as unpleasant a decision as anyone could have to take. But I don't see any way round it. He's got to be silenced."

"Yes," said Colonel Lavery. He said it so flatly that it sounded meaningless. It implied neither agreement nor dissent.

"Even if he's right about Coutoules," went on Baird—"and I think it's a very nice point as to whether he pushed his face into the sand or whether he just stood by and watched it being done—to my way of thinking he's got the blood on his hands of every prisoner who's lost his life trying to escape from this camp."

"He wasn't in the camp during the Colley escape," said Goyles mildly, "or the McFadden business. The only 'break' since he's been here was the last one—"

"I should have thought three deaths was enough," said Baird.

Goyles flushed. "It hasn't been proved, sir," he said, "that he gave it away."

"Does it need proof?"

"It might be a good idea to ask the person chiefly concerned," suggested Colonel Lavery. He looked at Baierlein, who came back to earth with an obvious effort.

"I beg your pardon, sir," he said.

"Did you," said Colonel Lavery, "come to the conclusion that your escape attempt had been betrayed? You must have thought about it since."

"I've thought about little else," said Baierlein. After a pause, he went on, speaking quietly, almost as if he and Colonel Lavery were the only people in the room. "The way we arranged it, Overstrand was to go up the ladder first, then Grimsdale. Desmond Foster was next, and I was last. We were all lying out in the deep shadow, between the theater hut and the chapel. It's one of the places no searchlight can reach. We had fifteen yards of open to cover before we reached the wall. We lay in reverse order—that is to say I was nearest the wall, Overstrand furthest away. That was so that when we came to the wall the first man could throw the ladder up and steady it, while the back men went up first. Immediately the arc lights started to dim we got going. I don't know how long there was between the arc lights and the searchlights going out, but I swear we had the ladder in place before the searchlights started to go out."

"Only about two seconds, I thought," said Goyles.

"Then it proves you can go fifteen yards in two seconds if you really try," said Baierlein. "I felt at that moment we were going to pull it off. I was half crouching under the ladder, holding it, and Desmond was standing on the foot of it. Grimsdale was halfway up and Overstrand—he could have got away altogether, you know, if he'd just been thinking about himself—was lying on the wall, holding the top of the ladder. Then the fresh searchlight came on."

He paused.

"I don't think any of us moved a finger while you could count five. The searchlights were flicking about all over the place, but not systematically, and too fast to be much use. I couldn't see what happened next, but I fancy Overstrand got up to jump—anyway, he must have made some move. All the lights swung round at us, and then the shooting started. Overstrand rolled off the wall, right on top of me. I think he was dead before he fell. Grimsdale tried to go up onto the wall—he got up about three rungs before they finished him. Desmond was beside me on the ground. I didn't even know I'd been hit till I tried to move."

"Your conclusions from that?" said Colonel Lavery.

"I've thought about it, on and off, sir, ever since. I can't honestly think of any other explanation. They weren't expecting us. They were jumpy, as usual, and quick on the trigger—and when they did spot us they did a lot more shooting than was necessary. But I don't think they were waiting for us. If they had been—if they'd known what was happening and where it was going to happen—they'd have had a couple of searchlights trained on the wall where we were going to put the ladder up."

"I suppose Long knew where you were going to try," said Colonel Baird.

"Yes, sir. He knew every detail of the plan. He was doing one of the small helping jobs. Then again, even when the spare searchlights came on—it stuck out a mile that they hadn't a cue what to look for. But it was more than that. I was listening to the sentries on the nearest platform when the lights first went out. They were surprised out of their wits. No. I'm sorry. If you want me to say that we were framed, I shall be a bad witness."

"Even if that's true," began Colonel Baird, "I don't see—"

"Just one moment, if you don't mind," said Colonel Lavery. "I want to clear my mind on this point first. It may help us later. The suggestion is that Long was doing an ordinary military intelligence job. That he didn't step aside to betray escape schemes or such like. He told Benucci and a few others about the Hut C tunnel, because that happened to come into their Coutoules scheme. Incidentally, he was also perfectly prepared to see Byfold made the scapegoat for it. Apart from that particular scheme, it's suggested that he stuck to his job, which was to gather intelligence and did no more incidental harm than was necessary. That seems to be his only real defense. That's the line, isn't it? All right, then. You knew him best, Goyles. What do you think of that? Is it true?"

"For the life of me," said Goyles, "I don't know. He was easily the most wholehearted actor I've ever met. I really think he was speaking the truth about that and he meant to keep it up for the rest of the war. Even afterward, perhaps, who knows? If we were packed off to Germany, and he came with us, he'd have the most perfect credentials. All of us would have vouched for him without a second thought. He actually jumped off a train, remember, with Byfold and me, and got his coat peppered with buckshot while he was doing it. There was no pretense about that. And he was easily the best of the three of us during the trek that followed. In an escape of that sort, on foot, in winter, there's apt to be a time when the cold and the lack of proper food and the lack of sleep work on you to such an extent that you either give yourself up—or neglect precautions so stupidly that it really comes to the same thing. Your mind surrenders, even if your body goes on making a pretense. Well—all I can tell you is that it wasn't Long who gave in first. I think he'd have gone on for days more. We might even have reached the frontier. I don't quite know what would have happened then."

"Your view, then," said Colonel Lavery, "is that he did his job according to his lights."

"You must remember that it's very difficult for me not to be prejudiced in his favor," said Goyles.

"You mean that you were a friend of his?"

"By no means," said Goyles. "All things being equal, that would have made me feel worse about him, not better. What I have to discount is the fact that he saved my life when the tunnel collapsed."

"I see," said Colonel Lavery. "That, I take it, represents the case for the defense. Now, what about the prosecution?"

He looked at Colonel Baird, who said, unsmilingly, "We're playing with this. We're not looking the main fact in the face at all. We're sliding round on sentiment. There's only one thing that matters at this moment. That's the tunnel in Hut C. I think it's a fact—it's certainly a miracle—that the secret is still ours. I should think that everybody knows that there *is* a tunnel—but exactly where it starts and how it works is known only to our side, to some of the Fascists, who aren't here any more and—to Long."

"That may have been true," said Colonel Shore, "at the moment when Benucci and Butsi and the other top Fascists cleared out. Is it still true now?"

"I think so," said Baird. "If that search in the kitchen of the wrong hut was a bluff—well, as I said at the time, it was rather a pointless one. Another thing. You all heard the question I put to Long and the answer he gave. I asked him if he'd been in touch with the management since Benucci left. He said 'No.' All right. He's a good actor. He could have been lying. But why should he lie about something that was going to put his own head in a noose?"

"I don't think he was lying," said Colonel Shore.

Colonel Lavery said nothing.

"Very well then. What in God's name are we arguing about? We all know what's happening outside these walls. There's a British Army about to land. Some say it's landed already. The Italian armistice is round the corner. The Germans—who in hell knows what the Germans are going to do? Either they're going to fight in Italy, or they're going to fall back on the Alps. Either way they're not going to leave us here, if they can help it. If we stay in the camp, we're sitting birds. Ten men with a couple of machine guns could round us up and put us on board a train for Germany, and we wouldn't be able to lift a finger to save ourselves—"

Quite unconsciously Baird's voice was rising as he spoke. Everyone in the room could feel the force of his personality. It was like the hot breath of a furnace.

"Perhaps the Commandant intends to turn us loose. All right, perhaps he does. I wouldn't trust him, myself. If there was the slightest chance that he might get hurt himself, I'd guess he wouldn't lift a finger to save us. And why should we rely on him? By a miracle—by a series of miracles—we can save ourselves. The tunnel's still intact, and it's practically ready for use. To my way of thinking our duty's absolutely plain. Not everyone who gets out of that tunnel's going to get home, but a fair number will. Say we only save fifty—that's fifty trained officers back in the fighting line, instead of spending the next three or four years lying on their bunks in a camp in North Germany—or Poland. And there's one man standing in the way."

Still Colonel Lavery said nothing.

"We might keep him under guard until the tunnel breaks—" began Colonel Shore—and then realized the futility of what he was saying.

"How should we explain his absence from roll call?" said Colonel Baird. "Or do you suppose we should have someone standing next to him with a knife at his back? He's not a person who'll frighten easily, if I'm any judge of character. He'd laugh at you—"

No one had anything to say. In the silence Goyles felt his heart bumping uncomfortably. The heat in the room seemed suddenly unbearable.

At long last Colonel Lavery spoke, very quietly.

"A moment ago," he said, "you talked about Long putting his head in a noose. Were you speaking figuratively, or did you really mean that we should hang him—"

"I hadn't got down to the details," said Colonel Baird.

"Then please get down to them now. If that is going to be our sentence, how exactly do you suggest we carry it out? We are rather short of the amenities of civilization here. We have no public hangman. Or do you suggest that we take a leaf out of Benucci's book, and hold him face downward in a box of sand?"

Colonel Baird started to speak and then thought better of it.

"Another point. Who do you suggest should carry out the sentence? I am in command here. I give orders. On the whole they get obeyed because public opinion is behind me. But is this an order that I can give?"

He turned to Goyles.

"If I ordered you to kill Long, would you do it?"

"No, sir, I shouldn't," said Goyles.

"That's not fair," said Baird. "He's his friend."

"What do you suggest then? That we should draw lots for it? Isn't that robbing a judicial execution of some of its dignity? Doesn't it become uncomfortably like a murder—?"

The word hung in the air. It was the truth. And the truth had only to be spoken once to be recognized. Goyles said to himself, over and over again, "It's a dream. I've started something, and I can't stop it. It's a dream. I shall wake up soon."

There was a sharp knock on the door.

"See who it is, Pat," said Colonel Lavery. "I said we weren't to be disturbed."

The Adjutant went out. Everyone was silent, with his own thoughts.

The murmur of voices outside went on.

The Adjutant reappeared.

"It's Meynell, sir. I think you ought—"

"What is it?" said Colonel Lavery.

Tim Meynell looked with some surprise at the crowded room. Then he said, "I'm sorry to butt in, sir, but I thought you ought to know this at once. I was under the Commandant's office about half an hour ago. If everything's just right, it's possible to hear what's being said. Anyway, you can pick up scraps of conversation. The Commandant was talking to someone. I guessed it was some sort of foreigner, because he was speaking so slowly and clearly that even I could understand most of it—and I'm no wizard at Italian. Then the other chap said something and I caught that too. It was German—"

"German?"

"Yes, sir. German's one of the things I know. I got the gist of it quite easily. This German is C.O. of an armored-car unit in this area. Apparently they've got wind of the fact that the Allies are going to announce the Italian armistice at eight o'clock tomorrow evening. At one minute past eight the Germans are going to take charge here. I'm afraid there's no doubt about it, sir. The Commandant has sold us up the river."

Chapter 15

The Great Crawl

1

Those who possessed watches looked at them.

It was exactly eight o'clock.

"Well now," said Colonel Lavery. Something in his voice made everyone look up. The change was remarkable. It was as if ten years had fallen off his shoulders. "Fate," he said, "is a much abused lady. She's played the hand for us this time, all right. Bring in Long. We've got no time to waste, so we might as well dispose of him at once. That's right—the guard can come in too. Shut the door behind you, please. Now listen to me, Long—"

Long said nothing, but Goyles could see him starting to draw in a long breath.

"We were trying to come to a decision about you, but it's been taken out of our hands. We've just learned that the armistice is due to be announced tomorrow evening. Also, that the moment it is announced, the

Commandant has arranged to hand the camp over to your fellow country-men. That means that anything that we may do has to be done before tomorrow night. Which, of course, simplifies the problem of disposing of *you*. Before we get on to that I've got two questions to put to you, and you'd better think pretty carefully before you answer them. First, are you going to tell us the name of the orderly who has been helping you?"

"*Ausgeschlossen.*"

"Very well." Colonel Lavery did not appear to be disconcerted. "I expect we can manage without knowing, though it may be a little unfair on the other orderlies. Second question then. Are you prepared to give us your parole until tea time tomorrow—anyway, let us say, over roll call tomorrow morning?"

"*Ausgeschlossen.*"

"If you don't," said Colonel Lavery calmly, "I have Dr. Simmonds next door. I shall have him put enough drugs into you now to keep you unconscious for twenty-four hours. At roll call tomorrow morning the guard will find you in the infirmary—under medical supervision."

There was a moment of silence. As duelists touch their swords, the two strongest wills in the room met, and withdrew.

"Very well," said Long, speaking in English for the first time. "Until tomorrow night."

"Take him over to Hut C," said Colonel Lavery. "Keep him in his own room—that's not a room that looks directly onto the walls, is it? All three of you are to stay with him, until I can have you relieved."

As soon as they had gone, Colonel Lavery turned to the Adjutant. "I shall want the hut commanders over here," he said. "Tell them not to come in a bunch—I think the Quartermaster is in his room. You might pass the word for him. Oh, and tell R.S.M. Burton I shall want him—but he's not to come before nine o'clock."

As Colonel Lavery spoke, Goyles realized one thing very clearly. Any chance that they had lay in the fact that the S.B.O. was a man who had mastered the technique of command. This did not imply that he was a captain of men or a leader of forlorn hopes—but simply that he was a professional soldier who by long practice and usage had acquired the ability—that deceptively easy, much underrated ability—to formulate a plan and put it into operation.

"I don't think we need you any more, Meynell—thank you very much. You won't say a word about this to anyone, of course. That's right. You can stay, Goyles. We shall want someone who knows the ins and outs of that tunnel. Now then, Baird. How long's it going to take you to break out?"

Colonel Baird pondered. "It's easy to be too optimistic about a thing like that," he said. "I should say, at least four hours—not more than eight."

"Shoring it as you go and making a decent exit hole at the end?"

"Certainly. I'll guarantee we'll have the whole of Hut C out of it before roll call tomorrow morning."

"That you won't," said Colonel Lavery. "I'm not going to throw away eighty per cent of this camp unless I have to."

There was a moment's silence.

"I don't quite see, sir—" said Colonel Shore.

"You might get half a dozen people from the other huts across in the dark tonight," said Colonel Baird. "Particularly if the sentries aren't especially alert. I don't think you'd get more—"

"No one's going to stir out of their hut tonight if I can prevent it," said Colonel Lavery. "I shall evacuate the camp—tomorrow—"

"But—" said Colonel Baird.

"How—" began Commander Oxey.

"By Christopher Columbus," said Colonel Shore. "That'll be something, won't it?"

"See here," said Colonel Lavery. "You told me that, with any luck, you could get that tunnel out over the brow of the hill—out of sight of the sentries—right?"

"I think so, yes."

"Then Hut C shall do that, tonight. They've got the whole night to do it in. It doesn't matter where they put the sand—that's not important now. They can store it in sand bags under their beds. They can use any woodwork they like. We must have a perfect job. If you can bring it out somewhere that'll give us a hidden crawl right down to the river, so much the better. As soon as you cross the river, you're in the wood, so you'll be all right."

"By Christopher Columbus," said Colonel Shore again. "Four hundred men—in broad daylight."

"Why not?" said Colonel Lavery.

"Why not indeed," said Colonel Baird. He brought his big hand down with a gentle smack onto his knee.

"There's a lot to be thought about," said Colonel Lavery. "Oh, come in, Hugo. This is an orders party. Find somewhere to sit down. As soon as the others are here, I'll start."

With a queer pang Goyles was suddenly reminded of hundreds of orders parties he had attended during the war. The Colonel talking. The quiet men sitting round him busily writing it all down in little notebooks. How much tragedy and comedy, how much destiny, how much death and destruction, how many famous last words had been scribbled down into little notebooks.

"Now we're all here," said Colonel Lavery. "I ought to say one thing. And that is that I lately received—in the usual way—an order from the War Office that in the event of an armistice everyone in prison camps was to stay put. I think—I hope and believe—that that order is now out of date. I think it was given under a misconception about the tactical situation. I intend to disregard it anyway—but I think perhaps you ought to know of its existence. Now then, there's a lot to do before lockup tonight. And a lot to do after lockup for that matter. This isn't a formal party, so I'm going to welcome suggestions—though I'll make the final decision. The first thing is that if the plan's going to work everyone will have to go through Hut C. That means that everyone in the camp has got to go into Hut C in broad daylight tomorrow. There's no reason they shouldn't, but it's going to take some organizing. First of all, quite clearly, they won't be able to take much equipment with them. Even the dumbest sentry's going to begin to get ideas if he sees squads of men filing into Hut C in full marching order—"

"If I might say so," said Colonel Baird, "I don't think anyone needs to take anything except a small reserve of food, a good pair of boots, and compass and map if he's got them. After tomorrow night it's going to be a reasonably friendly countryside. You can pick everything else up as you go."

"That's what I feel," said Colonel Lavery. "I'd like hut commanders to inspect every man in their hut tonight in the outfit *he actually proposes to go out in*. There are bound to be some fools who'll give the game away by trying to take too much. The next point, I think, is this. We're not going to send out a complete hut at a time. We'll have ten serials—call them A to J—each composed of a mixed bag of people from all huts."

Out of the corner of his eye Colonel Lavery saw Goyles move and said, "Yes. I know what you're going to say. I'll tell you what I've got in mind about orderlies in a moment."

"Timings for serials," suggested the Adjutant.

"I don't think we can be too rigid, Pat. We've none of us any idea how long it's going to take forty men to crawl through a tunnel and disperse—"

"Longer than you think—always," said Colonel Baird, out of his experience of tunnels.

"I agree. I think that the answer is that we stick up a letter on the main notice board immediately we're ready for the next serial. The Italians are used to seeing a crowd round that notice board—and with things as they are a bit of an extra crowd won't look out of place. I'll leave it to each hut to decide what men go in what serial because quite obviously the men in A and B are going to be a lot happier than the ones in I and J."

"Draw for it."

"Something like that. The only party whose composition I'm going to lay down is the rear party. I'm afraid it won't be a very popular party. I shall be in on it. I'd like you to stop, Pat. Also the Escape Committee—and a few men who know the ins and outs of the tunnel. That better be you, Goyles and Byfold."

"Yes, sir," said Goyles. He tried to sound cheerful about it.

"Also a provost section. I don't anticipate trouble at the tunnel mouth, but it's as well to be sure. We shall want about eight tough and willing types. They'll be armed with sticks. They can operate from Goyles' room.

They'll have three jobs. First to control the entrance to the tunnel. Secondly, to look after Long—"

Colonel Lavery looked up. "Some of you don't know about that," he said, "and there's no time to explain. But Long is under close arrest in Hut C. He won't be coming with us."

"You said three jobs," said Colonel Baird.

"Yes. They'll also have to deal with any Italian who wanders into Hut C. I don't want that to happen—but if any Italian does stick his nose in he'll have to be dealt with. Any weapons he has on him can go to the provost."

"If we get at all far with this," said Colonel Baird, "one of the things is going to be to prevent the camp looking empty."

"The last serials out will have to keep busy," said Commander Oxey. "They'll have to show themselves all over the shop."

"Like a stage army," suggested Colonel Shore.

"I'll put something in orders about it," said Colonel Lavery, making a note. "The last serial about must organize two open-air classes and half a dozen pairs to walk round the circuit. If we get that far it'll be late afternoon, and the camp's pretty dead by then. The serials before will put on two games of basketball and a cricket practice. The serial before that can play rugger—they'll need time to change back and cool off before they go out. Now—the orderlies. There's a snag here." Colonel Lavery turned to the hut commanders. "We were discussing it just before you came in. We've got reason to suppose that one of the orderlies is in touch with the Italians."

"Keep all the orderlies until last," suggested Baird.

"I think that'd be a bit unfair," said Colonel Lavery, "and it might start trouble—which it would be very difficult to put down without drawing attention to ourselves—"

"Send them out first, in one party," said Colonel Shore, "and get them as far away from the camp as possible."

"They'd be very difficult to control once they were out," said Colonel Baird. "I think we'll have to compromise. Here's R.S.M. Burton. He's just the man we want. Look here, Burton, I'd better put you in the picture—"

"Do I understand, sir," said the R.S.M. finally, "that from now on I'm to take my orders from you and not from the Italians?"

"That's it."

The R.S.M.'s chest expanded about four inches and his shoulders became miraculously even squarer. "Sir," was all he said.

"Now, then. I think the orderlies had better be told after lunch tomorrow. There's no need for them to know before that. If they spot anything out of the ordinary they'll just think it's a normal escape. Parade them after lunch in their own hut, R.S.M. I'll give them their orders myself. They'll go out together as one complete serial—we'll call it serial O so as not to confuse it with the others, and we'll give them a timing—let's think—if we allow one minute per man—that's forty minutes a serial— say fifty to allow for accidents. If we start at nine o'clock we should do five complete serials before lunch. We'll have one more after lunch, then the orderlies."

"Serial O after Serial F and before Serial G," wrote R.S.M. Burton in his little notebook.

"My orders will be that when they are out, they must travel in parties of not less than six for the rest of the day. If anyone tries to leave his party of six before nightfall the other five will have to stop him—by force if necessary. After tomorrow night they can please themselves."

"Very well, sir," said the R.S.M. He had no idea of the reasoning which lay behind this order, but it seemed quite straightforward—indeed, a good deal more reasonable than many orders to which his service in the Brigade of Guards had accustomed him.

"Do they think they'll do what they're told?"

"They'll do what they're told, sir," said R.S.M. Burton.

"Now the other parties—once they're out. They must keep their heads well down until they are across the river and in the wood—they won't need telling that."

"After that it's going to be a bit more tricky, isn't it?" said Colonel Shore. "We don't want an aged Italian peasant tottering up to the front gate of the camp at about midday saying he met a file of escaping *Inglesi* in the wood and what is the Commandant going to do about it."

"I think that's one of the real snags," said Commander Oxey. "And I don't honestly see how you're going to get over it."

"I do," said Colonel Baird. "Make everyone travel in parties of five and six for the first day. Any Italian they meet, they kidnap him."

"We don't want to start by—"

"I don't think there's any choice," said Baird. "The Italians won't know about this armistice until tomorrow evening. Technically, until then, we're enemies. We ought to keep out of sight as much as possible, but if any party *does* run into an Italian—they should, I suggest, persuade him to accompany them for the rest of the day."

"I don't like it," said Colonel Lavery. "But I agree it's the best we can do. What next?"

"Food."

"That's the Quartermaster's department. I don't think anyone should bother to take perishable food. Things like tea and coffee and tinned porridge might be useful—I suggest that Serials A to E draw what they can at breakfast. The rest at lunch."

"I'll have it taken over to huts first thing tomorrow," said Captain Porter. "Luckily it's a distribution day anyway, so the orderlies won't get wondering—"

"All right," said Colonel Lavery. "Has anyone else got any points? I don't want to hurry you, but I've got to get out written orders, and that's going to take time. I don't think it's avoidable though. Once things start tomorrow we shan't be able to hold conferences to sort it all out if it goes wrong. It's got to work automatically or not at all. If I haven't got the orders ready by lockup I'll need a volunteer from each hut to carry them across after dark. It's a risk but it's one I'm prepared to take."

"Invalids," said someone.

"Hell, yes," said Colonel Lavery. "I'd forgotten all about them. How many are there?"

"There's only one at the moment," said Baierlein. "That's me."

"Are you able to move yourself?"

"Put me in an early serial," said Baierlein with a grin, "and I'll manage."

"Anything else?"

"Synchronize watches, sir," suggested the Hut C commander happily.

2

It was two o'clock on the following afternoon and Goyles and Byfold were sitting in the Hut C kitchen. Goyles had never before realized that time could stand still. He had appreciated that there might be some difference in its apparent duration—a minute in the hands of the Spanish Inquisition might be longer than an hour in the arms of a lover—but he had never before realized that time could actually stop—that the sun and the moon could stand still and the chronology of the human race be suspended.

There had been minutes in the previous twelve hours which no one was ever going to forget.

Night in Hut C. Hot, sticky darkness. The lights were turned out at eleven and the hut commander had banned all torches. Into one room, carefully screened on the blind side of the hut, they had come, in batches of twenty, to hear their orders. Later they had come back to the same room, one at a time, to have their escaping kit inspected. Some of them had been sent back more than once before the hut commander would be satisfied. "Since you have the good luck to live in Hut C," he had told them, "you will be able to take more with you than the other chaps—they have to walk here across the compound under the eyes of the sentries. But that doesn't mean you can dress yourselves like Christmas trees. You've got to crawl, remember, at fair speed, through a tunnel nearly two hundred feet long. If you stick, or bring part of the tunnel down, you will wreck the chances of every single man behind you in the queue. Go back and think again."

Goyles had seen very little of this. He had been down in the tunnel itself with a select band of experts. They knew roughly where they were in relation to the slope of the hill, for metal rods, thrust upward, had shown daylight at decreasing distances for the last few days, but precise calculation was still impossible.

"It isn't an even slope," he said. "We may be running under a level patch or even into a small piece of uphill. We must reckon on eight feet of digging, and allow for more." After that they had worked; in nightmare, nonstop shifts. As the sand came out it was packed in bags and laid, first, in a wall up the side of the entrance shaft; after that it was carried out and stacked under beds.

It had been just after three o'clock in the morning that they made a perfect outfall. Goyles was at the face when it happened. His trowel ran first into a layer of packed flints, then into pebbles and thin dirt; then a spout of gloriously fresh air, and a star had appeared. He had given the order to dowse lights and as they had worked on in the gray dimness of the tunnel mouth the extent of their luck had become apparent. If the choice had been in their hands they could not have chosen better. They had come out underneath a considerable boulder actually in a dry stream bed, at a point where a small vertical drop must have made a little water-fall during the winter rains.

In the end Goyles had decided to stop all shoring about three feet short of the boulder. He realized that it was a choice of evils. If no props were put in, the boulder might collapse under use. If the entrance was shored, there was a chance it would be spotted from the opposite hillside when day came.

"Better leave it as it is," he thought.

When everything was ready, and in the last moments of dimness be-fore the true dawn, he had crawled out, down the stream bed, to the river at the bottom. The lips of the tunnel, he was pleased to see, were masked almost all the way down with tufts of low scrub and grass. He sat for a moment, trailing his hand in the water, and wondering what would hap-pen if he disappeared into the silent woods opposite—woods behind which lay freedom.

He had no illusions about his own chances. If he was to be one of the last out of the tunnel he had, he considered, no chance at all. The question in his mind was not whether the scheme would work—it was how many would get away before it was stopped. Places in the early serials, he knew, were already being bought for large sums.

He had come to the conclusion that if he had any sense he would cut straight off into the darkness. Nevertheless as he crawled back along the tunnel, made some last adjustments, helped to close the trap, and got into bed, he felt obscurely pleased with himself and he slept soundly until eight o'clock—and was one of the few people who slept at all that night.

On roll call that morning, Long, standing between two of his guards, had given no trouble. As the parade cleared Colonel Lavery gave the agreed sign that meant "All well—so far." The Italian orderly officer left the camp at ten minutes past nine. At a quarter past nine Major Gibb posted a news bulletin on the intelligence board. It was evidently intended to be the first of many, for it had a large letter "A" in the top left-hand corner.

After that, time stood still.

As Goyles realized, one thing alone had saved them that morning, and this was that the sentries themselves had something else to think about. Some whisper of the coming armistice was already in the air. It was known, too, that there were German forces in the neighborhood. The soldiers on the walls must have been wondering what the immediate future would bring forth. Otherwise, being trained guards, they could not have failed to notice the signs that were displayed before them—the purposeful coming and going of prisoners—the steady dribble of men toward one hut—men who went in, but never came out again—the crowds round the notice board—the self-conscious groups, who suddenly realized that they might be attracting attention and scattered for no apparent reason.

Serials A and B had run to time. Serial C had congregated in the hut when the first hitch occurred. The mouth of the tunnel was showing signs of collapse: against such a contingency Goyles had had two complete sections of boring cut and fitted and painted black. The tunnel had been cleared and while Serial C sat on the floor of the hut and sweated through a hideous hour the new sections had been installed. After that the pace had been increased and some time had been made up until an irresponsible pair in Serial D had tried to take out a homemade cooking stove. They were now under open arrest in the kitchen.

Lunch had been a nightmare meal. Half the places had been empty. The occupants of the other half had eaten with little appetite.

"It's the first time in a prison camp that I've ever seen food sent away from a meal," said Goyles.

"Did you see Rolf-Callender?" said Byfold.

"No—I missed him—he was dressed as a girl, wasn't he? What was he like?"

"Gorgeous," said Byfold. "I hope he got through the tunnel without wrecking his corsage. He said he was making for the Vatican City."

"Should give the Pope something to think about," said Goyles. "How are we doing?"

Byfold looked at his list. "Halfway through E," he said. "That's half the camp. They ought to give Lavery a gong for this."

"If the whole camp gets out," said Goyles, "you can make it a knighthood. It wouldn't be excessive."

3

At eleven o'clock that morning Joseph Rocca, farmer, received a fright.

He went straight home and reported it to his wife. Together they considered the matter, and came to the reluctant conclusion that they should do something about it. Joseph got onto his bicycle and rode downhill toward the village. There he stopped to consult with his brother. His brother proved skeptical. A second brother and a cousin were summoned. They thought there might be something in it. "You must ride to the camp and tell the Commandant," they said. "It is your duty."

"It is uphill to the camp," pointed out the first brother—"and it is now half past twelve. Let us eat."

At two o'clock Joseph arrived outside the gate of the camp and attracted the attention of the guard. He had, he said, information for the Commandant. He was allowed inside the wire and given a seat. A messenger went away, and came back to say that the Commandant was having his siesta. Could Signor Rocca wait? Joseph hesitated, but having come so far he decided he would wait.

At half past three he was taken in to see Colonel Aletti, whom he knew slightly. Signor Rocca was a well-known local farmer, and the camp purchased provisions from him. "This morning at ten o'clock—" he began.

The Commandant listened patiently. At the end, he smiled and said, "See for yourself."

The two men stood at the window of the Commandant's office and looked down on the camp. All was peace. Groups of prisoners lay out, listening to lectures. A game was in progress on the sports field. The sentries paced the walls.

"They looked like prisoners," insisted Joseph. "Five of them—large men—definitely of Anglo-Saxon type—a sort of criminal look, you understand."

"All were present at roll call," said Colonel Aletti. "None have been through the gates or over the walls. They could hardly dig their way out in broad daylight."

Signor Rocca felt that honor had been satisfied. He shook hands with the Commandant and departed. Lieutenant Paoli, who had been present at the interview, was not so sure.

As soon as he could he excused himself, and wandered into the camp. Once he was inside, every police instinct that he possessed told him that he was right. There was a current of feeling which hit him as soon as he got inside the gates.

Every group that he passed shouted a silent warning at him. He wandered slowly toward Hut C. Here the feeling was stronger still. He considered for a moment whether he should fetch some assistance and start an immediate search. Something was going on. That was plain. But what? Better to make sure first. He opened the door of Hut C and walked slowly down the corridor. He made his way to the kitchen and opened the door. The time was exactly four o'clock.

4

At twenty minutes to five Colonel Lavery, accompanied by the Adjutant, came out of the senior officers' hut. He made his way slowly across to Hut E and went in. He walked down the corridor, noticing that every door was propped open with a chair or a bench. It had been the duty of the last man out in every room to wedge the door open. The two of them left the hut and walked to the next one. They visited each hut in turn.

It had been their custom, for some weeks, to make an unofficial inspection of this sort during the evening meal.

As they passed the notice board they stopped for a moment to look at the bulletin. It was Bulletin No. 12 and had the words "Rear Party" in small letters across the top. At the bottom an unknown hand had scrawled 'Arrivederci." Colonel Lavery smiled.

He and the Adjutant turned together and made for Hut C.

"Is it just my guilty conscience," said the Adjutant, "or do things feel not quite as they ought to be? The compound's often empty at this hour—"

"It's the silence," said Colonel Lavery. "No talking, no shouting, no jazz bands. I believe even the sentries are beginning to cotton onto it."

They disappeared into Hut C and shut the door behind them.

In the first room they found Colonel Baird. He had gone early into the hut to avoid attention and had stayed there all day.

"Operation Crawl completed," he said, as he stood up. He added, "Would it be in order for me to congratulate you?"

"Thank you," said Colonel Lavery.

They went down the passage. All doors were open except for the kitchen. Inside they found quite a crowd. Perhaps the most noticeable object was a bundle on the floor, that heaved and jerked from time to time like a fresh-landed salmon.

"It's Paoli, sir," said Goyles. "I think he's quite all right, really."

"Better be sure about it," said Colonel Lavery. "Some of us are going to be captured." He smiled for the first time that day. "We don't want another murder trial." Then he turned to the group round Long and said, "Tie him up."

"It's not necessary," said Long. He added, "You took a much greater chance with me on roll call this morning. You can accept my word that I won't call for help for an hour after you've gone."

"I took a chance on you this morning," agreed Colonel Lavery, "because I wasn't at all sure, at that time, that this scheme was going to work, and I didn't want to run myself into trouble by assaulting a German officer unnecessarily. Now, however, that a small miracle has been worked in my favor I don't feel disposed to take any avoidable chances. Tie him up."

"I was once foolish enough to imagine," said Long, "that the Germans were the most ruthless people in the world."

"Gag him, too, please," said Colonel Lavery politely. "Then you chaps had better get going. After you, Baird."

He turned to Goyles and Byfold. "There's no means of shutting this trap behind us, is there? I'd like to give them the maximum trouble."

"I'm afraid not, sir," said Goyles.

"All right, down you go."

Goyles looked back for a second at Long. He carried with him the memory of a pair of blazing eyes.

Five minutes later he was at the edge of the wood. He turned to look back. From where he stood even the top of the camp wall was invisible: but he could see, a clear half mile away across the valley, the road which looped down the hill to the village at the camp foot.

He felt Byfold's hand on his elbow.

"It's them, all right," said Byfold.

Like six gray mice, each with its flickering tail of white dust, the German armored cars came creeping down the hill.

Postscript

The adventures of the camp during the next six months would afford material for at least two hundred books.

Goyles and Byfold crossed the British lines above Campobasso fifty days later and they were both back in Italy with their regiments in time for the battle of Cassino. Byfold got command of his old squadron and was killed in the assault on the Gothic Line in September. Goyles survived the war and it was from him, of course, that most of this story came.

Colonel Lavery received a mixed reception when he reached England. At first the authorities were inclined to feel that they should censure him for a plain breach of orders. Later, as other survivors of the camp arrived and told their stories—and as news of the fate of other camps with less strong-minded S.B.O.'s reached them—they changed their minds and awarded him a reluctant O.B.E.

What happened to Long is not known. Colonel Aletti was shot by the Germans on the day following the escape.

Rupert Rolf-Callender and the Honorable Peter Perse reached the Vatican after a number of remarkable adventures which they have recounted in a book which is to be published shortly.

The adventures of all these people belong to the private history of the war. A little of it gets into print but the greater part remains in the memory only.

The End